# the *House*
## *at Rose Creek*

# the House
## at Rose Creek

*the*

*a novel*

# Jenny Proctor

Covenant Communications, Inc.

Cover image: *1988 Diary* © SVGiles, courtesy of Getty Images, Inc.

Cover design copyright © 2013 by Covenant Communications, Inc.

Published by Covenant Communications, Inc.
American Fork, Utah

Printed in the United States of America
First Printing: July 2013

19 18 17 16 15 14 13     10 9 8 7 6 5 4 3 2 1

ISBN 978-1-60861-894-1

To my husband,
who never stopped
celebrating this journey

# *Acknowledgments*

IT WAS MY MOTHER, IN the earliest days of my childhood, who taught me to respect words, to use them wisely, and to recognize how powerful they can be. I'll always love her for that. And my sister—oh, my blessed sister—I never could have written anything without you. You were tireless, always willing to hash out story ideas and work wonders with your editing eye. I am a better writer because of you. My other beta readers—Lindsay Anderson, Valerie Walz, Kimberly Vanderhorst, DeNae Handy—your advice and counsel mean so much. Thank you for your willing, critical eye. I also owe a tremendous amount to my wonderful editor at Covenant, Samantha Millburn. As a first-time author, my questions might have been a bit excessive, but, Samantha, you were the epitome of kindness and patience as you led me through this extraordinary process. To my husband and children, thank you a hundred times. Your patience and, of course, your tolerance, were essential to my success. To my author friends, Melanie Jacobson and Annette Lyon, thank you for your endless advice, encouragement, and support. And finally, to my high school English teacher, Mrs. Gorsuch, and to all high school English teachers, thank you for inspiring young writers, for instilling love and respect for fine literature. Magic happens in your classrooms—I'm sure of it.

*23 June 1844*

*I do not know if I will ever find the truth I seek. I have grown weary of the searching, the sermons, the pastors and preachers all claiming to know the way to salvation. The way for whom, I ask them, your two hundred parishioners alone? What of the rest of us, then? When and if I find the truth, I believe I will feel peace and joy in my heart like I have never known. I will know of the truth because God will reveal it unto me. He has not let me down yet. I do not believe He will let me down this time either.*

*—Diary of Ian Wylie, 1801–1850*

# *Prologue*

MARY WALKER SAT IN HER quiet living room, trying to enjoy the soft light of late afternoon. A large oak tree stood outside the bay window, filtering the sunlight and casting small leaf-shaped shadows onto the pages of Mary's book. Her restless mood seemed at odds with the tranquility of her surroundings. Distracted, she set her book aside with a sigh and reached for the family photo album she kept on the end table, hoping perhaps to dispel the feelings of unease and discomfort embedded like nettles in the margins of her consciousness. Mary slowly turned the well-worn pages of the album, each one a catalog of memories and moments long gone. She smiled at one picture in particular and gently touched the faces of each of her three children. The tip of her finger lingered for a moment longer on a fourth child in the photo—a wild, dark thread woven into the lighter fabric of her own fair-haired offspring.

"Kate," she whispered softly. Kate was Mary's niece. It still stung Mary to think of the sudden and tragic accident that had left her without a sister and orphaned Kate when she was just seven years old. Even now, more than twenty years later, Mary missed her sister every single day. The accident was difficult for everyone, but Kate suffered the most. To lose a mother and father all at once, move to a new house, start a new school—it still made Mary's heart hurt to think of Kate's first years in their home. The one thing that helped Mary through the difficult time following the accident was knowing she had to be strong for Kate. It had been easy to love her. Her place in Mary's heart had been immediate and permanent. But the little girl held herself apart, Mary thought, in fear of forgetting her own parents, afraid to love a new mother out of loyalty to the first.

Mary's middle child, Leslie, had been Kate's saving grace. Only six months apart in age, it hadn't taken long for the girls to become completely inseparable. When Kate would retreat into the quiet corners of her own suffering, it was Leslie who could always pull her out again. Eventually, the raw edges of Kate's heart healed, and she settled into the comfortable patterns and rhythms of the Walker household.

Mary shook her head in disappointment as she thought of the cousins, once so close, now locked in a bitter and painful battle. Kate hadn't been home in years, not even when Leslie's husband had died.

"Foolish girl," Mary said to herself with a sigh. It wasn't her battle to fight, though she would love to see reconciliation. She had tried to encourage the girls, but she couldn't make them talk, couldn't make them listen to each other. She knew they would have to talk eventually. Life would require it. Of that, Mary was certain.

She stood and stretched, trying to shake the weariness from her bones. The doorbell rang.

Mary moved to the door and greeted the mailman, returning his friendly smile through the screen of the storm door.

"You'll have to sign for this one, Mrs. Walker," he said. "Certified mail."

She took the thick legal-sized envelope to her desk in the sunroom. At first she did not sense the fear and suspicion that softly tiptoed in behind her, but as she opened the envelope and started to read, they quickly took hold of her heart. She read silently for several minutes, one hand clasped tightly over her mouth, her eyes wide with disbelief.

It couldn't be true; not after all she'd done, all she'd endured in her fight to keep the house. The nightmare wasn't over after all.

The pain started slowly—a heaviness just below her sternum that pushed upward then over into her left arm. With each breath, Mary found it more and more difficult to fill her lungs. She clung to the side of the desk, the room spinning around her. She lurched forward, trying to reach the phone, but it was too late. When she hit the floor, the papers in her hand slipped under the heavy mahogany desk.

No one would ever look for them there.

Who would think to look when no one even knew they existed?

# *Chapter 1*

THE LOBBY OF BLANTON ADVERTISING was designed so that even on the cloudiest of days, the space still seemed full of crisp, clean sunlight. Tall mirrors stretched from floor to ceiling all along the back wall, and large triangular skylights beckoned upward, pulling the light down into the expansive room below. It was Kate's favorite part of the building.

The morning Aunt Mary died, Kate still went to work. She was screaming, nearly falling apart on the inside, but as she struggled to process the news of her aunt's death, work seemed the easiest option. There, Kate could pretend her world was still perfectly normal, unaffected by loss or sadness. But it was pretending, and Kate eventually found herself in no position to keep up the charade. As she walked through the lobby of the building, she didn't appreciate the patterns of light reflecting and bouncing off the mirrored walls and marble floor. She didn't see the faces of her coworkers or hear their friendly chatter as she passed by. As she pushed deeper and deeper into the people and patterns she knew so well, the foolishness of coming to work finally began to catch up with her.

Desperate to be alone, she raced toward the peace and solitude of her own private space. Her latest promotion had come with a corner office—the biggest one on the floor and, much to Kate's sudden annoyance, the one most distant from the elevators. She pushed blindly past unsuspecting coworkers, waving her hand in dismissal to anyone who dared notice her discomposure.

Kate's personal assistant, Veronica, met her at the door to her office, ready to hand her a cup of coffee and a copy of the morning schedule.

"Good gracious, Kate!" she exclaimed. "You're white as a ghost."

"Not now," Kate hastily whispered. "Not now."

She swung open the large walnut door and slammed it shut behind her. Leaning into the door, she slid to the floor and pressed her forehead against the smooth grain of the wood, clinging to its surface, trying to anchor herself against the spinning room around her. Her heart pounded in her chest, and her breath came in shallow gulps until, finally, the tears dammed up behind fear and guilt and shame burst through—a torrent of raw emotion Kate could not control. She wept for her aunt Mary. She dug into her soul's deepest corners and wept for her cousins who'd just lost their mother and for her own mother and father, lost years ago. And then she wept for herself.

When the tears stopped, Kate sat in weary silence, a crumpled shell of a person on her office floor. For years, she'd been trying to convince herself that she had managed to change her reality, but clearly, all she had done was ignore it. Now the past had roared back into her life with a vengeance, like razor-sharp fangs piercing the most tender spot of her flesh. Mary was dead. Kate couldn't ignore that. It was time for her to go home and face her past.

It saddened her to think that death was the only thing that could shake her into realizing her paradigm needed to shift. Slowly, the haze that hung over Kate's heart began to clear. For the first time, she recognized the excuses she'd clung to so desperately for so long as nothing more than trivial hang-ups. But was it too late? To ask for forgiveness and mend the broken, battered fences with her family seemed a nearly impossible feat. But if those fences weren't mended, Kate wasn't sure she could handle the pain of losing Aunt Mary. She needed her family. She wasn't sure they would want her, but she had to try. Mary would have wanted her to try.

Kate sat in quiet, inward reflection until a soft knock sounded behind her.

"Kate," Veronica called gently through the door. "Are you okay? Can I come in?"

Kate stood up and moved to her desk.

"Come in," she called.

"I just lied to half the people in the office," Veronica said as she shut the door behind her. "Your schedule's clear until noon. Shall I clear out your afternoon as well?"

"What did you tell everyone?" Kate asked as she circled her desk and sank into her chair.

Veronica hesitated. "Well, I told them your mother was dead. I figured that was a pretty safe lie since no one really knows you lost your mother a long time ago . . ." Her words trailed off when she saw her boss's reaction. "Oh no, Kate," she said softly. "Someone really did die, didn't they? I'm so sorry."

Kate nodded her head in quiet affirmation. "My aunt Mary died of a heart attack last night."

"Were you really close?" Veronica asked.

Kate was silent for a moment.

*Not as close as we should have been.*

"I guess so," she finally said. "We hadn't talked in a while."

Kate started searching through her desk drawer for some tissue. She had no mirror but imagined how dreadful her tearstained, swollen face must look. "My cousin Leslie called me this morning to let me know."

"Kate, why are you here?" Veronica moved across the room and sat down across from Kate. "People don't work when family members die. They get in the car and go home. They spend time with family and friends and eat casseroles the neighbors bring over. You shouldn't be here. Let me clear your schedule and talk to Mr. Blanton for you."

Kate managed a weak smile and then sighed as she leaned her head into her hands. "You're right," she said quietly. "I don't know why I'm here. I just . . . I didn't know what else to do."

"Go home," Veronica said again. "Blanton will understand. He won't deny you the right to a weekend away for something as important as this."

Kate nodded her head. She knew it was the right thing to do. "Go ahead and clear my schedule." She sighed. "Keep me informed if anything comes up or if Blanton needs me for anything that can't wait."

Veronica nodded, acknowledging Kate's need to be continually in the loop. Kate did not spend a great deal of time away from the office and had never been really comfortable doing so. But Veronica had been her assistant for nearly three years and had proven herself capable of handling things. She could manage the next few days without her.

"Thank you, Veronica," Kate said. "I appreciate your help this morning."

"Just doing my job," she said. She walked to the door then hesitated. "Do you want me to tell Steve?" she asked.

"Steve?" Kate said. "No. I'll go by his office before I go."

Veronica nodded one more time then slipped silently out the door.

Kate was grateful it was only Veronica who had seen her in such a vulnerable state. It would have been much more difficult had it been Mr. Blanton who'd discovered her, tearstained and upset . . . Worse yet, it could have been Steve.

He often came to see her first thing in the morning. It made Kate tired to think of how he would have responded. They had been dating off and on for almost a year, but in the past few months, Steve had pushed for a more serious relationship. But something held Kate back. Steve Carson was the kind of guy who always said and did the right thing. On the surface, he was perfect. But Kate always found herself questioning his sincerity. She couldn't shake the feeling that deep down, the person Steve cared about most was and always would be Steve.

Kate found the little travel pouch of tissue she'd been looking for and, with a bottle of water and the compact from her purse, attempted to clear the mascara from her red and splotchy face.

*Let Steve get a look at me now*, she thought to herself. *See how he feels about puffy eyes, swollen cheeks, and a red, runny nose.* She wiped away the last of the mascara from her cheeks and put on some powder, then pulled the clip from her thick chestnut hair. She used her fingers to loosen it, then shook it out around her shoulders, hoping it might conceal a bit of her morning suffering. Noticing her sunglasses in her bag, she toyed with the idea of slipping them on.

*No*, she thought. *Better to look sad than hung over.*

She stood and looked around. With Veronica taking care of work, there was nothing left to do but say good-bye to Steve and go home to pack.

Steve's office was two doors down from Kate's. Though they worked for the same company, they were, in many respects, rivals: like two football players competing to play quarterback for the same team. They claimed it didn't affect their relationship, but each secretly knew the other would love to be the one who brought in the next big client. Steve talked about working together, forming a partnership that would be even more powerful and persuasive than their individual efforts, but Kate didn't buy it. She suspected that given the opportunity, he'd boot her out of her corner office as quick as he could move himself in.

She stopped outside his door and listened before knocking, not wanting to interrupt anything.

"Gosh, Ms. Sinclair, you look awful!"

Kate turned and looked at Lacey, Steve's assistant, who sat wide-eyed behind her desk. "You musta had a rough night, huh? Were you and Steve out late partying?"

Kate sighed, suddenly grateful for the tact and kindness of her own assistant. Lacey had never been known for exemplary people skills and had a habit of believing that anyone's business ought to be her business as well. On any other occasion, Kate probably would have said something to her about discretion and professionalism, but after the morning she'd had, she just didn't have the energy.

"Is Steve busy?" she asked. "I'm on my way out and need to speak with him before I go."

Lacey glanced at the phone on her desk. "He was on the phone, but, oh, wait, there he went. He just hung up. Shall I let him know you're here?"

"No. I'll just go on in." Kate walked into Steve's office and closed the door.

"Sometimes I wonder where you found that exasperating woman," she said.

Steve looked up from his desk. "Oh, she's not that bad." He smiled. "I like her Southern charm." He stood up to greet Kate with a kiss on her forehead. "Kate, what happened to you? You look awful," he said.

"A fact already well established this morning," she said tersely. Looking into his eyes, pale blue and piercing, Kate saw that he was confused by her tone. He wasn't trying to hurt her and had no idea what her nerves had been through that morning. He didn't deserve her rudeness. She took a deep breath and tried to soften her tone. "I'm going to North Carolina for a week or so. My aunt just passed away. I've got to go to the funeral and spend some time with my family."

"Oh, Kate, I'm so sorry," Steve said. "Were you and your aunt close?"

Kate closed her eyes in exasperation. *Why must everyone ask that question?*

"Yes, we were close," she answered simply.

"Do you . . . do you want me to come with you?" Steve asked.

"No!"

Steve was obviously stung by her hasty rejection, but Kate was not moved. The idea of returning home was complicated enough. The pressure of having him along would only make things more difficult.

"Kate, I wish you'd let me be there for you," he said softly.

"It's not exactly the best place for you to meet my family, is it? A funeral? What would everyone think?" she said.

"I'm not really concerned about your family," he said. "I was thinking more about you and I being together. Work has us so busy; it might be nice to get away for a while." He backed up and sat on the edge of his desk. "Or maybe not."

Kate struggled to hide the irritation in her voice. "Seriously, Steve? A romantic getaway that just happens to include a family funeral? Please don't try to make this about us," she said. "This trip has to be about me.

Things with my family aren't very good right now. I've got to work some stuff out, and I don't really know how it's all going to go."

Suddenly, Steve was in front of her. He took both of her hands and turned her to face him. "You know how I feel about you, Kate. I love you. I want to be here for you, but I can't wait around for you forever."

Kate closed her eyes and internally cringed that now, faced with death and funerals and feelings she could scarcely endure, this man was pressuring her for a commitment. The words *I love you* hung heavily in the air between them. Kate had yet to return the sentiment. "I know you do." She pulled her hands away. "Just let me do this. Let me take some time and work through some things. I'll call you in a couple of days."

Steve ran his fingers through his hair and moved away from her. "You'll call me," he said flatly. "It's always you'll call me, and I'm just supposed to be here smiling and happy when you do."

"My aunt is dead, Steve. Do we have to talk about this now?"

Steve sighed and pressed his fingers against his eyes in frustration. "No, we don't. I'm sorry I said anything." He turned and walked around his desk, flipped open a folder, and studied its contents with feigned interest. "Please offer my condolences to your family."

As he disengaged from their conversation, his demeanor changed like the flip of a light switch. His love and compassion, when not returned in kind, were immediately replaced with intentional indifference.

Kate shook her head. It wasn't supposed to feel this much like a game. "We'll talk soon, okay?" She turned and left without waiting for a response.

*Chapter 2*

THE WALKER HOME WAS A large two-story farmhouse, originally built by Kate's great-grandparents in 1907. It sat in a little glen just outside a tiny pocket of a town called Rose Creek. The town was surrounded by a sea of lush farmland and expansive valleys buffeted on all sides by the smoky blues and greens of the Appalachian Mountains.

The old house had been there for so long, it seemed a permanent and completely natural part of the landscape. Nestled on two acres, with fruit trees and vegetable gardens, it seemed the perfect place to raise a family. A large wraparound porch covered three full sides of the house, welcoming friends and strangers alike with an abundance of rocking chairs, potted plants, and hanging baskets brim full with spring blooms. As a little girl, Kate had loved to sit in those chairs and think of her own mother growing up in the very same house. She imagined her climbing the same trees and picking tomatoes from the same garden patch in the backyard. She loved it when Aunt Mary would tell stories about her childhood, detailing the many things she and her sister had done as little girls. Kate and Leslie would listen to the stories and then, the next afternoon, go out to play the same games and search for the same hiding spots that had sheltered and entertained their mothers years before.

The house, for all of its generations of occupants, was still in remarkably good condition. It had undergone several modernizing renovations over the years, but it had never lost the look of an old farmhouse, and Kate was glad. It would have ruined it, she thought, for the house to be anything other than what it was. Mary's husband, Grey, had done much to maintain the old house, replacing floorboards, mending shutters, and updating fixtures. After he died, Mary had done the best she could to keep things up, but Kate still noticed a few signs of disrepair. The worn wooden siding could use a fresh coat of paint, and several of the steps on the porch needed replacement. Notwithstanding, the house felt unmistakably like home. The familiar sounds and smells were warm and welcoming as Kate climbed the old porch steps.

*It's good to be here*, she thought.

She stood on the porch and wondered if she ought to knock before going in. The house hadn't stirred when she'd pulled up the gravel drive, though the cars parked in front of the house indicated someone was home. Still, she couldn't be certain who might be inside. Losing her nerve, she turned and sat down on the top step of the porch. She leaned her head against the railing and turned her face to the warm afternoon sun.

Spring had invaded the little valley in all its beauty and splendor. The day, even in the warmest hour, was still pleasant, much nicer than the hot, summerlike temperatures she had left behind in Atlanta. She closed her eyes and let the warmth wash over her, bringing with it the memories and emotions that linked her to the house. Sitting there on the porch, she wondered how she had ever stayed away for so long.

*If only I'd come home more often. If only I'd seen Mary one more time. If only I had called. If only . . .*

There were too many reasons to say it. She wiped her tears away and turned at the sound of the front door opening.

"Katie! Is that you?" Mary's sister-in-law Linny came out on the porch and sat down next to Kate. "My gracious, child! How long has it been since I've seen you?" Linny wrapped her arms around Kate's shoulders and pulled her close. "Now tell me why it has to be something sad as this to bring you home. Oh, I've missed you, Katie!" She squeezed her shoulders again.

No one had a more Southern accent than Linny. Words dripped from her mouth like honey falling from a biscuit. She was Uncle Grey's youngest sister and Mary's closest friend. Kate knew how Mary's death must be affecting her, but as long as there were others who needed her, Linny would be strong.

Linny was a first responder—the woman who, come hell or high water, showed up with a casserole and a pan of brownies just in the nick of time. When Aunt Mary broke her leg, it was Linny who took care of everyone until Mary was back on her feet. When Leslie's older brother, Sam, ran away, it was Linny who found him behind the old Holly Springs schoolhouse and talked him into coming back home. Linny and her husband, Charles, had never had children of their own, but they happily spent their entire lives taking care of everyone else's.

She was a small, pleasantly round woman, with thick gray hair she wore pulled up in a loose bun at the base of her neck. Her eyes were a light green and had little specks of yellow that added a bit of mystery to her otherwise simple features. Of all the people Kate could have seen first, she was glad she saw Linny.

"Hi, Linny." She smiled. "It's good to see you too." She sniffed and wiped again at the tears collecting on her lower lashes.

"Have you seen anyone else, dear? Did you just arrive?" Linny asked.

"No, you're the first," Kate responded. "I wasn't sure . . . I didn't know if I should just . . ."

Linny sensed her hesitation and reached for Kate's hand.

"It's not an easy time for any of us, Katie, Leslie especially. She's been through so much loss these past few years. But whatever the two of you have to work out, you're still part of this family. You belong here whether you feel like you do or not."

Kate looked at her aunt, grateful for her straight-shooting assessment.

"I'm sorry I stayed away for so long. It just . . ." Kate looked down at her hands. "It just seemed easier, you know? But I should have come back. It wasn't right what I did."

She kept her eyes down, her head feeling heavy with shame. Her thoughts had mostly focused on Leslie during the drive up from the city. When her cousin had called that morning to tell her of Mary's passing, it was the first time they had spoken in over two years.

"Mother's dead, Kate," Leslie had said icily. "The funeral will be this weekend if you're not too busy to make it."

The animosity in her voice hurt nearly as much as the news of Mary's passing. Kate knew it was punishment she deserved, even wished for, to help assuage her guilt. She carried it with her always—like a small pouch of iron pellets hanging around her neck. It was heavy enough for her to remember its presence and grow weary of the constant tugging on her shoulders but not quite heavy enough to motivate her to action. But now, it was time to end it—time to take off the burdensome necklace of guilt and seek forgiveness.

It didn't seem that long ago that Kate could hardly pass an entire afternoon without wanting to talk to her cousin. As children, they had been inseparable. They had been in first grade when the wicked reality of Kate's parents' death dropped her square in the middle of Leslie's life. The sudden arrival of a new sibling would be an adjustment for anyone, most especially a child, but Leslie had handled it with far more grace than had been expected.

Aunt Mary and Uncle Grey had picked Kate up from the hospital the morning after the accident and taken her home with them. When they arrived, Leslie already had a spot cleared for Kate in her room. She gave Kate the top bunk, but that first night, and most nights after that, the girls slept side by side, leaving the bottom bunk empty. Leslie would wait until she heard the muffled sobs escaping from under Kate's pillow then quietly climb up the ladder at the foot of the bed and slide under the covers next to Kate. She would search for her hand and hold it tightly until the crying stopped.

"Don't tell anyone how much I cry," Kate whispered one night a few weeks after she arrived.

"I won't," Leslie promised. And she never did.

The girls remained close through childhood, but as they grew, their choices and goals began to take them down very different paths. That was enough to create distance between them, but Kate had done more than just take a different path. In the years after she left home, she placed a wedge between them, cold and deep, that splintered their relationship right down the center. In Kate's eyes, the damage was irreparable.

"You're not the only one who's ever made a mistake, Katie," Linny said. "I can't say I haven't been disappointed over some of your choices— confused even—but what's done is done. You're here now, so you best put one foot in front of the other and start moving forward." Linny stood and held her hand out to Kate. "Come on," she said gently. "Let's get you inside."

Kate shook her head. "Leslie doesn't want to see me." She remained seated on the porch, her shoulders slumped forward. "She won't forgive me, and I don't blame her. She was there for me when my world fell apart. But then when she needed me, where was I?"

"You're right about one thing." Linny placed her hands resolutely on her hips. "She doesn't want to see you. But it's got to happen sooner or later. And you're wrong in thinking she won't ever forgive you. She's got a good heart. You just have to give her a chance. There's still a bit of time before Sam and Bryan get in—use it!"

Sam and Bryan were Leslie's brothers. Both lived out of town.

Kate looked up then finally let her aunt pull her to her feet. "Linny?" She paused before they went into the house. "Was Aunt Mary alone when she died?"

Linny frowned. "She was. As far as we can tell, the heart attack happened around dinner time. She didn't call 911, so it must have come on suddenly. Leslie called her that evening, and when she didn't get an answer, she came over and found her. That was last night about 8:00."

Kate shook her head. "She was so young. It doesn't make sense for it to have happened so quickly. And for Leslie to lose her like this," she continued, "after all she's been through."

"It's been hard on her, that's for sure. She's still pretty shaken up about being the one to find her." Linny stopped, her hand resting on the knob of the front door.

"She needs you, Katie. And you need her. She might not know it yet, and you may not be willing to admit it, but that's the way it is. And nothing's going to change it either."

Kate sighed and looked out at the afternoon shadows dancing across the lawn. "Let's go in, then," she said softly.

## Chapter 3

LINNY USHERED KATE INTO THE familiar living room. Everything was just as she remembered. The outdated furniture still sat in the same spots, the pictures all hung in the same places, and the back of the couch was still covered with the same patchwork quilt from her childhood. Kate remembered the summer she and Leslie had helped Aunt Mary put it together. Mary gave the girls the assignment of deciding where all the different patches would go. They studied and moved each piece around tirelessly until each one was perfectly placed, a blissful union of complementary colors and patterns on all sides. Aunt Mary oohed and ahhed over every decision, congratulating the girls on their excellent taste. It was years before the cousins realized that with patchwork, it didn't really matter where each piece went.

A long bench sat by the front door, with a row of hooks hung directly above, presumably for coats and keys. Instead, Mary had filled the hooks with odds and ends—a macaroni necklace made by one of the grandchildren, a misplaced Christmas ornament, and a little wooden sign that read, "Home is where the heart is." Only the last hook was used for its intended purpose. Mary's sweater hung there, her purse sitting on the bench just below.

It was almost too much for Kate. She braced herself against the doorjamb as memories flooded her mind. She saw Mary, walking ahead of her through the garden with her pale pink sweater tied around her waist in the heat of a spring afternoon. She heard her laugh and smile and saw the tiny red roses that detailed the collar and sleeves of the sweater. She looked at the purse and remembered the faint smell of wintergreen that always clung to the inside.

*Wintergreen breath mints*, she thought. *She always had wintergreen breath mints.*

Kate took a deep breath and looked across the room at Leslie, standing stone still in front of the fireplace. Leslie made little effort to hide her disdain. Obviously, she hadn't been expecting Kate's arrival.

"Kate," she said curtly. "I wasn't sure you would come."

"Hello, Leslie," Kate replied softly. "It's been a long time." Kate didn't want to argue with her cousin. Though she wouldn't take all of the blame for the disintegration of their relationship, she knew she'd acted poorly and had been the first to sow seeds of unnecessary hurt and heartache. She could not begrudge Leslie's animosity. After all, how did you forgive someone for skipping your husband's funeral?

It was 5:30 on a Tuesday evening when Kate had learned that Leslie's husband, Tom, had finally succumbed to the harsh and unforgiving cancer ravaging his body. Kate had just left the office and was on her way to meet some friends for a drink when Aunt Mary called and told her the news.

Even as she'd said the words, Kate had realized she was making a mistake. But so much time had passed. She hadn't had a real conversation with Leslie in months. "I can't come home, Aunt Mary," she had said. "It's my first major presentation, and I'm team leader. If I miss the meeting, I'll lose my job."

Aunt Mary knew as well as Kate that it wasn't true, but she'd never been one to argue.

So Kate had missed the funeral.

Instead, she'd gone to work and nailed her presentation, landing her company one of its most profitable clients. That was two years ago.

Linny pushed Kate from behind, urging her farther into the room.

"Well, come on now, girls," she said. "You'll work nothing out just staring at each other."

Kate looked down in embarrassment. Leave it to Linny to jump right in and get to the point.

"I'll take the kids into the kitchen, and the two of you just sit right here for a spell." She walked across the room, pausing before she pushed the kitchen door open. "Mary wouldn't want you fighting, girls," she said calmly. She turned to Leslie's children. "Come on, then, children. Are you hungry? Let's see if we can find any cookies."

Leslie interrupted. "Actually, Linny, I promised the kids Happy Meals tonight. Please, don't bother with cookies or anything." Leslie reached for her purse and started digging for her keys.

"Happy Meals? Well, how 'bout I take them into town to get Happy Meals? Would you kids like that?"

The children cheered at the prospect of dinner with Aunt Linny. Leslie was visibly frustrated that her attempt at departure was thwarted, but grudgingly shrugged her shoulders in acquiescence and dropped her purse back onto the chair. Kate sat down on the sofa and watched as Leslie picked up the youngest of her children and helped him slip on his shoes. The baby, Tommy, was born just six months before Leslie's husband passed away. That would make him nearly three years old. Kate lowered her gaze, biting her lip in shame. *Three years old and he's never met his aunt Kate.*

"You have fun with Aunt Linny," Leslie whispered into Tommy's ear. "Nicholas," she said, looking up at her oldest. "Help your aunt with Tommy, okay?" Nicholas nodded his head and reached for his little brother's hand.

"I'll help too, Mamma," the middle child, a little girl, said sweetly.

Leslie smiled. "I know you will, Emily." She reached up and refastened a bobby pin behind Emily's ear. "You have fun too, and don't drink any Coke. I don't want you to be up all night."

Leslie looked up at Linny, who nodded her head in agreement.

"Let's go, Emily," Linny said, extending her hand. But Emily didn't take it. Instead, she walked over to Kate.

"You're Kate," she said, a statement rather than a question.

"Yes, I am," Kate replied, smiling at the little girl. "And you are Emily." Emily looked a lot like her mother. Thick blonde curls framed her petite face, and freckles dotted her nose and cheeks. But her eyes—they didn't look like Leslie's at all. Emily's eyes were a perfect reflection of her aunt Kate's: green, like moss, Aunt Mary always said, or maple leaves just after a good, hard rain.

"I don't really remember you," Emily said.

Kate's face flushed with the heat of regret as she looked into the wide eyes of her niece. "I . . . well," she stuttered. "I live in a different city."

"Do you have a family?"

"No," Kate said. "It's just me."

"My mommy always says you're too busy to visit, so I thought you must have lots of kids or something. If you don't have a family, what do you have?"

"Emily," Leslie interjected. "Aunt Linny's waiting for you. Hurry to the car now."

Emily nodded to her mother but turned back to Kate, waiting for her answer.

Kate found herself feeling defensive. "I have a job," she said.

"Is it important?"

Suddenly, Kate wasn't sure. She shook off her doubt. "Yes. It is important."

"Okay." Emily smiled and patted Kate's hand.

The little girl disappeared out the door and left the two women in the living room alone.

"She's beautiful," Kate said, watching from the window as Emily danced her way down the front stairs and into Linny's station wagon. "She's grown so much."

"Of course she's grown. It's been three years, Kate. You haven't been here since before Tommy was born." Leslie's words, while laced with bitterness, were still heavy with the exhaustion and pain of the past twenty-four hours.

Kate's eyes welled with tears as she looked at her cousin. She had always been the classic beauty—blonde hair, large blue eyes, and a perfect heart-shaped mouth. In stark contrast to Leslie's fair complexion, Kate's dark hair and mysterious eyes did little to establish a likeness between the two. While Leslie favored her mother's side of the family, Kate looked like her father. As a little girl, she loved it when people would stop and comment on the similarities—a shared nose, high cheekbones, and the same engaging smile. Kate would laugh and smile and climb into her father's lap, rubbing the rough whiskers on his cheeks.

"How can we look alike when you're so hairy?" she would ask.

After her parents died, she would sit in front of the mirror for hours, searching for her father's face in her own reflection.

The last ten years had aged Leslie little. She barely looked old enough to have three children and most certainly didn't seem old enough to have lost a mother, father, and husband. As Leslie sank into the soft, overstuffed chair and leaned her head back on the cushions, only the dark circles under her eyes and the worry lines creased across her forehead bore witness to her age. When Kate looked at her, she still saw the doe-eyed sophomore pointing at Tom Greenwood across the gym during a homecoming dance and saying, "That's the man I'm going to marry." Kate had laughed and rolled her eyes, but Leslie never had a doubt in her mind. She and Tom had danced together four times that night and never dated anyone else but each other. Kate was still in college when, just a year after their wedding, Nicholas was born.

Ten years later, parenthood was still a foreign concept to Kate. It made her head spin just thinking about that sort of responsibility. But it was exactly what Leslie had always wanted.

Kate wiped her tears away and moved over to the couch and sat directly across from Leslie.

"Leslie," she began. "I'm so sorry. I'm sorry about your mom, and I'm so sorry about Tom, and I'm just . . . I don't know what else to say."

"Words can't undo what's been done," Leslie replied coolly, her eyes closed. "They won't bring Mother back, and they most certainly won't bring Tom back. I don't know your reasons for staying away"—she finally looked up to meet her cousin's eyes—"but we've all been through a lot around here—me, the children, Sam and Bryan, and Mother too. Not to mention Linny. That poor woman has worked harder than anybody to keep this family from falling apart. And we did it all, Kate, we did it all without you around. I'm glad you're here. Mother deserves that much after all she's done for you and how much she cared about you. But just know we're not expecting anything else. Stay for the funeral and then go back to your job, to your life in the city."

Kate sat silently as the weight of her cousin's words settled upon her. It seemed simple, really. Stay for the next two days and finish out the funeral services then drive back to Atlanta in time for work on Monday morning. But it wasn't simple. Work would call her back eventually, but she could not leave without making an effort to pick up the scattered pieces of the relationships around her and painstakingly put them back together.

"Sam and Bryan should be here any minute," Leslie said wearily, interrupting Kate's pondering. "I expect they'll be staying here at the house, but they won't need our old room. You can stay there if you like. We've got to be at the funeral home early tomorrow to make all the arrangements—the viewing tomorrow night, I guess, and then the funeral Sunday afternoon. There's no reason for you to bother with going in the morning though. We'll be able to manage just fine without you." Leslie rose at the sound of gravel crunching outside. "I bet that's one of the boys," she said, moving to the door.

Kate felt like a stranger as she sat and listened to her cousins' heartfelt greetings in the driveway. When the voices moved toward the house, she rose and snuck into the kitchen. Noisily, she busied herself with making a pot of coffee to justify her disappearance. She pulled a serving tray down off the top shelf of the pantry and filled it, just as she had seen her aunt Mary do so many times before with the coffee pot and cups. The old blue coffee cups of Kate's childhood had been replaced, she noticed, with four shiny new ones, each one decorated with a smiling photo of each of Mary's four grandchildren. Kate looked at each of the smiling faces: Leslie's three children and then Sam's daughter, Kenzie.

Sam was Mary and Grey's oldest son—a physician living in Asheville, an hour east of Rose Creek. His wife, Teresa, was also a doctor. Just a few months before Tom found out about his cancer, Sam and Teresa had been in Atlanta for a medical conference. Kate met them for a quick lunch but hadn't been able to stay long. She had a client waiting for her at the office, she'd told them. She hadn't seen Sam since and had spoken to him only a handful of times. After Kate skipped Tom's funeral, she hadn't heard much from anyone in the family. Anyone, that is, except Mary. Mary had always called.

Kate picked up the small dish of sugar from its customary home on the kitchen table and added it, with the cream from the refrigerator, to the tray. She lifted the tray and walked toward the living room, pausing when she heard Sam's voice through the door.

"Who's in the kitchen?" he asked his little sister. "Is Bryan here already?"

"No," Leslie responded. "That's Kate."

"Really? Kate is here?"

Sam sounded incredulous, and Kate half expected him to stick his head into the kitchen just to verify Leslie's claim. She backed through the doorway carrying the coffee and greeted her older cousin.

"Hello, Sam," she said. "It's nice to see you." Kate set the tray down on the coffee table and crossed over to where Sam and Teresa stood. "Hello, Teresa."

Sam exchanged glances with his wife and sister before greeting Kate, surprising her with a big hug. "Hi, Katie." He took Kate by the shoulders and looked into her eyes. "It really is good to see you. I'm glad you're here."

Kate was touched by his sincerity. "Thanks. It's good to see you too. I made some coffee," she quickly added. "I thought you might need some after the drive over."

"I'd love some," Teresa finally spoke. "But I'm going to put this little girl down first." She hoisted the sleeping child higher in her arms and headed upstairs.

"How old is she now, Sam?" Kate asked.

"She'll be two next month. Growing like a weed, that little girl." He smiled and accepted the coffee his cousin offered him.

Bryan arrived not long after Sam. Bryan was Mary's second son and youngest child. A bit of a wild hair, Bryan had often tested his parents' patience and faith as he'd chased his dreams from one corner of the earth to the other. And yet, he managed with such optimism and spirit that one could hardly argue the path he'd chosen wasn't perfectly suited for him. He'd backpacked across Europe, spent six months on the Appalachian Trail, and even spent a season working as a fisherman off the coast of Alaska. Until recently, when he settled down just a few towns over from Rose Creek, no one could remember the last time he'd had a permanent address. Kate admired his ability to live so freely without managing to upset anyone in the family. It seemed her efforts at self-discovery had never been quite as successful.

Bryan greeted Kate with a big hug, acting as if her extended absence from family gatherings was nothing more than mere circumstance. Kate was happy not to feel on the defensive, but she couldn't help but wonder how the men really felt about her past actions.

Leslie spent much of the evening avoiding Kate's gaze, focusing on her brothers instead. Kate worried that her presence was perhaps making things worse for her cousin, adding awkwardness to the already difficult process of grieving. She reminded herself, though, that she was also grieving. Aunt Mary, for the largest part of her childhood, was just as much a mother to her as she had been to her own children.

*She was my family too*, she thought.

The stories came one after another. Some were sad and tinged with regret, while others were of a happier, reflective sort, looking back on memories created by a happy childhood and a pleasant home. Kate made a few meager contributions to the conversation but was drawn more and more into her own thoughts. She found herself wishing she had an entire evening's worth of conversation with which to remember her own mother. The space in her mind where she cherished the bits and pieces of her parents seemed but a small and dusty corner.

Much of what Kate did remember came in broken chunks: tiny pieces of indistinguishable moments, slivers of memories too fragmented to combine into one singular event. There were a few tangible moments Kate could recall—a trip to the zoo when she spent the entire afternoon sitting on her dad's shoulders and dinner the night before her parents died. They'd gone to Pizza Hut, and Kate's mother had let her order an entire pizza with pineapple on it just for her—no one liked pineapple pizza but Kate. As she watched the matching eyes of her cousins look to one another for solace, seeking and finding comfort in knowing that they shared their suffering and endured together, she longed for a sibling—for someone else who knew what it was to have your heart ripped from your child-sized chest, to have nurses tell you your parents were gone, that family was on the way to get you, to take care of you. Pain washed over her anew as she thought of that miserable night.

Bryan noticed her distress and reached across the couch, placing his hand gently on her back. "Losing people we love is never easy," he said. He looked up and watched as Leslie and Teresa stood and carried the empty coffee cups into the kitchen.

"It hasn't really hit her yet, has it?" Bryan asked, speaking of Leslie.

"Of course it has," Sam responded. "But she's a mother. She's keeping it together because she knows she has to."

"She always has been a fighter," Bryan said. "If this doesn't knock her down, nothing will."

## Chapter 4

LESLIE AVOIDED KATE ALL WEEKEND, effectively dodging all unnecessary conversation. The lack of communication was frustrating, but Kate reasoned it could have been much worse. Rose Creek was a small town. People knew she hadn't been home in years and remembered her notable absence during the months of Tom's illness and death. Her mere presence was enough to get people talking, reigniting discussion about her and Leslie's feud all over town. Through it all, Leslie was polite and respectful, responding to questions and comments about Kate with grace and charm. Any ill will Leslie harbored, she did so secretly. Still, the constant scrutiny made Kate uncomfortable, and she found herself itching to get back to her home and life in the city. All the reasons Kate had stayed away from Rose Creek—from Leslie—came flooding back.

It hadn't always been that way. At first, it was only physical distance that separated them. But as life progressed, it became more and more difficult for the two women to relate. While Leslie was making cupcakes for Nicholas's preschool class and hosting playdates, Kate was getting an apartment in downtown Atlanta and starting her first job as a junior marketing specialist for an advertising group. Leslie went to PTA meetings and well-child checkups while Kate attended gallery openings and wine tastings. When a second child and then a third joined Leslie's family, it felt as if Kate were on a completely different wavelength from Leslie.

Kate was happy with the decisions she had made in her life and didn't judge Leslie for the path she had chosen, but *Kate* felt judged. She found it difficult not to feel like her small-town friends and family were all waiting for her "real" life to start. They assumed Kate's job in the city was simply something to pass the time until she got married and moved back to Rose Creek to start a family. On the rare occasions when Kate returned home for weekend gatherings or holiday events, everyone would touch her gently on the arm and say, "It's all right, Katie, you'll meet someone soon, and then you'll have a family just like Leslie."

The trouble was that Kate didn't *want* what Leslie had. But to explain as much made her come across as jealous and bitter. So she stopped explaining. And then she simply stopped going home. Work was often to blame, but more times than not, Kate didn't have a reason beyond her own discomfort to stay away.

When she was feeling most sorry for herself, she was convinced that things would be different if her own parents were still alive. They would accept her and love her for who she was and the choices she made. It was just too hard, she decided, too hard in the Walker household to forget that she wasn't a daughter or sister. She was only a cousin.

*Only a cousin*, Kate thought, *and a poor one at that.*

But not this time. She would not run away from Leslie again. There was still far too much that needed to be said.

When Sam came to her Sunday evening after the services and asked if she could stay in town for one more day, Kate was happy to do so. Though it wasn't Sam's reason for asking, Kate hoped it might give her another opportunity to talk to Leslie.

"We've got an appointment to meet with the attorney on Monday morning," Sam said. "He'll read the official version of Mother's will. We all need to be there for that."

Kate called her office and easily secured a few more days off. Blanton had even encouraged her to take the week if need be, though she had no intention of staying away from the office that long.

Early Monday morning before the rest of the house stirred, Kate rose and put on her workout clothes and running shoes. They'd been a last-minute addition to her packing. She'd thought at first that exercising would be last on her list of priorities the weekend of a funeral, but running was a great way to relieve stress and was, on that morning, exactly what she needed. She sat down on the front porch steps to tighten her laces and pull her hair up into a ponytail, then started off down the gravel drive. The sun was just beginning to peek over the mountains, which were light green with early spring. The air was clean and crisp, still lacking the heavy humidity that would soon fill the summer months. It was invigorating to Kate as she headed onto the main road. There were no sidewalks, so Kate hugged the shoulder and watched for oncoming traffic. But this was Rose

Creek, she remembered. Even at the busiest time of day, these roads would see only a handful of cars.

A half mile into her run, Kate turned left to jog one of her favorite stretches of road. On one side, a steep, hilly pasture stretched upward, full of grazing cows that studied Kate quizzically as she passed by. On the other side, acres and acres of freshly planted tomato fields filled the valley. Beyond the fields, rolling pastures climbed the hillsides, reaching toward the mountains that rose majestically into the pale blue of the early-morning sky. Kate watched as a small army of workers maneuvered their way through the dewy plants. The scene was timeless. Replace the brightly colored baseball caps and the soft cotton T-shirts of the workers with rough homespun and straw hats and Kate could be back in time two hundred years. It was one of the things she loved most about Rose Creek.

Kate's thoughts turned to her cousin, home with her kids, probably just waking up and starting breakfast. She wondered what it would be like to be a familiar part of the children's lives. She imagined them welcoming her as she stopped by on her morning run, grabbing a water bottle from the refrigerator, and stealing a bite of pancake off of Emily's plate. For a moment, it almost seemed possible. As she ran the streets of her old home and imagined the happy scene among her niece and nephews, she surprised herself by thinking maybe there *was* a life for her in Rose Creek. Of course, you couldn't have a table full of happy children without someone there to make the pancakes. Leslie's presence in the kitchen quickly dashed Kate's daydream right into the pavement beneath her feet.

Glancing at her watch, Kate turned again and ran toward the elementary school, another mile down the road. The running was physically therapeutic, loosening the tightness in her muscles accumulated through the tense and anxious weekend, but it did little to slow the circuitous spinning in Kate's mind. Her thoughts jumped from Leslie's kitchen to Mary to her mother and father to Linny and then back to Leslie. When she tried to push Rose Creek from her frame of consciousness, her brain jumped to Atlanta and involuntarily focused on Steve. Just before setting out that morning, she'd checked her voice mail and had three separate messages from him. It almost made her ashamed to realize how little she'd thought of him the past few days.

*That can't be a good sign*, she thought to herself. Except, maybe it was a good sign. Kate realized she would never feel for Steve what he felt for her. She was weary of his mind games and his constant pressuring. It wasn't fun anymore. She would have to talk to him, though Kate dreaded the mental energy that conversation would require. Turning up the volume on her iPod, she sped up, trying to outpace the arduous weight of her own thoughts.

Pumping her arms, Kate pushed her way up the last stretch of hill before reaching the elementary school. The little brick building had one of the best views in the entire valley. Nestled among sprawling oak trees and flowering dogwoods, it overlooked acres and acres of protected farmland. The richly colored mountains climbed in the distance, creating a picturesque, almost enchanted setting for the little school. And then the best part, if you asked the children: the back side of the school overlooked the little runway to Rose Creek Airport. Kate remembered standing on the playground during recess, watching the small, single-engine planes take off and land, often circling right over the school. On rare occasions, something bigger would fly into Rose Creek, and all of the kids would race to the windows of the school to watch, wondering what important person warranted such a large plane.

Kate paused at the top of the hill to catch her breath. The school was out of session for spring break and was quietly unoccupied. She pulled off her headphones and stood alone in the parking lot, looking down toward the airport, also still in the early-morning hour. She took a slow, deep breath and noticed how at odds the scene seemed with the general nature of her life. There was little simplicity in a big city. She missed this—the solitude and serenity.

"I've never seen anyone else running here before."

Kate turned, startled by the voice of a man now standing next to her. He was bent over with his hands resting on his knees. He was obviously trying to catch his breath, likely after making the same steep climb that led up to the school.

"No, I, uh, I don't run here often . . . I live in Atlanta," Kate responded.

"Wow. That's some run, all the way up from Atlanta," he joked.

Kate rolled her eyes. "Ha, ha," she said sarcastically.

He stood then, and Kate saw his face clearly. She didn't think he'd grown up in Rose Creek. He looked to be about her age, and Kate thought she would have recognized him had they gone to school together. No, she was certain she had never seen this man before. He was tall, with brown hair and chocolate eyes so dark they almost looked black. Kate realized she was staring and quickly turned away, hoping the pink of exertion would cover the blush now warming her cheeks.

"Well, I do run here," the man said, "every morning, and that stupid hill hasn't gotten any easier yet."

"Oh, it's not so bad," Kate teased. "I was actually thinking of running it again just for fun."

The man laughed. "Yeah, well, you have fun with that. I'll just stay here and be exhausted."

Kate looked at his finely muscled arms and well-worn running shoes and guessed perhaps he was feigning a bit of his exhaustion. "I ran cross country growing up," Kate said to the stranger. "We'd run over from the high school and run sprints up and down this hill for practice."

"Oh, that's brutal!" He paused. "Wait, I thought you didn't live here."

"I grew up here," Kate replied. "But I moved away a long time ago." For a moment, Kate had forgotten why she was here in Rose Creek, why she was running, what she was running away from, but it all came back, settling nicely in her stomach like a solid, immovable piece of lead.

"I'm Andrew Porterfield," the man said warmly.

His smile drew her in, lifting her up from the inside out. She shook his hand. "I'm Kate," she replied. "Kate Sinclair."

"Well, Kate Sinclair, it's a pleasure running into you this morning. Are you in town for long?"

"Um, no," Kate answered, hoping her disappointment wasn't too obvious. "I'm actually heading back to the city tonight."

"Oh, that's too bad," Andrew replied. His voice was casual, uncommitted, but Kate thought she sensed a bit of disappointment on his end as well. "Maybe we'll see each other the next time you're in town."

"I hope so," Kate replied, and she meant it. She hoped he would ask for her number or even her e-mail address before running on, but he didn't.

He smiled one more time, and then just as quickly as he appeared, he took off running down the road. Kate watched him for a few moments and then turned, making her own way home.

One thing was certain: she no longer had any doubts about ending things with Steve.

# Chapter 5

WALTER MARSHALL'S LAW OFFICE SAT in a little corner building adjacent to the courthouse, squeezed in between an insurance agency and a little lunch café. Kate waited with the rest of her family among the dusty plastic plants and heavy leather-upholstered furniture that filled the small lobby of the office. Everyone was weary after the weekend, and little conversation passed among the siblings. Sam, as the executor of his mother's estate, assured everyone the will was simple and straightforward. No surprises, nothing complicated.

Aunt Mary and Uncle Grey had lived a relatively modest lifestyle and had been very diligent in their savings. Mary's untimely death left a generous sum behind that everyone assumed would simply be divided among the children. Kate wondered where she would fit in. It wasn't that she needed the money. She had a good job and was quite capable of providing for her needs. She feared the sting of exclusion more and the loneliness that would surely accompany such a slight. Sam said the attorney was very clear in requiring that all family members be present, but Kate still felt uneasy.

Mr. Marshall's secretary led them back to a large conference room. A massive oak table sat in the center of the windowless room and was surrounded by large, square-backed chairs. Floor-to-ceiling bookshelves packed tightly with stuffy law volumes and county record books lined the walls. The room was void of decoration or warmth, with the exception of a plastic fern in the center of the table and velvet-trimmed purple cushions on the seat of each chair. Kate immediately noticed the cushions and was struck by how ridiculous they looked in the otherwise characterless room.

"Sorry to keep you waiting," Mr. Marshall said as he waddled through the door. He was a small man, just over five feet tall, with a round protruding middle and a round balding head. What little hair he had stuck out in silvery tufts above each ear, circling down and around the base of his scalp. His nose seemed entirely too small for his face and barely held up the wire-rimmed spectacles perched delicately upon it. Kate thought he must be near sixty and wondered how he managed to keep up in a courtroom. But then, this was Rose Creek—hardly a hotbed for criminals or high-profile divorce cases.

*Let's hope the reading of one Mary Ellen Walker's will is as low key as the rest of Rose Creek*, she thought to herself.

Sam had met Mr. Marshall on one other occasion and, after greeting the attorney, introduced the rest of his family. Mr. Marshall smiled, his eyes disappearing into the folds of his face, and invited everyone to take a seat. Kate moved to the opposite side of the table and sat down next to Bryan, across from Leslie, Sam, and Teresa.

"Where are the matching curtains?" Bryan whispered as he settled onto his purple cushion.

Kate smiled at her cousin as Mr. Marshall started to speak.

"Well, should we just get started, then?" He pushed his spectacles up on his nose, then pulled a handkerchief out of his pocket, dabbing gently at his brow. "Your mother, Ms. Walker," he said, "came in many years ago with her husband and worked out her affairs right here in this office." His words were slow and thick, with the gentleness of typical Southern delivery. "Her will is simple and straightforward," he continued, "and stayed the same, even after the death of her husband. She did, however, make one amendment since then that I'll include in the reading." He looked up and glanced around the room. "Does that suit everyone?" he asked.

When everyone nodded, Mr. Marshall began.

"'I, Mary Ellen Walker, of Harrison County, North Carolina, declare this to be my last will and testament. My residuary estate, being all of my real and personal property, wherever located, not otherwise effectively disposed of, shall be disposed as follows:

—To my children—Samuel, Leslie, and Bryan—I leave my residuary estate to be divided in equal shares in fee simple.'"

Mr. Marshall looked up from the file before him and then pulled out another sheet, handing a copy to each of Aunt Mary's immediate children. He motioned to Sam. "As executor, Mr. Walker was relatively aware of what your mother's estate contained. Though it will not compensate for your loss, each of you, her immediate children, will receive quite a generous sum of inheritance. The sheet before you indicates this amount."

Kate looked down at the sheet of paper in front of Bryan—$37,000. It was a generous sum—a sum left specifically for Mary's children. Not for her. It hurt worse than she had anticipated. Bryan reached under the table and grabbed her hand, then turned to Mr. Marshall and his older brother.

"Surely the will doesn't indicate that Kate be excluded, Sam. She's a part of this family."

"Bryan, it's all right," Kate said quickly. "You don't need to—" She stopped as Mr. Marshall raised his hands.

"That actually brings us to the amendment Ms. Walker filed shortly before her death," he said.

Kate looked up, searching the faces of her cousins for any indication of awareness. They all looked as startled as she did. They turned in unison to Mr. Marshall.

"'To my niece, Katherine Isabelle Sinclair, I leave the property, in its entirety, 728 Red Dogwood Lane, including the land and structure and all that is contained therein.'"

Leslie spoke for the first time. "There must be some mistake," she said, rising from her chair. "That's the house . . . That's Mother's house. That house is included in this, in this that she left to all of us!" She held up the paper that had been sitting on the table in front of her. The color rose quickly in her pale cheeks, her eyes wide with astonishment and anger. She turned to her brother. "Did you know anything about this, Sam?"

Sam shook his head. "No, Leslie. Mother didn't tell me she made any changes, but she had that right. You didn't expect her to exclude Kate, did you?" he questioned. "She is part of this family."

"Mr. Marshall," Leslie pleaded. "Really, this must be some sort of mistake. I really feel my mother would want that house to be for her grandchildren . . . for my children."

"I'm sorry, dear," Mr. Marshall responded. "Your mother was certainly of a sound mind when she came to me and requested I add the specification. There is no mistake. The house belongs to Ms. Sinclair."

"But it was my mother's house! It was my house!" Her voice was shrill, intensified by her disbelief.

Kate had been silent through all the debating, motionless as waves of shock, sadness, and utter amazement took turns washing over her racing heart. But Leslie's words struck a chord deep within Kate's conscience. When she spoke, the words came from a place so deep and dark inside her she hardly recognized them as her own. "It was my mother's house too, Leslie," she said calmly.

"What?" Leslie asked.

"My mother." Kate's voice rose, thick with emotion. "She lived in that house too, grew up there, just like your mother did. Please don't forget about her. Perhaps it would have been her house had things been different. It would have been her growing old, watching her grandkids play in the yard, drinking lemonade on the porch. But that will never happen, Leslie." Tears suddenly erupted, flowing freely down Kate's face. "That will never happen because my mother is dead. She died long before she ever had the opportunity to build up an inheritance, to leave me anything but a few fragments of memories, fuzzy photos, and ticket stubs from the circus. That's all I have—hardly enough to fill a shoebox. Do you know what that feels like? I lived in the house almost as many years as you did. It was the family's farmhouse. And even though you seem dead set on forgetting, I am a part of this family."

No one spoke. Leslie stared at her cousin, eyes wide. She slowly lowered herself back into her chair and looked down at the table. The silence was finally broken by Mr. Marshall, who cleared his throat.

"Well then. Shall I just continue on?" He pushed forward, leaving no time for any objection.

"There is one thing in regard to the house that I imagine you are all aware of," the attorney continued. "It seems it is one of the properties listed as 'under negotiations' with the State Department of Transportation regarding a highway going through the valley. Was your mother in the process of negotiating the sale of this home?" He looked first to Sam for an answer.

Sam immediately shook his head. "No, that must be old information. The house was in danger at one point. There were two possible routes for the highway, only one of which came near the farmhouse. It's been going on for years, the town meetings, the petitions. Mother fought with all she had to keep her house off that list. And it worked. Just, oh, I don't know, two months or so ago, she received a letter indicating the state's decision to use the route that did not include our house." Sam paused, smiling at the memory. "It was the happiest I've seen my mother in a long time. She was so relieved."

Kate looked down at her hands, embarrassed that something as critical as the potential loss of the farmhouse had plagued the family for years, as Sam had mentioned, and yet she'd known nothing of the impending danger.

*Why would Mary fight so hard to keep the house and then give it to me? I don't deserve it.*

"Ah," Mr. Marshall said. "Well, that would roughly coincide with the final change Mary made to her will. Perhaps her assumed victory inspired her to think of Ms. Sinclair." He smiled in Kate's direction. "What that doesn't explain," he continued, "is why, if two months ago the house was no longer a property of interest, the deed would still be flagged. This paperwork all seems current, dated just last week. Has your mother received anything else, then, from the department of transportation or perhaps from the county board of commissioners?"

Sam looked at Leslie and shrugged his shoulders. "I don't know of anything. Leslie, did Mother mention anything to you?"

"She told me everything about the house," Leslie answered. "I knew everything that was going on. I even read the letter that told her the house was no longer in question. If she received anything else, I would have known about it. She would have told me." Leslie was answering Sam and the attorney, but it was clear her words were meant for Kate.

"Mr. Marshall, it must be a mistake," Sam reiterated. "Surely the state would send notification if something had changed."

"You could be right, Mr. Walker, and I hope you are. At any rate, I feel it my dutiful responsibility to make certain. I will make some calls this afternoon and see what I can find out. Ms. Sinclair, would it be all right if I contact you directly if I am able to learn anything further?"

Kate suddenly felt very overwhelmed. Not only was she a brand-new homeowner, but she was a homeowner in a potential battle with the State Department of Transportation.

"Um, well, sure. I . . . Yes. That would be fine," she finally concluded. "I can leave you my cell number before I go."

Mr. Marshall read through the remaining portions of Aunt Mary's will and then led the family through the consent and agreement of all parties involved, the signing, and the explanations and definitions as required by law. Kate was barely aware of the proceedings. The only thing she felt was the heavy pounding of her own heart and the intense heat of Leslie's insufferable stare bearing down on her.

# Chapter 6

LATER THAT AFTERNOON, KATE SAT on the porch of the old white farmhouse, now empty, and wondered what on earth she was going to do. Sam and Teresa had come back to the house for lunch, but they'd left shortly after for Asheville. While a little surprised at their mother's decision to leave the house to Kate, they hadn't seemed bothered by it. For that, Kate was grateful. Bryan left for Maggie Valley directly after the meeting with Mr. Marshall but had assured Kate he was okay too as long as she didn't touch anything in his old room until he'd gone through it himself.

"You think I want to find what's hidden in that room, Bry?" Kate had joked.

She sighed deeply and leaned her head back against the worn slats of her rocking chair.

The house, of all things, was the last thing she had expected. Suddenly, she was faced with so many choices and had little idea of where to begin. Selling wasn't an option. And she most definitely didn't have any intention of moving back to Rose Creek herself. It seemed silly that the house should sit empty. The logical part of Kate wondered if she should have accepted Leslie's offer made shortly after the meeting with Mr. Marshall. Once the fireworks had all fizzled out, Leslie had approached Kate, offering a simple exchange.

"I'm sure Mother had the best of intentions, whatever her reason for doing it this way, Kate. But it just doesn't make much sense, you, alone in this big house. And with your job in the city, I just think it's more practical for me to have the house," she had said.

And for all that seemed good and practical, she was right. It did make more sense for her to have the house. The old house would fall apart quickly without someone to tend to its needs. Leslie could do that. Her children could fill it up, bring friends over, and crowd around the kitchen table. They could climb the trees and plant vegetables in the garden. They could keep the house breathing.

For a moment, Kate nearly conceded. The words sat on the tip of her tongue as she thought of the house alive and cared for.

But the old walls seemed to beckon her, taking hold of her heart and making it impossible for her to relinquish her claim. The house was hers. It had to be hers. For some reason she didn't understand and some purpose much bigger than she could presently comprehend, the house on Red Dogwood Lane was a permanent part of her future.

She'd been adamant in her rejection of Leslie's offer. "I'm sorry, Leslie," she'd said firmly. "Aunt Mary wanted me to have this house. I may not understand why, but I can't let it go."

Kate couldn't fathom why her aunt would ever feel compelled to give the house to her. Leslie did not understand either. In her estimation, the house was always destined to be hers. But the only thing Kate could conclude was that Aunt Mary remembered that, as Kate had so vehemently shared in the conference room that morning, the house did, at one point, belong to Kate's mother as well. Whatever the reason, and as confused as Kate felt about the house's future, she was grateful to her aunt for remembering her in such a magnificent way. It was much, much more than she felt she deserved.

Kate looked up as she heard the sound of an approaching car. She smiled as she watched Linny's old blue station wagon wind its way down the gravel drive. Kate was glad to see her. Linny had a way of making any situation seem, at the very least, optimistically tolerable. She stood and walked down to greet Linny.

"Hello, dear," Linny said gently. She reached up and pulled Kate into a warm embrace. "Are you all right?"

"I'm fine, Linny," Kate responded. "A little overwhelmed, but I think I'll be okay."

The two women crossed the driveway and climbed the steps to the rocking chairs, where Kate had been sitting on the far side of the porch.

"Let's sit a spell," Linny said as she relaxed into the nearest chair.

Kate had loved these chairs as a little girl, and she still loved them. They were made of a simple oak and had extra curves to make them more comfortable.

"You talked to Leslie, then?" Kate asked.

"Leslie?" Linny responded. "No. I talked to Sam. He called me from his cell phone just after he and Teresa left town . . . told me everything." She looked at Kate, and Kate saw the sincerity in her eyes. "It's a good thing, Katie. I can only imagine how furious this has made Leslie, but she'll see in time. It *is* a good thing."

"Did you know about this, Linny? That Mary had changed her will?"

"I didn't know about it, but I can't say that I'm really surprised," Linny answered.

"I don't understand," Kate said.

"Katie, Mary cared about you. It killed her to see you and Leslie at such odds with each other. She worried every day about you never coming back. Maybe she's trying to tell you something," Linny said emphatically.

"But it doesn't make sense, Linny," Kate said, finally voicing the struggles she'd been volleying around in her mind. "I don't live here. I don't have a family to fill this big house. I don't know how to take care of a house like this! I have a job in the city—a job I'm supposed to return to in a couple of days." Once she began, the words of uncertainty and doubt tumbled out in a heap. "What am I supposed to do with this house? What am I supposed to do?"

"Well, if that's how you feel, why don't you just give the house to Leslie?" Linny fired back. "I'm sure she'd take it in a heartbeat. Just be rid of it and go back to your life, your job in the city. It need not be complicated, that's for sure."

Kate sighed and looked at Linny. "She already asked for it . . . for the house. I know she wants it," she said dejectedly.

"Well, there you go." Linny leaned back. "Problem solved."

"But it isn't solved! In my head, all that logic makes sense. Leslie is here. Leslie wants the house. But I can't. My heart can't do it. I don't know why Aunt Mary did this. Surely she knew the trouble it would cause. But she did anyway, and I just can't help but feel there's a purpose to it all."

"I thought that's how you felt." Linny reached over and patted Kate on the knee. "You did the right thing, Katie, and it will all work out. Why don't you take some time off from that job of yours? Stay in the house for a week or two, think things through, and make some plans. A little time in the country never hurt anybody, did it?"

Kate almost immediately shook her head. "No, I really couldn't. There's so much to do back at the office."

But Linny wasn't convinced, and if Kate was honest with herself, neither was she. It made her feel good to think that her presence was mandatory in order for Blanton Advertising to function, but it wasn't necessarily true. There were others who could cover her workload, and since she'd never used her vacation days before, she had at least three weeks' worth saved up and ready for the taking. She was surprised at how quickly she took to the idea. In fact, she thought perhaps it was exactly what she needed. She leaned back in the old rocking chair, one leg pulled up under her as she silently made her plans.

"Did you know anything about the highway project?" she asked Linny after a few minutes.

Linny barely flinched. "Everybody in Rose Creek knows about that blasted highway. They've been stomping around, threatening people's property, for years. Word is they're set to start construction this summer."

"But the farmhouse, it isn't in danger, is it?"

Sam had assured Kate time and time again at lunch that he was sure the house was fine, that his mother would have said something had there been a change of plans, but Kate still felt uneasy.

"Well, I certainly don't think so," Linny responded. "It was a question for quite some time . . . which way the highway would run, this way or that. I think those old highway people just got so tired of hearing your aunt make such a stink about things, they changed their original plan so they wouldn't have to listen to her anymore." Linny chuckled at the memory.

Kate smiled. "I'm sure you're probably right. It just worried me what the attorney said."

"Oh, don't worry about that silly road," Linny said lightly. "I'll come chain myself to the front porch if that's what it takes."

Linny continued to rock, head leaning back, eyes gently closed.

"Stay around and see it through, Katie," she said. "Things will work out with the house, and Leslie won't stay mad forever. Things will work out. You'll see soon enough."

She spoke her reassurance with such quiet fortitude Kate couldn't help but feel hopeful. After a few more minutes of quiet rocking, Linny spoke again.

"The boys don't seem to be struggling with your having the house. That must be encouraging," she said.

"They've been very sweet," Kate agreed. "They never spent as much time here as Leslie. It probably doesn't change much for them."

"True, their lives aren't quite so enmeshed with the house as Leslie's was. Those children of hers were over here almost every day. You know, I think Teresa's pregnant again." she said, changing the subject. "She's been looking a bit fuller in the face, if you know what I mean, hair all shiny and thick looking. I'd bet money on another baby coming."

Kate smiled. "I'll remember you said that. What about Bryan? Do you think he'll stay in Maggie Valley?"

"Your aunt Mary thought it might be a woman that's keeping him there. He hasn't said anything one way or the other, but I reckon she could be right."

"I hope so," Kate said. "Bryan deserves to be happy."

"What about you, Katie? Is there anyone special in your life? You deserve to be happy too."

Kate looked at Linny. "I've been seeing someone, someone I work with, but I don't know. I don't think it's going to work out."

"Hmm," Linny said. "Working and loving mix about as well as oil and water, if you ask me."

"It's not that. I just . . . I don't feel much of a connection, you know? He's nice, attractive, successful. But I shouldn't have to convince myself that he's right for me, should I? It should just feel right."

Linny leaned her head back and smiled. "When I met Charles," she said, "you couldn't have convinced me with a shotgun to give him up."

## Chapter 7

AUNT MARY AND UNCLE GREY inherited the old farmhouse from Mary's parents, George and Jeanette Wylie. Kate remembered doing a report about the Wylie family heritage when she was in the third grade. She'd drawn a family tree with her own name on the trunk of the tree and then her parents' names above hers, followed by the names of her grandparents on each side of the family. Around the tree, Kate had drawn elements of each family's country of origin—Scotland for the Wylies and England for the Sinclairs on her father's side. Big Ben and the British flag had been easy, but Kate still remembered how hard she'd tried to draw a man in a kilt, playing the bagpipes. No matter her effort, the picture never really looked quite right. When Leslie came and looked over her shoulder, she asked Kate why the woman in the picture was holding an angry goose.

Aunt Mary and Kate's mother, Jenny, were George and Jeannette Wylie's only children. Mary always said her mother would have filled every room of the house with children had she been able, but only the two daughters came—Mary, the oldest, and then Jenny, younger by four years. When Mary married Grey, there was little question as to whether she would want to keep the old house. By that time, it had been in the family for close to a century. When Grey casually suggested they build a newer, more modern house in an upstart neighborhood across town, Mary nearly left him. Instead, they poured their heart and soul into the upkeep of the old house. They renovated and restored and modernized all they could without removing the charm and simplicity that gave the house so much character.

And it *did* have character.

Kate thought the house seemed wise and mysterious and full of secrets no one would ever know. *If only walls could talk*, she thought. Kate was sitting at the desk in the sunroom, a modern addition off the kitchen Mary and Grey had added when she and Leslie were in high school. It was a lovely room, windows on all sides, with pretty views of the vegetable garden and the mountains off in the distance. When the sun came up behind the mountains, the delicate rays of early-morning light hit this room first, filling it with a soft yellow glow and a comfortable warmth.

The desk, thanks to Sam's efforts, was well equipped with a computer, a flat screen monitor, and a high-speed Internet connection. Kate felt fairly certain Aunt Mary had little use for the Internet and assumed Sam's efforts were more for his own convenience when he and Teresa visited his mother. Just the same, as Kate sat down to check her e-mail, she was grateful Sam had kept the house technologically up to speed. Earlier that morning, Kate had made the two-hour trip to her home in Atlanta. She had collected a few weeks' worth of clothing, called the post office about forwarding her mail, and stopped by the office to see Mr. Blanton about her vacation time.

When she arrived in the familiar lobby of Blanton Advertising, the routines of her work life seemed to beckon. The sights and smells of the city, the click of her shoes on the clean marble tiles of the floor—they were familiar, comfortable to Kate. And yet, they seemed to lack a certain luster. It wasn't the city or the building that was different; it was Kate's own life that appeared dull, suddenly mundane and meaningless.

She spent a few minutes in her office, sorting through her messages and mail, but found herself anxious, ready to drive back to the mountains and escape from the near-suffocating busyness that swarmed around her. It was disconcerting when, just a few days before, she'd felt the opposite: anxious to get back to work and itching to escape Rose Creek. Kate didn't understand the change.

Veronica, well-intentioned, followed her around the office, filling her in on every detail she had missed in the few days she'd been gone. Though Kate would have been interested in the news and gossip of her coworkers a week ago, she now found it inconsequential and tiresome.

Mr. Blanton himself was more than accommodating, even encouraging Kate to take as much time as she needed. He even went so far as to scold her when she offered to continue fielding her own e-mails and phone calls and handling what she could from North Carolina.

"Vacation is *not* vacation if you are still working, Kate," Mr. Blanton said.

In the end, Kate at least convinced Veronica to send daily e-mail updates so she could stay informed, even if she wasn't allowed to actually do any work. Veronica promised to call if anything hugely significant (Steve moving into her office, for example) deserved Kate's immediate attention.

*Ah, Steve*, Kate thought. She made it through the office without running into him and thought she'd be home free, but he ran after her, catching up to her just as she reached her car in the parking garage. He pulled her into a tight embrace, totally oblivious to Kate's less-than-welcoming body language.

She sighed. "Hi, Steve," she said. "How are you?"

"Better now that you're here." He grinned. "How was your weekend?"

"It was a funeral, Steve. Not really all that great," she answered. "I'm actually going back. I'm taking a little bit of vacation time. I think it will be good for me."

"Vacation?" Steve asked. "In Rose Creek? What is there to do there?"

"It's not that sort of a vacation," Kate told him, already a bit exasperated. "I just want to spend some time with my family."

"What if I come see you this weekend?" he asked.

Kate bit her bottom lip, not really wanting to hurt him but certain he did not need to make an effort to come see her—not in Rose Creek and not anywhere else.

"I don't think that's a good idea."

He didn't catch on. "Oh. Well, how about next weekend?"

"No, Steve," Kate said. "Not any weekend. You're a nice guy, and I do care about you. But not like you care about me. I have to be honest with myself, and I thought a lot about life and, I don't know, just everything, over the weekend. It's not going to work out between us. It just isn't right for me."

Steve stood still, hands on his hips, jaw set. "Have you met someone else?" he asked, obviously incredulous that someone would just decide independently that they didn't want to be with him anymore.

"Seriously?" Kate asked. "I went home for a funeral. Do you think I was out bar hopping right afterward?"

He couldn't have seen the momentary flash of truth in her eyes as he asked the question. Kate hardly thought conversing with a stranger for five minutes in the middle of her workout constituted meeting someone.

Still, Andrew Porterfield's face had immediately come to mind when Steve suggested such a notion. She shook Andrew out of her head. She would probably never see him again. Even if she did, it didn't change the ridiculousness of Steve's question.

"I'm sorry, Kate," he said. "That was uncalled for. I just don't think I understand. This felt right to me."

"I'm sorry," she said again. "I never meant to hurt you." She wondered how many more classic breakup lines she could deliver in one conversation.

*It's not you; it's me.*

*The timing just isn't right . . .*

Or how about, *You're not really in love with me . . . just with the idea of me.* Kate might actually believe that last one. She didn't think Steve really was in love with her.

"Well, that's great, Kate," Steve said. "Really great. All I'm saying . . . You'd better watch that client list of yours *really* close."

Kate rolled her eyes and added another breakup line to her list. *I don't think you love me, just my corner office.* Getting into the car to head back to Rose Creek, she felt lighter than she had in months.

When she got to the farmhouse, it was late afternoon. She scrolled through her inbox to see if anything caught her attention. She hesitated before reading a message from Steve.

She sighed and opened the message.

*Kate . . . I miss you and hope things are okay. Are you coming home soon? Still waiting for your call . . . Steve.*

*He must have sent that before we talked.*

As far as breakups went, she thought Steve had actually handled things pretty well. He was a no-nonsense kind of guy. If he learned he couldn't get what he wanted from Kate, he would find someone else—probably sooner than later. And he would not have trouble doing so. Kate could think of three or four women from the office who would be thrilled to hear she and Steve were no longer dating. He'd bounce back quickly, Kate was sure, and would be dating by the end of next week at the latest.

If only Kate could figure out what she wanted.

*Andrew Porterfield would be nice.*

Kate's cheeks flushed at the unbidden thought that had surfaced for the second time that day. She quickly pushed the idea from her head.

*I'll never see him again. It's a waste of time to even consider it.*

After a few more mundane but necessary tasks—checking her bank statement, paying her power bill—Kate was ready to tackle the list in front of her. The night before, Kate had walked through the entire house with a pad of paper and a pen, writing down anything that needed repair. Her heart had swelled with emotion when she thought of Aunt Mary walking through the house just as she had, hiring Mr. Brumfield from down the street to come fix and mend and take care of the things she could no longer handle on her own. Mary's efforts had left the house in remarkably good condition, and Kate's list was much smaller than she had expected. Still, there were a few things that ought to be taken care of. Kate still wasn't sure what she would do with the old house, but she felt good about busying herself with a few minor repairs and simple improvements.

"The house needs paint," she said aloud, reading the first item on her list. "Both inside and out," she amended. "Bathroom sink drips, the front porch has three broken pickets, two steps need to be replaced, and the toilet in the downstairs bathroom doesn't flush." She decided to call a plumber for the issues in the bathroom and see if Mr. Brumfield could replace the pickets and fix the porch steps. But the painting she wanted to do herself. She wondered what paint supplies might be stashed away in some corner of the house somewhere. After a futile search in the storage room off the kitchen and in the garden shed outside, Kate climbed the stairs to the attic above her old bedroom to try her luck there.

The attic had always been wonderfully mysterious and magical. Leslie had never enjoyed the cluttered, dusty space, so it had become a private refuge for Kate as a child. The low-ceilinged room was lined with boxes and crates and trunks as old as the house itself—so old, it seemed, they simply faded into the lines of the walls, hardly discernible from surrounding items on either side. The center of the room was newly cluttered with the recent deposits of the years since Kate's childhood: broken strings of Christmas lights, discarded band instruments, and the horseback riding boots Kate had insisted on buying when she was determined to be a show jumper in the Olympics. A stack of Bryan's old CDs and cassette tapes, as well as a stack of Mary's old records, filled one box near the door, and a large basket of dress-up clothes overflowed in the small dormer space of the north window.

Kate looked around the cluttered room. It stretched the full length of the house, and small windows at each end filtered in soft sunlight, casting dusty shadows around the room. Much of what filled the attic was quickly discernible as junk—stuff Kate was sure she would, as soon as time allowed, clean out and simply throw away. But it couldn't all be junk. Kate found herself itching to dig through the long-forgotten boxes to unearth the history and happenings of years past. Drawn by old habit, she walked to the one corner of the attic, where she knew exactly what she would find. Most of what was in her parents' home when they died had been sold or given away, but before anything had been taken, Aunt Mary had walked

Kate through the house and told her to point out anything she wanted to keep. Her childlike vision of value did not extend to furniture or fine art or anything else a casual observer may have considered lovely and worth keeping. But to her, what she kept were treasures without price: a small porcelain figurine of a mother smiling down at an infant child in her arms, a gift to Kate's mother, she was told, when she was born; a smooth wooden bowl, brought back from her parents' honeymoon in Hawaii; her mother's purse; her father's reading glasses; and the soft, silky robe her mother put on when she made breakfast in the morning, among other things.

For the first few years after her parents' death, Kate kept her side of the bedroom she shared with Leslie full of her parents' belongings. Eventually, though, as she grew up, things that expressed her own personality replaced her parents' possessions: posters covered her walls, and music and books covered the surfaces of her dresser and desktop. Some things had remained—her mother's jewelry box, supplemented by Kate's own trendy offerings, and the shoebox that housed all of the pictures from Kate's first seven years of life. But everything else was eventually relegated to this quiet corner of the attic. Even into her teenage years, when Kate felt overwhelmed, she would escape to her small attic refuge, close her eyes, and imagine her parents close by.

Kate smiled as she looked through the old orange crate that held so many of her childhood memories and emotions. She picked up her mother's old robe and held it close to her face, breathing in the scent of the flimsy fabric. Any lingering scent had faded years ago, but the action alone was enough to trigger Kate's memory and fill her mind with the wispy scent of roses and sweet honeysuckle.

Kate returned the robe and noticed a single picture standing sideways in the corner of the crate. She picked it up. It was a snapshot of her parents standing next to a forest service sign for Morgan Falls Trail. Kate had hiked the trail numerous times herself. It was a short loop just a few miles outside of town, with a beautiful waterfall at the end. Kate's mother was pregnant in the picture, her father standing behind her, hands resting on her swollen belly. Kate wondered who had taken the picture. A stranger, most likely, willing to help the happy couple capture the moment, freezing their dreams and aspirations all in one single frame. She traced the outline of her father's dark hair that nearly touched his shoulders in the photo.

*It's so much like mine*, she thought, running her fingers through her thick and often unruly hair. *Thanks for that, Dad.*

She turned away from the crate, keeping only the picture with her, and remembered once again why she'd come up to the attic in the first place. "If I were a paintbrush, where would I be?" She spoke out loud, disturbing the stillness around her. After several minutes of fruitless searching, Kate gave up, deciding to go to the hardware store first thing in the morning.

## Chapter 8

THE NEXT MORNING, KATE STOOD in front of the large wall of paint colors at the hardware store, wondering why on earth there had to be so many different shades of white. She held sample cards of eggshell white and misty dawn white and picket fence white up to the light, searching for some variation. Finally, she settled on the aptly named farmhouse white and hoisted two cans of the mixed paint into her cart. Loaded down with brushes and rollers and anything else she thought she'd need to paint a house, Kate turned the corner and moved toward the front of the store. She passed the service desk, where several customers were waiting in line, and recognized Andrew approaching the counter. She ducked behind a large display of toolboxes so she was hidden from his field of vision but not so far away that she couldn't hear him speak. She listened as the old gentleman working behind the counter said hello.

"How are you, Andrew?" His tone was familiar, like that of an old friend. He shook Andrew's extended hand. "What can I do for you today?"

"I was hoping you could sharpen this for me, Bill." Andrew lifted a heavy ax and placed it on the counter.

"Sure, sure. You've got some wood to cut, then?"

"Actually, I just finished. I borrowed the ax from a neighbor and thought I'd sharpen it up before returning it."

Kate raised her eyebrows, impressed with his thoughtfulness. She could tell he'd been working outside. He wore blue jeans, dirt stained and ragged, and an old T-shirt with a soft flannel on top. He also wore a baseball cap turned around backward, which Kate thought made him look much younger than he actually was—unless, of course, he really was only fifteen. Kate smiled at the thought. Bill was nearly finished with his sharpening. She wanted to talk to Andrew but struggled to think of a graceful way to appear from behind the toolboxes without looking like she'd been hiding there on purpose, listening in on his conversation.

"There you are, son," Bill said as he handed the ax back to Andrew. "That's sure nice of you to sharpen an ax before returning it; seems stuff like that hardly happens anymore."

Andrew smiled. "It's a great way to guarantee my neighbor will always lend me his ax." He took the ax from Bill and thanked him again. Forcing her courage to the surface, Kate took her cart and wheeled out from behind the display. She caught Andrew's eye and smiled as he recognized her.

"Hey! It's Kate, right?" He walked over to her cart, looking curiously at the display of toolboxes from which she'd just emerged. "Were you looking for something?" he asked, glancing behind the toolboxes, eyebrows raised in question.

"Um, no," Kate stumbled. "I mean, yes, it's Kate, but no, I wasn't looking for something. I was um . . . just looking at the toolboxes," she continued. "I thought maybe the ones in the back were a different color."

*Good grief! This is a hardware store, not the shoe department at Macy's!*

"What are you doing here?" she asked, quickly changing the subject.

"Just getting this sharpened for a friend." Andrew held up the ax. "I thought you were leaving town yesterday. Did your plans change?"

Kate muffled a small laugh as she thought of how much her plans had changed in the past week. "I . . . well, yes. They did," she answered. "I'm going to be in town for a few weeks after all."

Andrew looked over the items in her cart. "So what are you painting? A fence?"

"A house," Kate replied. She held up the color sample she'd deliberated over for so long. "See? Farmhouse white."

For a brief moment, Andrew looked completely incredulous, but the surprise on his face was gone as quickly as it had arrived. Kate wondered if she had been seeing things.

"It must not be a very big house," he said sheepishly. He removed his hat and ran his fingers through his tousled hair.

Kate paused. She wasn't an expert, but she knew enough to know a house as big as hers would require a much larger amount of paint than two cans. She must not have been thinking but quickly backpedaled to keep Andrew from realizing her misjudgment. "It's a really big house, actually. But I thought I'd start small, make sure I really like the color before I buy all that I need."

"That makes sense. You'll probably need upwards of ten gallons, maybe more depending on how big your 'big house' actually is. Better to be sure on your color before you spend money on that much paint."

Kate could tell he was still calculating and wondered how "really big" translated into number of required paint cans in a man's head. He turned back to her, smiling, something she decided he really needed to stop doing if she was ever going to maintain her composure.

"So, painting a house seems like a big job for just one person," he said.

Kate took a deep breath. "Well, it's my house," she answered. "Newly acquired, and it needs paint. That's really as far as I've thought it through. I guess I'll have to get help eventually, but it feels good to get started."

"Simple enough," he said as they started walking toward the checkout. Andrew shifted the ax from one hand to the other and glanced at his watch.

"I've got to run," he said. "I'm due back at work in half an hour, and I still have to return the ax. It was nice bumping into you again."

"Same to you," Kate said. "Maybe we'll run into each other again—while we're running, even."

Andrew paused for a moment. "That would be nice," he said.

Later that afternoon, Kate stood on the front porch and prepared herself and her supplies for painting. As she worked, she thought back over her conversation with Andrew and was thoroughly embarrassed. It was bad enough she had told him she was looking for a different color toolbox—as if they came in various shades of lavender or pale pink. But then, to practically beg him to go running? She sighed as she filled the rolling pan with the clean, crisp farmhouse white then started to paint the square of house in between the front door and the large living room window. The color looked refreshingly white against the weather-stained boards of the old house. It encouraged Kate, and she happily started painting what little house she could reach just standing on the porch. It was weary work, and though in some ways it was therapeutic, Kate quickly realized painting the entire house was, just as Andrew had predicted, a job much too large for one person.

"Katherine Isabelle! What in Sam Hill are you doing?" Kate hadn't heard Linny arrive and was startled by her boisterous and very sudden question. She turned, paintbrush in hand, with a smear of white across her cheek and several streaks woven into her hair.

"I'm painting the house," she answered simply.

"Well, I can see that clearly, but by yourself?" Linny asked, validating Kate's concerns. "Your uncle Grey would hire an entire team of men to come paint this house, and it would still take them all day. You got plans to do anything else while you're here?"

Kate put down her paintbrush and stretched her tired muscles.

"Oh, I don't know, Linny. I just thought the house needed new paint." Kate sat down on the porch steps and yawned. The drive and determination she'd felt to paint the house was quickly fizzling out. "I've got a list of other things I was going to have Mr. Brumfield fix for me. Does he paint too?"

Linny scratched her forehead and pushed a few loose strands of silvery hair out of her face. "You haven't seen Mr. Brumfield in a while, have you, dear? He's good for a bit of mending here and there, but he's much too old for something like painting this big, old house. I'll check with Charles to see if he knows someone who could do it for you without charging you too much. He'll know somebody, I'm sure."

"Speaking of Charles," Linny continued, "our heat just went out at the house, and I'm worried about him getting cold in the evenings when the temperatures drop a bit."

Several years older than Linny, Charles's health had declined rapidly in recent years. He was a gruff and stubborn old man, and only the women in his life knew he had a softer side. Though his mind was still sharp, he struggled physically and didn't get around as much as he used to. Linny took it all in stride, caring for Charles with the same iron devotion that bolstered her efforts all over the community. She was good at taking care of people—most especially Charles.

"Would you like to stay here?" Kate offered. She thought she would actually enjoy the company. After Sam and Bryan left, she managed her first night alone in the house just fine but still found the silence of her solitude in the big house a bit heavy and overwhelming.

"Are you kidding me?" Linny remarked. "And ask an old man to move himself and his favorite chair and everything else he needs in order to be comfortable? Maybe if it were twenty degrees, dear, but not for just a touch of spring chill." Linny smiled at Kate. "Thank you for offering though. Your aunt Mary would've done the same thing. I was just thinking I could grab those space heaters up in the attic. Would you mind if I borrowed them?"

"I saw them up there yesterday afternoon when I was looking for paintbrushes. I'll go get them for you."

"Oh, come on now. Don't rush off on me yet. Just grab them before I go. I'll sit here for a few minutes if you don't mind it."

Kate leaned on the railing of the porch and looked down at her paint-stained hands, wondering again what she was really trying to accomplish.

"Have you talked to Leslie today?" Linny asked as she leaned back next to Kate.

"No. Have you?" Kate looked up, hopeful, but saw Linny's answer in her eyes before she spoke.

"I told her she ought to come over here, give you girls the chance to talk things out, but she's not having any of my suggestions," Linny said calmly. "Just give her time though, Katie. She can't stay mad forever."

"I didn't do this, Linny. I didn't take the house from her. It just happened."

"I know that, and so does she," Linny responded. "But she's got a lot of pain to work through. Just give her a little bit of time. If you keep reaching out, eventually, she'll reach back. I'm sure of it."

"It's not easy," Kate said softly.

"No one ever said it was."

The women sat in companionable silence for a few more minutes before Linny moved to leave.

"Well, I best get back to Charles," she said. "He hasn't had anything to eat yet, and you know how men are when they're hungry."

Kate hurried into the house and retrieved the space heaters from the far corner of the attic, where they sat on top of a large wooden trunk. She didn't recognize the trunk and, touched by curiosity, moved several other items off the top so she could open it. A small, rusty lock held the trunk closed, and it was unyielding to Kate's efforts. She thought perhaps with a bobby pin or a nail file she might be able to pick it open, but the thought of Linny waiting caused her to abandon her efforts and hurry downstairs.

"Do you ever go in the attic, Linny?" Kate asked as she returned to the porch with the heaters.

"Not in years and years. Why do you ask?"

"There's just so much stuff up there—stuff that seems centuries old," Kate responded. "I figure I ought to go through it all, see what's worth keeping and what's not."

"Who knows what you'll find up there, though 'centuries old' may be stretching a bit." Linny picked up the heaters and started walking to her car, but she turned back to Kate. "Just don't do too much too fast, okay? There's no rushing needed around here."

Kate walked over and gave Linny a quick hug and a kiss on the cheek. "Thanks, Linny. Will you come over tomorrow?"

"Of course I will, dear." Linny climbed into her station wagon and then, as an afterthought, rolled down her window to ask Kate one more question. "Did you ever hear back from the attorney?" she asked.

Kate shook her head. "I figure if the house really was in danger, he would have let me know by now. Everything must be okay."

"That's good. I'd hate to see anything happen to this old place. And you feel that way too, I can see. I can already tell you're invested."

"I was invested a long time ago. I just forgot for a while, that's all."

"It's nice to have you back, Katie." Linny smiled and then pulled away.

Kate watched Linny move down the driveway, the sun hanging low in the afternoon sky. In her haste to start painting, she had completely skipped lunch and found herself suddenly ravenous. She cleaned up the paint and took the brushes to the large outdoor sink behind the garden shed for rinsing. The sink sat next to a wooden workbench and storage table, where Mary had kept all of her gardening tools. Kate turned and looked at the garden behind her, freshly plowed and ready to be sown. It was nearly warm enough. Mary would probably have planted in the next few weeks, generous rows of green beans and tomatoes, squash and zucchini, and enough cucumbers to make pickles for all of Rose Creek. Kate had spent so many summer hours standing at this very sink with her aunt, cleaning cucumbers, scrubbing, and laughing. The tears came with little warning, the heat on her cheeks a stinging contrast to the icy water now running over her fingers. She shook the brushes and dropped them into a bucket stored under the sink then hurried into the house.

It was impossible to get away from it. Every corner, every sight, sound, and smell of the house reminded Kate of Mary. She angrily wiped away her tears and stormed into the kitchen. The process of Kate's grieving happened in waves. She would continue along at an even keel, calm and controlled, until, like the moment at the garden sink, the reality of life without Aunt Mary would wash over her anew, tormenting her every nerve and casting her into a miserable pit of desperation and loneliness.

"It's too much!" Kate cried. "This is just too much to endure!" Unable to stop the tears, she sank to the kitchen floor and pulled her knees up to her chest. She cried until her tears were all used up, then sat in the quiet stillness of her solitude. When the pain and sadness dissipated, all she felt was emptiness.

She sighed and stood up, wearily starting preparations for a light meal. Aunt Mary's kitchen was very different from the small, efficient space of her apartment in Atlanta. While Kate often enjoyed the process of preparing a solitary meal in the city, it hardly seemed possible for her own singular presence to fill a kitchen so used to the love and fullness of family.

This kitchen needed people crowding the table and leaning up against the counters, talking and laughing and carrying on well past the end of each meal. Kate wondered how many times the family had gathered in that very room in recent years. Countless times, she was sure. And yet, she had never been there. As she sat in Aunt Mary's kitchen, all alone, eating the fettuccine she'd made, the weight of her own selfishness felt heavier than ever before. She longed for her family, for the kind of connection that bound them together no matter what—making them strong enough to handle the highs and lows, the rough roads and choppy water that life brought.

Kate didn't want to be alone anymore.

She slid her half-empty plate of pasta to the side and pressed her forehead into her hands. She needed a friend, but there was no one to call. Her relationships in Atlanta were only skin deep and would provide little comfort in her present situation. She was saddened to realize that the person she generally talked to the most in the city received a paycheck for being her assistant. Disheartened and lonelier than ever, Kate did the dishes and cleaned the kitchen. The busyness of her hands, at least temporarily, dampened the sadness in her heart.

# Chapter 9

WHEN THE DISHES WERE PUT away, Kate searched the junk drawer in the kitchen for something she could use to pick the rusty lock on the old trunk she'd noticed in the attic. She wondered how it had managed to escape her notice until now and was curious about its contents. Armed with a slender nail file and a handful of bobby pins, Kate climbed the stairs to the attic and moved things aside until the trunk was fully exposed. In the darkness of the evening, Kate had to rely on the single bulb hanging from the attic ceiling to light the cluttered space. The light's performance was less than satisfactory. When Kate leaned in front of the trunk to try her hand at picking the lock, her body cast a shadow over the entire thing, making it impossible for her to see what she was doing.

She climbed behind it in frustration, sliding it as best she could toward the small circle of light pooling in the center of the room. With the lock now in better position, she wiggled the nail file around inside until she heard the little click she was hoping for. Kate laughed quietly to herself and thought of the time she'd lost the key to the lock on her storage unit in the basement of her condo. The super had picked the lock with surprising ease. Clearly, mimicking his technique worked for Kate as well. The bolt slid out of the rusty lock, and Kate gently lifted the heavy lid. The trunk was made of heavy walnut, with dovetailed edges and wrought-iron handles on either side. Its scratched and heavily weathered exterior made it obvious that this trunk had done a lot of traveling.

Kate reached in and pulled out a soft quilt, the fabric so thin she worried it might dissolve between her fingers. Under the quilt, she found a small wooden horse, a corn husk doll, a set of tarnished silver spoons, and a heavy Bible published in 1843. Kate marveled as she picked up each item, wondering who these things could have belonged to. In the bottom of the trunk, she found a small wooden box. Carefully, she lifted it out and tried to slide off the lid. The warped wood resisted her efforts, catching in the narrow grooves that guided the lid into place. After a few minutes of delicate struggle, the lid finally yielded its contents into Kate's hands. As she'd struggled with the ancient lid, she had imagined something of value, jewelry, perhaps, hidden inside. Instead, she found a small leather-bound book and a few pages of thick, tightly folded paper held together with a thin piece of twine.

Kate gently opened the small book and flipped through the first few pages. It appeared to be a journal, the date on the first page marked September 29, 1817. Carefully, she held the folded paper, picking the twine loose with her fingernails. It was a letter. Two letters, it seemed, written by the same hand. The faded ink of the slanted cursive was difficult to make out in the dim light of the attic, and as she puzzled over it, Kate realized the chill of the cool spring night had crept into the drafty attic space. Placing the other items back in the trunk, Kate took the letters and journal, as well as the old family Bible, downstairs to the family room for more comfortable reading.

Settled in her favorite chair next to the bookshelf, the reading lamp turned on above her, Kate picked up the first letter. The paper was thick but still felt fragile, almost brittle to Kate's touch.

*4 February 1818*

*My Dear Ian,*

*I received your letter this week past, and though I've put pen to paper many a time, I've stopped for fear of wetting the paper too heavily with my tears. Oh, how you've grieved my heart with such news. It's been most difficult knowing that all these months I've prayed and hoped for my husband's well-being, and he's been gone—buried beneath the ground. The thought of it has near ruined me, but now, Ian, my heart aches for you—alone in a strange land. Your letter made mention of friends—those who knew your father and are willing to help you. Don't trust just anyone, son. I know there are good people in this world, and your father would not have kept company with someone he did not trust, but be careful just the same. Keep your eyes and ears open; use your head, and, of course, take all of your decisions to God. God is with you. He will take care of you, just as Da always taught you. "Wherever you walk . . . walk with God." I know you will, and I know you will work hard. Your father isn't there to help you know what to do, so I want you to listen to me. I want you to save your money, and when you have enough, return to Scotland. I feel it unlikely your sisters and I will ever be able to make the journey ourselves.*

*Susannah has fallen ill these past few months. Doctor McGinnley doesn't know what ails her, but she is quite sickly and would never endure such a strenuous journey across the Atlantic. The news of Father's death has hit her hard, and I worry for her well-being. She is thinner than I've ever seen her, her skin so pale. The doctor is here to treat her regularly, but she makes little progress. He knows of a doctor in London who may be able to help, but we've not got the money to make such a journey. Instead, we place her life in God's hands and pray He will preserve and heal her little body. It hardly seems fair for such a young child to endure such a crisis. She misses you also and asks regularly to have the small part of your letter addressed to her read over and over. Mary is doing quite well and is tireless in the assistance she offers her sister. Things are difficult here, Ian, though your uncle does the best he can to help us. My worries are all for you though. I wait anxiously to hear from you again, to know what your circumstances are, and to know if we might expect your journey home. You are a man now, son. I've taught you for sixteen years and trust you to make wise decisions. Don't be imprudent. You represent your father, remember . . . and God. May He be with you always . . .*

*Mother*

"Ian," Kate spoke out loud as she finished the heartfelt letter. She was surprised at how deeply it touched her heart. A son, she determined, separated from his family, his father dead. She wondered what could have created such circumstances. The letter was obviously a response to one already sent by Ian—a letter that must have informed his family of the father's death.

*Sixteen years old and an ocean away from any family; who are you, Ian?*

Kate turned over the letter and found what she was looking for. There, in faded ink on the outside of the paper, was a name she must have missed in her haste to see the contents of the letter:

*Ian Wylie*
*Watson Home Bakery–Calhoun St.*
*Charleston, South Carolina*

"Ian Wylie!" Kate exclaimed. It made sense that a Wylie had penned these letters. It was a Wylie, after all, who had built the farmhouse so many years ago. He was her ancestor, then; she turned to the heavy Bible she had pulled from the trunk, hoping to find a family record on the first few pages. Sure enough, page three of the Bible contained a record of the Wylie family ancestry. The most recent name on the list, Kate didn't immediately recognize: Isaac Abraham Wylie, born in 1888. She counted backward, guessing that her grandfather, George Charles Wylie, was born sometime around 1920. It was reasonable to assume, then, that Isaac Abraham could be George's father.

Kate followed with her finger the Wylie paternal line: above Isaac Abraham, John David Wylie, born in 1866, and his father, Henry Sebastian Wylie, born 1845. Above Henry, Kate read James Ian Wylie, born 1825, and then she found what she was looking for. The first name in the old family Bible: Ian Edward Wylie, born 1801, in Edinburgh, Scotland. Kate had never seen such a detailed list of her ancestry. She was sure that had Mary known this Bible existed, she would have kept it close and cherished the record of her ancestors. She could not have known. Somehow, the trunk must have remained hidden in the attic, an undiscovered treasure.

*And I was the one to find it.*

Kate wondered if there was a way to confirm the lineage, though she really had little doubt. How else would such a specific element of family history have wound up in Aunt Mary's attic? Still, her mind kept searching for proof, some tangible connection that linked her to the Wylies on the page before her. Then it came to her: Grandpa Ike. Aunt Mary had told stories about going to Grandpa Ike's farm—Ike . . . short for Isaac.

Kate was amazed at the kinship she felt just reading the faded names off the page of the old Bible. She'd never thought much about her ancestors, beyond her basic awareness that the Wylies had come from Scotland, and she had never heard anything about Ian or the experiences his mother had made reference to. Kate turned back to the letter and shook her head in amazement. She couldn't imagine how desperate his mother must have felt, her husband gone and her son alone in a strange country. Even worse, how must have Ian felt? Kate picked up the small leather journal she'd found with the letters and gently opened the soft, worn cover. On the inside, she read *Property of Ian Wylie.*

The first entry was dated September 29, 1817, five months prior to the letter Kate had just read.

*Mrs. Watson says it will do me good to write about things as of late, though I don't much have a knack for writing. Even still, Mr. MacDonald was generous in giving me this book. Out of respect for him, I'll try. Perhaps I'll have family one day that will benefit from knowing my story.*

*I arrived in America near two weeks ago. Passage was easy, the weather mild. At once, the city reminded me of Edinburgh: busy, full of people. When I couldn't find Da, I didn't worry. I thought perhaps he'd not realized the Gloriana, that's the name of the ship I was on, came in that day. I wandered the streets of Charleston for three hours before I started to fear the worst. Soon, I came to a little square just up the street from a large church. The road rose steeply up from the square and provided a view of the ocean just beyond the harbor. I was listening to the sound of the church bells ringing the hour when my mind was suddenly filled with the memory of one of Da's letters. He'd written of the city, of the church just one street over from his shop and the view of the ocean from hilltop square. I was filled with new energy, for I knew I had at least found Da's part of the city. Instead of searching the faces of the people around me, I started searching the signs hanging in front of the shops that lined the streets. I searched until the darkness around me made it too difficult to go on. I'm not sure I should admit it, but I was scared and didn't know what I was to do. Finally, I arrived at a bakery, hungry and tired and worried too. It was Mrs. Watson, the baker's wife, who greeted me. I don't think she trusted me at first. I told her I meant no harm but was weary from the day and hungry too. I begged a loaf of bread and perhaps a corner, out of the way, where I might rest. We talked only a moment before she knew me, told me I had the look of my father, that our eyes were the same. I knew well enough when she started to cry that something was wrong. Mr. Watson, the baker himself, came into the front room to tell me. Da died three weeks before I arrived, an infection in his lungs. He got into bed, they said, and never got out again.*

*It's hard to imagine him so sick he'd not get out of bed. But so it was. The Watsons have been very kind. They tell me they were good friends with Da, their shop just down the street from his. They seem like good people, and know quite a bit about my father, which helps me trust them.*

*I've also seen the MacDonald family. They came across from Scotland on the Gloriana just as I did and have been very kind. I think I can trust them too. Abe MacDonald seems a kind man. He came to Charleston to work with his brother, who was already here running a printing press. That was Mr. MacDonald's business in Edinburgh as well. The best news is they've agreed to give me work so I can save money and bring Mother and my sisters across to be with me here in America. I think Da would have wanted us all together.*

*I don't remember much about the night I learned of Da's death, saving I thought most seriously about wanting to be dead myself. Never have I felt so alone. Mr. Watson, the baker, took me to Da's gravesite, still fresh, and left me there. I was angry—angry at God, at the world, at Da for leaving me here all alone. Finally, just before morning, I decided to pray. I felt peace after that. I felt Da's presence, felt his strength, and felt God's comfort. I remembered Da's words, "Wherever you walk, walk with God." Until that moment, they'd always been words, nothing more. But I realize now the only way I will make it in this city all alone is if I do walk with God. I need His strength and guidance. I miss Da and wish he were here. But I believe I will be all right. I live now to live worthy of the Wylie name, to honor Da's memory in all I do.*

Kate wiped a tear from the corner of her eye. "I don't know how you did it, Ian," she whispered. The difficulty she was facing in her own life suddenly seemed insignificant compared to the obstacles Ian must have overcome.

*I would have given up. How were you strong enough?*

Kate didn't realize it at first. She didn't hear a voice or feel the earth move. There wasn't thunder or a dramatic, bold realization. But suddenly, her question was answered, the words clear and distinct, filling her mind, reaching into her very soul and clutching her emotions from the inside out. She looked back at the journal, rereading the words Ian had quoted of his father: *Wherever you walk, walk with God.*

She read them again and again.

Kate wasn't a religious person. Growing up, she'd gone with Aunt Mary and Uncle Grey to the Methodist church across from the elementary school for Christmas and Easter services, and she'd attended vacation Bible school every July until she'd hit middle school. But God was always more of an idea to Kate. Nothing about church really felt *personal.*

She did remember one experience as a girl when she thought she felt something close to a kinship with God. It was Easter morning, the spring she turned nine. Just as they did every year, her family attended the Sunday-morning service at the Methodist church. When the service was over, everyone filed outside into the warm April sunshine. Kate realized she'd left her pink-and-white purse in the pew, so she hurried back inside to find it. She was alone in the spacious chapel. Her little black dress shoes clicked noisily against the parquet floors, so she moved onto the soft crimson rug that filled the center aisle, wanting to preserve the peace and stillness around her. She brushed her hand across the backs of the smooth wooden pews, glancing into each one until she found her little bag. She picked it up and turned to leave just as she saw the sunlight pouring in through the large stained-glass window on the far eastern side of the chapel.

It was beautiful. From where Kate stood, the floor-to-ceiling picture of Jesus holding His arms out, face looking toward the sky, seemed to radiate, the beams of sunlight extending directly from Jesus' hands. Kate stood, mesmerized by the majestic scene in front of her. Her heart seemed brim full of warmth that exuded outward through her entire person, even to her own fingertips. Leslie had found her just as a single tear spilled over Kate's lashes.

"Katie! We're waiting for you," Leslie had shouted as she burst through the doors at the end of the chapel. "Mama says it's my fault if you don't come, and neither one of us will get ice cream if you don't come now."

Kate smiled at the memory. It had been a long time since she'd thought of that moment in the church, though it was easy to recall, even twenty years later, how she'd felt in that moment. *Walking with God must feel something like that*, she thought. She looked back at Ian's letter. There were certainly parallels between his situation and hers: he, a young man in a strange city with a dead father and no plan. *And me*, Kate thought to herself, *with a dead mother, a dead aunt, an estranged cousin, a big house . . . and no plan.*

Kate knew the big Methodist church she'd attended in her childhood was still there. She'd passed by several times on her way in and out of town. She wondered if the stained-glass window on the eastern wall was still there and contemplated the possibility of going to see it, but it was a silly idea. It was just a window.

She stretched and glanced at her watch, gently closing Ian's journal. She reached for the second letter but was interrupted when her cell phone rang from the other room. She put everything aside on the coffee table and ran to catch the phone, picking it up just before it went to voice mail. It was Linny.

"Oh, Kate," Linny said. "I'm so glad I caught you."

"What is it, Linny?" Kate could hear the stress in her voice and knew immediately that something was wrong.

"Well, I'm at the hospital, but I'm all right, so don't get too worried. I slipped on the blasted stairs leading down to the basement, and I broke my ankle."

"Oh no!" Kate said. "Is there something I can do?"

"Well, they brought me into the hospital in the ambulance, 'bout scared Charles to death seeing them haulin' me off like some invalid. Apparently though, ambulance services are only one way, so I got to find myself a ride back home." Kate smiled at Linny's unfailing wit and humor.

"I'd be happy to come get you, Linny. I'll be there in ten minutes."

*Chapter 10*

KATE DROVE THE FAMILIAR ROADS to the hospital and pulled into the small parking lot beside the emergency room entrance. She half expected to see Linny hobbling out to the car on her own, waving her crutches above her head, daring anyone to keep her from walking without assistance. But she was pleasantly surprised to find Linny sitting comfortably on a bed in one of the exam rooms, her ankle heavily wrapped and splinted and propped up on a pillow.

"Well, it looks like they've taken good care of you," Kate said as she walked in and took Linny's hand.

"I don't know why I didn't break my ankle sooner," Linny joked. "I could stay here all night and not worry one bit about the dishes getting done." She squeezed Kate's hand. "Thank you for coming." She motioned to her ankle, lifting her leg just an inch. "They say I have to come back next week for a more permanent cast. I'm thinking pink. What do you think?"

Kate smiled. "Pink would definitely suit you. How does it feel? Does it hurt at all?"

Before Linny could answer, Leslie came bursting around the exam room curtain. "Linny! I came as soon as I heard! Are you all right?" She froze when she saw Kate standing next to Linny. "Oh," she said curtly. "I guess you don't need me, then."

"Well, now, Leslie," Linny said. "Of course I do. I didn't want you to have to leave the children, so I called Kate to come take me home. I just didn't want to worry you. I said that in my message, didn't I?"

"Tommy was up," Leslie responded. "I was just trying to get him back to sleep when you called."

"Well, I'm glad you did come. The more the merrier when bones have been broken!" Linny winced as she shifted her weight, cautiously repositioning her ankle on the stack of pillows at the foot of her bed. "You know, girls, I think I'm goin' to have the doctor look at this one more time," she said as she waved a hand in the general direction of her ankle. "I think it's pinching me on one side. Since you're both here, why don't the two of you go down to the cafeteria and get some coffee, maybe talk awhile?"

Linny didn't even try to hide her scheming. It was obvious what she was trying to accomplish. Leslie protested first.

"Actually, if you're all right, I think I'll just get back to the children. I hate to leave the babysitter too long."

"Your neighbor does not count as a babysitter. Beatrice is a friend. I guarantee she's snuggled on your couch right now with a bowl of popcorn and an old movie on the television, listening to the sweet stillness of all your children sound asleep. Just go get some coffee."

Kate blushed at her aunt's persistence. She looked up at her cousin and shrugged her shoulders as if to say, "I didn't know about this either," then motioned hopefully in the direction of the cafeteria. Leslie sighed her acquiescence then turned and walked away.

"Be patient with her, Katie. It'll be all right. Oh, and if you see a doctor on your way out, send him in here, would you? I wasn't kidding about the pinching."

"I will," Kate assured her. "I'll be back in a little while to take you home, okay?"

"Don't hurry on my account. I'm quite comfortable right here. Get on now. You let Leslie get too far ahead of you, and she's sure to just slip out the door and go home."

Kate hurried after her cousin, catching her just as she arrived at the hospital's small cafeteria. The two women silently filled their coffee cups and sat down across from one another, their metal chairs scraping on the worn linoleum of the floor. They sat silently, awkwardly, filling their cups with cream and sugar, waiting for the other to speak first.

Finally, Kate began. "Leslie, I swear I didn't know anything about the house. Aunt Mary never said anything about it. I just . . . I had no idea."

Kate looked at Leslie, who had her arms folded across her chest, shoulders hunched forward. Kate could almost see the thick shroud of anger and resentment Leslie held tightly around her. Feeling she may have no other opportunity, Kate continued anyway. "What else do you want me to say, Les? I'm sorry. I'm sorry about the house. But more than that, I'm sorry I wasn't here for you when Tom died and sorry I stayed away for so long. It was selfish and wrong and just so stupid of me." Kate shut her eyes and took a deep breath. The words tumbled around in her head, and she struggled to pull them into complete sentences. Even still, she pressed on. "Leslie, it's the one thing I regret the most, more than anything else. I should have been there for you. I should have been at Tom's funeral. I should have been there to help . . . been there for the children. I don't think I can ever make it up to you, but I am sorry. I'm so sorry I hurt you."

Leslie didn't move. Her eyes focused downward on her Styrofoam cup while her hands fiddled with the drawstring of the pale blue windbreaker she wore. Kate noticed the jacket and recognized it as the one Tom had given her the Christmas after they'd gotten married. The weight of the many losses in Leslie's life swelled in front of Kate—a monstrous mountain of grief and loneliness near impossible to climb.

"Kate." Leslie's voice was calm and distant. "You already tried to apologize once before, but it's not that easy. You can't just fly back into town when someone dies, spread your apologies like wildfire, and expect everything to be like it was. You hurt me. You abandoned me, you rejected me, and now you've taken the one thing that could keep me connected to my mother."

"I never wanted to hurt you," Kate said, color rising swiftly to her cheeks. "I wasn't trying to reject you."

"But you did. You went off to your fancy college and then landed your big important job, bought a fancy car, lived a big, impressive life in the city. Everyone knows why you stopped coming back, Kate. This life, this small-town life, my measly little high school diploma, it isn't good enough for you anymore."

Kate was dumbfounded. "Is that really what you think? That I didn't come back because I thought I was too good for you? I didn't come back because I was tired of everyone making me feel like a failure because I didn't have *your* life. You and Tom were so happy; it was like everyone was just waiting for me to finally get my act together so I could be just like you." Kate pressed her head into her hands in exasperation. "And then, once I missed the funeral, I was just so ashamed. I . . . I didn't really feel like I had any right to come back."

"That's just an excuse. We're your family. You always have a right to come back."

"How could I come back? It was awful what I did, jumping ship on everybody just because things were hard. I was afraid of this, Leslie, of this conversation." Kate sighed. "It just . . . it was just easier to stay away."

"It would have been easier to not bury my husband and then my mother three years later. It would have been easier to not raise three children by myself, wondering if I have the strength to get out of bed in the morning, to hug and comfort my children when I am screaming on the inside because I don't know if I can do it for one more day. Any road but this one would have been easier, Kate. But we don't get to choose the road our life takes. Sometimes it just happens, and it stinks, and there isn't anything we can do to change it." She sighed and leaned back in her chair. "And we can't run away from it either," she added.

Kate knew Leslie was right. She had run away, and it had been an awful, cowardly thing to do. But she wasn't running now. It wasn't that she didn't feel the urge. She could have given the house to Leslie and made it back to her life in the city in time for work on Tuesday morning. But that wasn't who Kate wanted to be anymore. Somewhere deep within her, she realized it wasn't who Aunt Mary wanted her to be either.

"That's why she gave me the house," Kate whispered softly to herself.

"What?" Leslie asked.

"Aunt Mary," Kate explained. "She wanted me to stop running, to stop ignoring this part of my life—the most important part."

"How is a house going to teach you that?" Leslie sounded weary.

"I'm here, aren't I?" Kate smiled timidly at her cousin.

Leslie didn't smile in return, but Kate thought she noticed the deep frown lines between her brows lift just a little.

"Kate," Leslie said carefully. "I'm glad we had this conversation, and I'm grateful to hear your apology. But you're still going to have to give me some time, okay? This whole house thing—it's still really hard for me to comprehend."

"I understand," Kate said softly.

Leslie rose from her chair. "You better get Linny home. Charles is probably worried about her."

Kate glanced at the clock hanging above the door of the cafeteria. "You're right," she agreed.

They walked in silence back toward the emergency room. Leslie left without talking to Linny again, asking Kate to give her a hug and relay her promise to check on her the following afternoon. Kate did so and then helped her aunt into the wheelchair the hospital staff had provided.

"Ready to go?" a nurse asked. When Linny nodded, she steered the wheelchair down the hallway toward the hospital exit. Kate could sense

Linny's impatience as she walked beside her aunt. She was obviously anxious to hear how Kate's conversation with Leslie had gone. They had barely made it through the hospital doors before Linny stomped her one good foot on the ground, halting their progress and thoroughly startling the nurse.

"Well?" she finally questioned. "I'm not going another inch in this thing until you tell me how things went with Leslie."

"The coffee was very good," Kate teased.

"Katie, don't you start with me."

Kate laughed and reached down to touch Linny's shoulder. "It went much better than I had expected. Thank you for your not-so-subtle assistance."

"Yes, well, you know what they say . . . broken bones mend broken homes."

"Really, is that what they say?" Kate asked.

"I just said it," Linny said with a grin. "I think it's got a nice little ring to it. That counts for something, right?"

## Chapter 11

THE NEXT MORNING, AFTER A quick run and a long shower, Kate sat down in the sunroom with scrambled eggs, toast, and a tall glass of orange juice. She checked her e-mail, ignoring several from her office, determined not to be sucked back into work mode just yet. She laughed at the thought of how hard she had pushed to have daily updates and reports e-mailed to her so she could stay in the loop. And now here she was, ignoring them on purpose. She was just getting used to being away and was a bit surprised at how much she liked it. But even her newfound freedom from work couldn't hedge her curiosity in one regard. She couldn't keep herself from opening a message from Veronica with the subject line, "Steve." He had eaten lunch with Francine Weston from third-floor public relations the day before and had had flowers delivered to her desk that morning.

*Ha*! Kate mused. *He was much faster than I thought.* She was actually relieved that she didn't feel even a twinge of jealousy at the idea of Steve dating other women. He really wasn't the right person for her.

Just then, the house phone rang, disturbing the stillness and startling Kate so drastically she sloshed orange juice all over the front of her shirt.

"Well, that's just lovely," she said to herself, reaching for the phone. It was Mr. Lewis, a friend of Charles's and a painter who was happy to take care of the rest of the farmhouse. Kate willingly accepted his offer, and then, while it was on her mind, called up Mr. Brumfield about the rest of the needed repairs. Grateful to have the burden of home improvement lifted from her shoulders, Kate decided she should start sorting through the years of accumulated clutter that filled the closets and corners of the farmhouse. It was a dangerous job with a house so full of memories and emotions for so many people. She hoped that before her three weeks of vacation were up, Leslie would be willing to come over and help, but Kate reasoned it was still too soon to issue such an invitation.

The attic, however, felt safe enough for her to start on her own. Little of what was in the attic had anything to do with the family members who were still living. To be safe, she decided she wouldn't throw anything away until her cousins had had the opportunity to look it over. Before getting started, she went upstairs to change her orange-juice soaked shirt.

Kate yawned as she climbed the stairs to her room. She had stayed up late the night before and had hardly mustered the energy to climb out of bed that morning, much less put on her running shoes to run four miles. Still, she'd forced herself to go. How else might she run into Andrew? She'd left the hardware store optimistic that they would run into each other again, but even after twenty minutes of unnecessary stretching in the school parking lot, he had never made an appearance. For a moment, she wondered if he'd stopped running in hopes of avoiding her, but then she chided herself for thinking such things. She hardly knew the man. She probably gave herself too much credit in thinking he even thought of her enough to avoid her. More likely, he simply wasn't thinking of her at all.

As she picked out a new shirt, she thought of Ian's journal, the reason she'd been up so late. After she'd returned from the hospital, she'd stayed up reading, working her way through each page of the journal. It was slow and tedious. While a number of the entries were perfectly clear, much of the journal was faded and barely legible, requiring patience and good light to be read. Kate didn't mind the extra effort. She was captivated by Ian's words. Though day-to-day living was obviously very different two hundred years ago, Kate had found it surprisingly easy to relate to his words.

*People are people no matter the century*, she had concluded.

In several of Ian's entries, he mentioned a girl named Jennie. Kate was fairly certain Jennie was the daughter of Abe MacDonald, the gentleman Ian mentioned in his first entry and his employer. The family Bible indicated that Ian married Jennie, and Kate was thrilled every time she read of their developing romance. Ian's accounts were generally straightforward and practical, making Kate wish she could read Jennie's version of the story. But she did find one entry that revealed the intensity of Ian's feelings. It was only one, but it was enough. Back in her bedroom, Kate opened the journal and, finding that specific entry, read it one more time.

*29 April 1820*
*I've asked Jennie to marry me. I don't deserve her, but she's*
*agreed to have me just the same. I could not be happier, for*
*surely there is no woman more capable and lovely than she.*

*She was just a lass, though a bonnie one, the first time I met her. I thought little of her those first years, my head too full of myself to see how lovely she really was. But then one day, my eyes opened, and there she stood, same as she always was but, suddenly, completely different. Now that she is part of my life, I hardly imagine how I managed to get along without her. Her father has been generous in teaching me the skills of his trade, and though I never would have imagined, I seem to have a knack for it. He's agreed to have me work by his side, taking over the business completely in time. I'm grateful and hope to honor his generosity by taking care of his daughter, treating her as best I can, as best as she deserves.*

*Oh, to find such love,* Kate thought. She believed her parents had experienced such love. She didn't remember much about the dynamic of their relationship, but what she did remember was full of warmth. Mary had told her once that they had been soul mates. "I've never known a couple more devoted to each other than they were," she had said.

Leslie and Tom, on the other hand, had always been a bit more volatile in their relationship. They loved each other, of that Kate was certain, but from what she remembered of their early courtship, there was little middle ground between passionate love and outright loathing. The pair seemed to bounce between the two extremes as quickly and as frequently as the sun and moon changed places in the sky. Apologies were numerous and intense and generally resulted in a rekindling of emotion that turned the stomachs of anyone unfortunate enough to be around.

Years ago, Kate asked Mary if Leslie and Tom had mellowed out any as their marriage had progressed into parenthood. Aunt Mary had laughed and told her the only difference was that now they waited until the kids were asleep to battle things out. It must have worked for them. Kate was never aware of Leslie ever having been unhappy in her marriage.

At the same time, Kate was sure she didn't want that sort of a dynamic in her own relationship. She hoped that instead of someone who would capitalize on her hotheadedness, she might find someone who balanced her out—someone who ran and sharpened axes for neighbors and had a really great smile and amazing forearms. It still surprised her how readily her brain turned to Andrew. *Who is he, anyway?*

Shaking the thought from her mind, she changed her clothes and headed upstairs to the attic. After several hours of sorting, the heat and dust of the cluttered space overwhelmed Kate's senses. She retreated to the kitchen for a glass of water. While there, she decided to call and check on Linny. When no one answered, she thought it best to just go over and make sure she was all right. Surely she wouldn't be out and about with a newly broken ankle. Kate slipped on her shoes and put her keys and cell phone in her purse. On the front porch, she met Mr. Brumfield, who was arriving to start work on the repairs.

"Well, if it isn't little Katie," he said warmly.

Kate smiled and took the old man's extended hand. "It's nice to see you again, Mr. Brumfield. Thank you for your help today."

The kindly man closed his other hand tightly around hers and looked in her eyes, his own filled with sadness.

"Katie, I didn't have the chance to talk to you at the funeral. I'm most mighty sorry what's happened to your aunt. She was a good woman, the best I may have ever known, save my own dear wife. It's a shame this had to happen so soon after Tom died." He took a deep breath and patted the back of Kate's hand. "I reckon God has a purpose in it all," he finished, finally releasing her from his grip. "My prayers are with you, I want you to know."

"Thank you," she responded softly. "That's very kind of you to say."

"Well, I mean every word of it." He smiled, pale eyes sparkling in the morning sunlight. "Now, I expect you'll tell me anytime you need help around here. You'll do that, won't you?"

"I'll be sure to. I promise. I'm going over to visit my aunt Linny now," Kate said. "Please stay as long as necessary. A crew will be here within the hour to finish the painting. I hope they won't be in your way."

"Oh, no," Mr. Brumfield said. "It's John Lewis and his boys, I suspect. He'll do a fine job for you."

Kate said good-bye then climbed into her car to leave. As she pulled down the drive, her cell phone rang. She pulled it out of her purse and was surprised to see Harcourt Insurance, the name of Leslie's employer, on the touch screen of her iPhone. She quickly answered the call. "Hello? Leslie?" She tried to sound casual, like it wasn't a landmark event for her cousin to call her voluntarily.

"Hi, Kate . . . listen, I need a favor. Are you busy?"

"No," Kate responded. "I'm just leaving the house. I was going to check on Linny, but those are my only plans. What can I do for you?"

"Actually, it's Emily. I just got a call. She's not feeling well and needs to be picked up. But I'm the only person in the office today, and I can't leave to do it. Normally, I would've called Mom or Linny, but with her ankle, she can't drive, and well, I just didn't know who else to call."

Kate was suddenly nervous to spend time alone with her niece.

*It's what you wanted, Kate—the opportunity to spend time with Leslie's children.*

"I'll be happy to pick her up. Is she at the school? Wait, it's spring break, isn't it?"

"Yeah, she's at a day camp over at the YMCA. They said they'd have her wait at the front desk."

"I'll go there first, then, and if she feels up to it, we'll check on Linny together."

"Thanks, Kate."

Kate hung up the phone and turned left toward town and the YMCA. She found Emily sitting in a swivel chair behind the counter, drinking apple juice from a juice box and reciting the fifty states and their capitals for the youth director.

"You don't look sick to me." Kate smiled as she leaned over the counter and looked at her niece.

"Hello, Aunt Kate," Emily responded, though she didn't smile back at first. "There were boys in my group who were mean, mean, mean to me. So I didn't want to stay."

Kate was surprised at her straightforward reply. She wasn't even going to pretend to be sick, not even for Kate's entertainment.

The director stood and quickly apologized. "I'm so sorry. She really did tell me she was ill. Perhaps I can talk to the children involved and we can work this out so she can stay."

"It's really okay," Kate replied quickly. "I think I'd actually enjoy her company. I don't mind taking her with me as long as she's up for it." Kate glanced over at Emily, half expecting her to change her mind and race back to the mean, mean, mean boys in her group. Instead, Emily nodded her head, slid down from the chair, and reached out for Kate's hand. Kate slid Emily's hand into her own and the two walked companionably to the car.

"I don't have a booster seat, Aunt Kate. What should I do?" Emily climbed into the backseat of Kate's sedan and looked at her expectantly.

"A booster seat?" This was new territory. Did Emily think she could simply pull a booster seat out of her back pocket or her trunk or the Mary Poppins bag people who were actually prepared to spend the day with children must keep with them at all times?

"I guess I don't have one, Emily. Can you just buckle your seat belt without a booster seat for this one drive?"

"That is against the law!" Emily was shocked at Kate's suggestion.

"Well, I guess you could go back inside to the mean, mean, mean boys in your group," Kate said casually. "And then your mom can pick you up when she gets off work this afternoon."

Emily pondered her aunt's words and then said quietly, "Grandma had a booster seat in her car."

Kate's heart broke at the sound of those tender words and all that they implied.

"Would you like to pick up your booster seat from your grandma's car?" she asked gently. "Then we can go see Aunt Linny."

Emily was pleased with the plan and quickly buckled her seat belt. Kate was sure Mary had been a rock for Leslie's children through their father's illness and passing. She hadn't thought about how much Mary's death had affected them.

She pulled up to a stoplight two blocks from Main Street in downtown Rose Creek and looked at the surrounding buildings. Kate noticed a few small changes, but overall, the town seemed just as it always had. The light changed and Kate pulled forward, turning right onto Main Street. It was a narrow, one-way road that climbed upward until it reached the courthouse in the center of town. The surrounding shops and restaurants were squeezed in tightly, brick-and-mortar fingers clinging to the sides of the road as it descended sharply away from the town center.

Kate stopped at the next light. To her surprise, she noticed Andrew Porterfield leaving the courthouse, a large roll of papers in hand. He was dressed as he had been the day before—casual work clothes and thick, heavy boots. At the bottom of the courthouse stairs, a large golden retriever stood up and joined him as he walked toward a white truck parked just a few cars up from where Kate sat. She watched as he opened the passenger door for the dog and then, crossing over to the driver's side, climbed in behind the wheel. This was the third time in four days that Kate had run into this man. Even in small towns like Rose Creek, residents didn't run into the same people that often. Yet their meetings were so spontaneous; there was no logical way to deem them anything other than strange coincidence. But coincidence or not, Kate wished her interactions with Andrew could involve more than just staring after his car, now pulling ahead of her into the flow of traffic.

"Aunt Kate?" Emily's tiny voice piped up from the backseat.

"Hmm?" The light turned green, and Kate pulled across the intersection, glancing one last time at Andrew, who was now turning down a side street and moving out of Kate's range of vision.

"Do you know that man you were staring at?"

Kate blushed. Was this girl really only five years old?

"Um, no, not really," she said. "I met him once before, but I don't know him all that well."

"He looked like a nice man," Emily said sincerely. "He had a pretty dog."

"It was a pretty dog, wasn't it? Do you have any pets, Emily?"

"No," Emily said. "Nicholas is allergic to cats, just like Daddy was. And Mommy says dogs are too much work."

Kate smiled. She remembered the countless conversations Leslie had had with her parents the summer after sixth grade when she was desperately trying to convince Uncle Grey to get her a puppy. He had finally conceded, and Leslie had brought home a scruffy little terrier she named Ralphy. Ralphy was cute for about three weeks, until he started barking and chewing and causing trouble all over the house. Kate still remembered the look on Leslie's face when Ralphy chewed through her brand-new pair of white cheerleading shoes she hadn't even worn once. Uncle Grey never said I told you so, but within a week, Ralphy found a new home with someone much less sensitive to chewed shoes.

Back at the house, Kate pulled the car onto the gravel drive and ran in to get Mary's keys, which were still hanging on the hook by the door. Sam was planning on taking the car. He had been driving the same old Honda since before med school and could benefit from something newer, but the wounds had been too fresh when he'd left on Monday to take it then. It had seemed almost disrespectful to drive Mary's car away from her home so soon after her death. So he'd left it, planning to return in the next few weeks to drive it home. Kate walked over to the tan Subaru and retrieved the booster seat from the back. She was ill prepared for the ensuing emotional assault on her senses. The inside of the car smelled of fresh vegetables and lavender, coriander and honeysuckle. It smelled of Mary. Kate sat down in the backseat, still holding on to the booster seat, and spent a moment just breathing it all in. "Oh, Mary," she whispered gently. "If you only knew how much we miss you."

Remembering Emily, Kate stepped out of the car and walked quickly back to her own. It wasn't a big, fancy car, as Leslie had accused the night before at the hospital. It was a Volvo, albeit a nice, more-on-the-expensive-side, fully equipped Volvo. But still, it wasn't a Mercedes or BMW, though she technically could have afforded one if she'd wanted. She did have some modicum of modesty when it came to how she spent her money. Her salary wasn't out-of-the-ballpark impressive, but because she had only one person to spend her money on, it was a bit easier to pamper herself with the niceties of life.

Kate thought of Leslie and the meager salary she earned working as an administrative assistant at Harcourt Insurance group. She wished the sum of money Leslie had just inherited had been a bit more so Leslie didn't have to continue working at a job she probably didn't enjoy. After all, Leslie had only ever wanted to stay at home with her children, but working had become necessary after Tom's death.

"Here you go, Miss Emily," Kate said as she handed the booster seat to her niece. "Are you hungry? What do you say we pick up some lunch and take it over to Linny?"

"Sounds good to me," Emily said. She settled into her seat, obviously more comfortable with the law-abiding booster firmly beneath her.

## *Chapter 12*

ALL WAS WELL AT LINNY'S house, though the phone had gone unanswered all morning. Charles was sleeping in his recliner, and Linny, with her broken ankle, was unable to get to the phone in time to answer each time it rang.

"If you had a cordless telephone, you could just carry it with you everywhere you go," Kate suggested, knowing Linny would not agree with her.

"Why would I buy a new phone when this old phone works perfectly well? If I talk on the phone so much I need to carry it around the house with me, well, then I'm talking too much, and I'd be better off without a phone at all."

Kate shook her head, exasperated with the lovable, stubborn woman. "It's a matter of safety, Linny." Kate tried again. "I'll even buy the phone for you, and then we can donate your old one to Goodwill, where someone else, someone without a broken foot, can stand up and walk across the house to answer the phone every time it rings."

"Or I'll just do fine for the next few weeks until I get to feeling better."

"How are we supposed to know you're doing fine if every time we call, no one answers?"

"Well, I . . . oh, humph." Her shoulders slumped in defeat, but she still managed to have the last word. "It better not be some fancy, hard-to-operate thing, or I'll throw it in the trash as quick as you buy it."

Kate hugged Linny and sat down across from her on the couch. "I'll pick the simplest one I can find. I promise."

The two women talked while Emily ate her Happy Meal and watched cartoons.

"I dare say, it is good news she called you to get Emily, isn't it? I'm not sure that would have happened if not for last night," Linny said.

"I'm sure it wouldn't have happened. I'm glad she did call me. I really like Emily, and the more time I can spend with any member of Leslie's family, the better." Kate ate a handful of fries, feeling totally indulgent in making lunch out of french fries and a large Coke.

"That's the right attitude, Katie. You know, it really is good to have you back here. I wish it weren't just temporary."

"There's little need for advertising work in a town like Rose Creek," Kate said.

"Well, no, but there's other things you could do," Linny argued. "It would be good for you, don't you think? Small-town living is good for the soul."

"Hmm, I won't deny that." Kate smiled. She finished her food and stood to gather the trash, carrying it over to the kitchen before sitting back down with Linny.

"Linny? Do you believe in God?" She'd been toying with the question in her mind, but hearing the words out loud suddenly made her nervous. She chewed on her lip and waited for Linny to reply.

Linny raised her eyebrows in surprise. "Of course I do, child. Why would you ask that?"

Kate thought perhaps she should rephrase her question. She pulled her knees up under her and leaned her head onto her fist, propping her elbow against the back of the couch. She had been thinking a lot about Ian's letters and what his relationship with God had meant to him.

"I guess what I mean is, what does your relationship with God mean to you?" She continued, not wanting Linny to answer before she explained more fully what she meant. "See, I remember going to church when I was growing up, a few times a year, because that was what people did, but it was never really a big part of our lives. I don't remember ever praying or talking about God or anything. And now, with so much death and suffering and so many saying they will pray for the family, I don't know, it's just got me thinking. Is it—Do you . . . Is it a part of your life in that way?"

Linny leaned her head on the sofa cushions. Kate could tell it wasn't something she had expected and wondered if it made Linny uncomfortable to talk about it. She didn't seem bothered though, just surprised.

"Well, I probably haven't relied on God as much as I should," Linny began. "But then, I like to think He's a part of my life anyway, helping me know right from wrong, giving me strength when times are tough. I may not get down on my knees and ask Him for help, but at the end of the day, I think He knows who I am, and I think He knows I know who He is too." She seemed satisfied with her answer and looked to Kate to see if she was satisfied as well.

"So have you ever gone to church on a regular basis?"

"Well, to be honest, it wasn't really the way I was raised, to be going to church all the time. Not that my parents were bad people. It just wasn't what we did. And it was probably Grey's indifference that stopped your aunt Mary from church goin' herself. He and I were alike in that sense. But Mary, I remember a time when she went every Sunday, felt horrible if she missed a day. I think she went down to the Methodist church up on the hill, with the big stained-glass windows."

"That's where we went as children," Kate said. "For Christmas and Easter."

"Are you thinking about going to church?" Linny asked.

"Oh, no," Kate said. "I was just curious, that's all." The thought of attending church hadn't actually occurred to Kate until just then. But now she wondered if it was something she wanted to try.

"Well," Linny concluded, "I don't think it ever does harm to work on your relationship with God. At least I know that much is true."

Kate and Emily stayed at Linny's house for most of the afternoon. When the day finally leaned toward evening, Kate thought she should return to the farmhouse to see how the painting and repair work were going. Emily came along, her mother planning to pick her up there when she got off work. The painting, in fact, was almost complete. The house looked clean and crisp in the orange glow of late afternoon, and Kate climbed out of her car, standing in awe at the sight. Emily followed Kate's gaze to the house.

"I think Grandma would be happy with how pretty it looks. I wish she could come back to see it," Emily said thoughtfully.

"I wish she could too, Emily." Kate reached down and squeezed Emily's hand.

"Aunt Kate?" Emily asked.

"Yes?"

"Are you and my mommy going to be friends now?"

"I hope so, Emily," she said gently. "I really hope so." She wondered what this wide-eyed little girl thought of her and her conspicuous absence over the past few years. Kate crouched down in front of her and put both of her hands on Emily's tiny shoulders.

"I was gone for a long time, Emily, and I was wrong. But I don't want to do that anymore. I want to visit more, if that's okay with everyone."

Emily tweaked her mouth over to one side and wrinkled her eyebrows, giving off an air of serious contemplation. Kate struggled not to smile and waited patiently for Emily's approval.

"Are you going to live in Grandma's house forever?"

"Well, I'm not really sure what I'm going to do," Kate answered. "But I promise I will always take care of the house, no matter what."

Emily let out a sigh of relief. "That's good," she said simply. "I really love this old house."

Kate smiled and silently agreed with her niece. The house certainly seemed to have that effect on people.

Leslie didn't stay long when she came to pick up Emily, but she was polite and gracious and openly grateful for Kate's help. Kate assured her it was a sweet pleasure to spend the day with her niece and she was willing to help out anytime Leslie needed her, at least for the next two and a half weeks.

As Kate imagined spending more time with Leslie and her niece and nephews, it was hard to think of living somewhere far away—hard, really, to think of living anywhere but right there in the old farmhouse. Her job and life back at home in Atlanta, the life that had seemed so big and important a week ago, continued to feel vacant and shallow to Kate, empty of the things capable of truly filling her up. Her niece, for example, and Leslie's boys. Kate knew so little about Nicholas and Tommy and suddenly yearned to know everything she could about each one of them.

And then there were the letters—Ian's letters. Kate found herself thinking about her ancestor frequently throughout the day, thinking about his words, "Wherever you walk, walk with God." Kate was comforted, she discovered, by the mere knowledge that God existed. It made her wonder what it would be like to actually seek God, learn more of Him, and perhaps even pray. When Kate had read Ian's words for the first time, she had thought to pray but felt silly and ignorant as to how to start or what to say. She imagined herself the last person God would actually be concerned with. With all the good, worthy Christians in this world, why would God have need of her? Would He even hear her prayer? She wasn't sure, and yet, she felt she needed Him. The question, then, was how to find Him.

Kate finished cleaning up the kitchen after her impromptu dinner of cereal and buttered toast. It was one of the things she appreciated about being single. When she didn't feel like eating, she just didn't cook. She thought of her cousin, who, weary after a day's work outside the home, was faced with three hungry little people every night. Kate's respect for Leslie was increasing by the minute. But then, to get to spend all of that time with kids like Emily—surely the work and weariness were worth it. Surely it was better than washing a few dishes in a big, empty house, all alone. Her work done in the kitchen, Kate turned again to Ian's journal.

> *8 November 1824*
>
> *I've never been as scared as I was last night when Jennie struggled so fiercely to bring our son into this world. About three hours in, when the screaming was so awful I thought I might near burst with my own agony, the midwife came to me and said, "Ian . . . I need you to pray. Only God can help her now." So I prayed. I prayed and cried for three more hours, tormented by Jennie's pain, wishing I could feel it for her instead. And then all was quiet, and the blessed midwife, tears in her eyes, told me I have a son. He's healthy and well and, though a bit worn out from his difficult entry into this world, has passed all examination and seems to be as perfect a baby as I've ever seen. And praise be to God, Jennie is fine too. The midwife says the baby was turned the wrong way, and no amount of maneuvering would help. But then when Jennie was out of strength and we'd all but given up hope, the midwife says it was like a miracle under her hands—like a giant knot in Jennie's belly unwound itself and out came my baby boy. An act of God, she called it. To Him I give praise and glory, my heart so full of gratitude for His love and mercy. My life is rich with His blessings. And now as I look into the tiny face of my offspring, my newborn son, I feel as if I'm looking into the very face of God. Surely there is nothing quite so beautiful as this. We named the baby James, after my father. I wish my mother were here to meet him.*

Kate had only ever considered children of her own as a vague and distant idea—something her family hoped her to have but that she'd never felt ready for herself. Never had she felt like her own biological clock was ticking. It wasn't that she was against the idea of a family, but she hadn't lost sleep wishing for it either. She hadn't, that was, until now.

## Chapter 13

THE NEXT COUPLE OF DAYS, Kate kept herself busy organizing and sorting through the boxes and piles of stuff in the attic. Much to Kate's delight, Leslie even brought the kids over one evening to help. The five of them ate pizza and drank Cherry Pepsi then had a hilarious time going through all of the old clothes in the guest bedroom closet upstairs. Leslie and Kate laughed as Emily and Nicholas paraded around in sweater dresses and polyester vests, circa 1974. Tommy fell asleep in Kate's arms, and while the older kids watched a movie, the two women sat in the family room and talked. It was tenuous and still a little strained, but it was obvious they were both making an effort.

The more time she spent with Leslie, the more Kate wanted to punch herself for all of the wasted time she'd been away from her family. Her heart burned with fresh agony every time she thought of Aunt Mary, of the face-to-face conversation she didn't get to have with her before she died. The pain was most easily soothed by spending time with Leslie and her kids. Kate fed off of their presence. Even with the fresh pain of losing Mary, Kate's life here in Rose Creek, with Linny and Leslie and the kids so close by, felt surprisingly rich. Work and life back in Atlanta had never felt so far away.

After her evening with Leslie, Kate called Bryan and Sam, inviting them up to have dinner and help sort through the last of what was in the attic. There was also a large pile of boxes and some furniture Kate had set aside that she wanted everyone to look through one final time before she donated it all to a local charity. And, of course, Bryan still had to look through his room. Kate kept her word and steered completely clear of the space. Really, she had no desire to see what he might be hiding in there. It would be a couple of weeks before Sam and Theresa could make it over, but they promised Kate they would come. Bryan was willing as well.

Without really realizing what she was doing, Kate was preparing the house for new occupants—visualizing improvements and updates. It was only a matter of time before her family asked if she was getting the house ready to sell. But Kate wasn't preparing for a sale. As she walked through each room of the house, it scared her to admit she was preparing the house for herself—for her own family.

When she wasn't sorting through closets or imagining plans for the house, she continued her efforts to piece together a little bit of Wylie family history. She studied Ian's journal, even copying by hand the entries that were too faded to read completely, piecing the letters and words together as best she could. It had become a bit of a project, and though she knew Ian was an ancestor of her cousins as well, she hadn't yet told anyone about her discovery. Perhaps she was being selfish, but a part of her felt as if some magical connection existed between Ian and her, some link between their stories. To tell her family about him might dissolve that connection.

She *would* tell them. But not yet.

Kate asked Linny if she knew if Mary had kept in touch with any of her cousins on the Wylie side, wondering if there might be a fellow descendant of Ian Wylie who may be familiar with his story. But Linny knew of no one. Aunt Mary's address book revealed a few Wylies living in Western Tennessee and one in Wisconsin, but Kate didn't recognize the names. Since they had not been at Mary's funeral, Kate guessed they must not have been close relatives. Mary's father, George Wylie, had three brothers that, if Kate remembered the story correctly, had all moved away from North Carolina when they were very young, establishing and growing their families in other parts of the country. George had been the youngest brother by ten years. A bit of a generational gap separated his kids from those of his siblings, and Mary had never been close to her cousins growing up. Even still, to find such a record of ancestry was worthy of looking up a long-lost cousin. Kate decided that before her three weeks were up, she'd have to make some phone calls to the Wylies listed in Mary's address book.

After a particularly dusty Sunday afternoon in the attic, Kate decided she needed a break. After taking a shower, she drove into town to pick up a few things for Linny, including the new cordless phone she'd promised her. Linny and Charles had friends dropping in that afternoon and had invited Kate to stay, but she declined the invitation. She was anxious to get back to the farmhouse, though, once there, she found herself suddenly listless, no longer in the mood to work.

She wandered aimlessly through the rooms, restless and unable to settle into any specific activity, though much needed to be done. A large box of pictures on the dining room table briefly captured her attention, but she left it so she and Leslie could sort through it together later in the week. Leslie and the children were spending the weekend in Knoxville with Tom's parents but were returning Monday afternoon and had plans to come over.

A large stack of documents the attorney had sent over was waiting for Kate's signature—deeds of trust, appraisals, and tax assessments—but Kate's heart wasn't in it. Passing by the phone, she remembered her determination to call the Wylie family members listed in Mary's address book and picked up the phone to make the calls. Grandpa George's brother, Russell, lived in Tennessee. The number listed was for Russell's son Harrison, but Kate spoke only with a grandson. Harrison had passed away a few years before. The son had little knowledge of the family's heritage and did not recognize the name Ian Wylie. He did promise to mention the name and the vague story outline Kate gave him to his other family members and call if anyone remembered anything, but Kate wasn't very hopeful. Ian had lived a long time ago. If anyone would have known about him and the details of his life, it would have been Mary. And if she knew, she would have told the story.

No, this story was Kate's and Kate's alone.

Finally settling on the couch in the family room, Kate picked up the journal to resume her study of its pages. She pulled out the notebook where she kept her transcriptions of the difficult passages, planning to pick up her work where she had left off. She flipped to the back of the journal, searching for the right page. Instead, she was surprised to find a nearly perfect and completely legible entry toward the end of the book. The ink was not faded, and the letters were clear and distinct. Kate wondered what conditions so perfectly preserved this particular entry. She speculated that perhaps the kind of ink used in the writing of each entry contributed one way or the other to purity in preservation. She made a mental note to do some research on the subject. Then she began to read.

*6 April 1837*
*My father-in-law, Abe MacDonald, has passed away. He*
*was an old man, and we give glory to God that he lived such*
*a full and rich life. I am grateful to the man for stepping in*
*and treating me like a son when my own father could not do*

*so. He saved me in more ways than he could ever imagine,
giving me the hand of his sweet daughter not the least of them.
He will be missed, his name forever honored in this house. His
death has also brought about a change of our more intimate
circumstances. Upon finding herself widowed, Jennie's mother
decided it best to move in with us. Our home is adequate
enough to accommodate her, and I'm sure with time my spirit
will make room for her as well. Don't understand me wrong. I
love the woman. Her kindness and compassion nearly matches
that of her husband. I have tremendous respect for her and
dare not speak evil of her character or goodwill. But we are
prone to our differences and find ourselves in contentious
disagreements quite frequently over the subject of religion.
Mother MacDonald is a faithful, dutiful Methodist who
attends church three times a week and feels it her obligation
to enlist her family in the same measure of devout service. And
here is where we disagree. I am a religious man. I give glory to
God for pulling me through those difficult years when I first
arrived in this country. He has blessed me in more ways than
I deserve. My life is rich with peace and happiness. But I do
not subscribe to any one particular faith. I find the minister
of Mother MacDonald's church stuffy and a bit pompous.
It does not seem a gospel of good news but one of fear and
condemnation. Are we not meant to be happy in this life? To
celebrate the joy that comes from righteous obedience to God's
laws rather than comply out of fear, out of an anxious desire
to keep our souls from the hellfire and damnation preached so
heartily from every pulpit in this city? I've acquired a group
of religious writings by one Roger Williams, a theologian and
pioneer in the establishment of religious tolerance and freedom
in this nation. He details in his writings his belief that the
authority to act in God's name is gone from the earth, that
until Jesus Christ comes again to call apostles to organize His
church as it was in the times of the New Testament, it will not
be on the earth. The intentions of the men leading the churches
surrounding me today are good. They are good men, though I
daresay some could improve their personalities a bit. But did
Jesus not call apostles to act in His name? Were they not given*

*authority to preach and to act for Christ after He ascended into heaven? What happened to that authority? Williams says the Christian church is in a wilderness of apostasy—that over time, emperors and rulers of state corrupted the religion of Christianity and that basic tenets and truths have been lost. There must needs be a restoration, he says. And Jesus himself must do it. To this, I align my own beliefs. I've spent a great deal of time reading in the New Testament and believe our God to be one of unity and love. I don't see the reason to have so many factions, so many different churches preaching one thing or another. I'll wait for that restoration, for a unification of purpose and spirit. Whether in this life or the next, I'll wait for it, all the while disagreeing with my dear mother-in-law. Though I feel I have no house of worship, no four-walled structure to house my praise, I have my heart, full of gratitude and love, a heart dedicated to raising my children to know God, love Him, and worship Him in all they do. I have walked with God as my own father prescribed all those years ago. And I have felt His goodness on a daily basis. I pray that one day He may lead me to the truth.*

Ian's words were changing something inside of Kate. It felt as if a part of her had been locked up and hidden from view for so long she'd nearly forgotten it was there. But now she was finding it again, feeling a desire to learn more about who that person was. Every time she read Ian's journal, she felt more and more certain that the person who would teach her the most about that hidden part of herself was God. Maybe it was time to visit the Methodist church after all.

## Chapter 14

THE FOLLOWING MONDAY MORNING, KATE almost didn't run. She had already logged more miles the week before than she had ever run back in Atlanta. But the cool, clean air of the mountains was much more invigorating than the wall-to-wall mirrors of the gym and the robotic hum of the treadmill. She followed her usual path, a four-mile circuit from the farmhouse to the elementary school and then back again. She'd all but given up on running into Andrew. She had not seen him out running since their first encounter, so she was surprised when she crested the top of the hill leading up to the elementary school and saw him circling the little dirt track around the school's playground. She glanced at her watch. It was still early, just after seven. She had started earlier on purpose to avoid the crowds of parents and children pouring into the school, which was now back in session after spring break. Perhaps that's why she'd missed seeing Andrew the week before. She was never there early enough to catch him.

She stopped at the top of the hill to catch her breath, bending over with her hands on her knees until the burn in her calves slowly faded. Andrew hadn't seen her yet. She watched as he circled the track once. Finally, he looked up and saw her standing there. He raised his arm and waved, motioning for her to join him on the track. She waved back and jogged over to the stairs leading down from the parking lot.

"I ran this track fourteen times hoping you'd show up." Andrew smiled as she approached him.

"Fourteen?" Kate questioned. "Would you have kept going had I not come?" She was silently thrilled with the prospect of him intentionally waiting for her.

"I set the limit at twenty-five," he joked.

Kate could tell Andrew was nervous. The air around them crackled with anxious, hopeful energy. Ironically enough, it seemed a scene appropriately suited for an elementary school playground. They stood, smiling awkwardly, toying with the gravel beneath their feet.

Finally, Andrew said, "Would you like to walk a little bit? We can head in the direction you're going if you'd like."

Kate readily agreed, and the pair set out, circling the track one final time before climbing the stairs and heading back down the hill away from the school.

"Tell me how you came to Rose Creek," Andrew said, beginning the conversation.

"I grew up here," Kate replied simply.

"Ah, I remember that," Andrew said. "But you've been gone a long time. What brought you back?"

Kate walked in silence a few moments, hands tucked into the pockets of her lightweight performance jacket. She'd been living the reality of her situation all week, but it was still hard to say the words out loud.

"My aunt passed away," she finally answered. "I came back for her funeral."

"I'm so sorry," Andrew said.

"She was like a mother to me. She was the only mother I can really remember. My own mom died when I was a little girl."

"I'm sorry to hear that too. How did it happen?"

She looked at him and saw the sincerity in his eyes. He hadn't asked out of mere curiosity; he was asking out of concern.

"A car accident," Kate said. "I was seven years old. Both of my parents were killed. I was asleep in the backseat. I remember being in the hospital after it happened and hearing one of the EMTs say it was a head-on collision. My parents absorbed the bulk of the crash, and I was pulled from the car with a few bruises and a cut above my eyebrow." Instinctively, she raised her hand to the scar, barely visible on her left brow.

Andrew took a deep breath. "I can't imagine," he said.

"Thank you. It . . . it's been tough, I guess. I don't know. Life isn't always fair. You just take it one day at a time, you know?"

"I know all about that," Andrew said softly.

Kate looked up. "That sounded like a loaded statement."

Andrew shrugged his shoulders. "Everybody's got a past, right?"

"Uh-huh," she said, smiling. "Some more shady than others."

Andrew didn't respond, eyes cast downward to the gritty pavement under their feet.

Kate changed the subject. "I saw you the other day while I was driving through town. You were leaving the courthouse. You had a dog with you."

"Yeah? That was Ruby. She's kind of the company pet. I was picking up a building permit for a new construction job." Andrew's mood obviously lightened with the change of subject.

"So that's what you do, then? You build . . . things?"

"Well, I guess for now, yeah. That's what I do. Spencer Contracting—Dan Spencer—he's my uncle, my mom's brother, so I'm working with him for a little while." Andrew seemed nervous, like there was more to the story than what he was telling. "It's a small local company, but they do pretty well for themselves—mostly commercial but some residential projects as well. This new project," Andrew went on, "is a big vacation home for some doctor in Atlanta."

Kate nodded in interest. "So what do you do for the company?"

Andrew shrugged his shoulders, arms folded across his chest. "A bit of everything, I guess. Honestly, it's probably just a temporary thing. I needed a change of pace, and my uncle's been kind enough to help me out the past few months."

"What did you do before you starting working for your uncle?"

Andrew was quiet for a moment before finally answering her question. "I was an architect . . . working for a firm in Virginia. It's sort of complicated. Let's just say we didn't exactly part ways on the most amicable of terms."

"That's got to be tough," Kate said.

"I don't know. I'd been thinking about going out on my own for a while anyway. I expect that's what I'll do eventually."

There was a slight edge to his voice, a distance in his tone indicating to Kate further probing would yield few results. Kate could tell he was uncomfortable, and though she was curious about whatever details might be hidden beyond the front page of Andrew's story, she didn't push him.

"Hey, you probably went to school with some of my cousins—Dan's kids. They grew up here too," Andrew said.

"Oh gosh! Tracy Spencer. I remember now. Her dad sponsored our summer swim team. We had Spencer Contracting written on the sides of our swim caps."

Andrew smiled. "Yeah, Tracy was a swimmer. And then her younger brothers . . ."

"Bradley and Ben." Kate finished his sentence. "Twins, weren't they? They were on the team too. Man! How is Tracy? I haven't thought about her for years."

"She's good," Andrew answered. "She's married, has four kids. She's living in Idaho, in Twin Falls."

"Idaho? What on earth took her there?"

"Her husband is from Idaho. He works with the family business, I think, so that's where they ended up."

"Wow, four kids. That's hard to believe. I always liked Tracy. She was always so nice to everybody, and she swam a killer anchor leg for our 4x100 relay." Kate pulled the sleeves of her hooded jacket down around her fingers. The sky, though clear when her run began, was now full of clouds, the air turning chilly.

"Yeah, that sounds like Tracy. Wait." Andrew paused, voice filled with sudden enthusiasm. "When Tracy's high school relay team went to state, you were on her team?"

"I swam lead leg," Kate answered, smiling at the memory.

"I saw you swim, then. I was there, watching with my family when you guys won. My family drove over from Charlotte for the meet."

"All the way from Charlotte to Raleigh? You guys must be really close." Kate was incredulous. It seemed like a big thing for a family to do—an extended family from a different town—to drive all that distance.

"Yeah, I guess so," Andrew said casually. "You know how family is."

Kate was quiet. She wasn't sure she really did know how family was. She certainly didn't seem very good at keeping things up with her own.

"How'd the house painting go?"

"It's finished," Kate said, "much to my delight."

"Wow. I need to hire you to paint my house," Andrew said.

"Very funny," she said. "I hired someone in the end. I'd still be painting had I tried to do the whole thing myself."

"Much easier that way, for sure," he agreed. "It was your house, then, that you were painting?"

"It was my aunt Mary's. I didn't expect it. She actually has children that I thought would have inherited . . ." Kate's words were nearing dangerously emotional territory. "I'm not sure why it's mine," she said simply. "But it is."

"And I'm sure it looks lovely with a new coat of paint," Andrew said. Kate was grateful that he didn't push for more information. Their conversation continued as they wound around the dusty roads of the valley. There was little traffic, little to interrupt the steady flow of conversation, the light laughter.

As they walked, Kate told Andrew about her work, about her home in Atlanta, about her cousins and her aunt Linny. Andrew told Kate about his family, how he grew up in Charlotte but often spent summers vacationing in Rose Creek. His family owned a cabin there, where he was staying now. With all of their talking, Andrew did not provide further details about why he'd left Virginia for Rose Creek, though he admitted he'd only been there just shy of a year. Kate was curious and casually probed into what prompted his move, but Andrew staunchly avoided the subject. It wasn't difficult to see that whatever his reasons for leaving his previous home, they were not something he wanted to discuss. Just the same, he was very easy to talk to, and Kate felt strangely comfortable in his presence, even though their acquaintance had been so short.

When Kate was dating Steve, he had always been careful how he said things in conversation, not because he was concerned about those around him but because he was constantly worried about how things made him look. But Andrew was different. He seemed to be aptly tuned into Kate's emotional barometer—his words not measured against his own comfort but against hers. There was a certain peace about him—a quiet confidence that was thoroughly intriguing. Kate didn't want their walk to end.

The clouds overhead rumbled a low but distinct warning, and the two decided they were better served by less talking and more running. Kate had no idea where Andrew's run had originated that morning, but the air was ominously thick and heavy with moisture. Since they had been walking in the general direction of the farmhouse, Kate motioned for Andrew to follow her home in hopes of finding shelter before the rain began. They were a half mile out when it started. It came with such force that by the time they reached the house, they were soaked to the skin.

They climbed the steps to the porch, laughing as they tried to catch their breath. Kate looked at Andrew, drops of rain clinging to his eyelashes and trickling down the end of his nose. Andrew ran his fingers back and forth through his hair, flinging water all over the porch and all over Kate.

"Good thing you're already wet." He grinned. They stood there looking at one another, eyes suddenly held by the other's gaze. While her breathing slowed as she recovered from their run, Kate's heart continued to race. Andrew looked great standing there, clinging wet T-shirt showing off the wiry definition of his chest and shoulders. Kate wouldn't deny a physical attraction, but in that moment, what she felt went far beyond the physical. She wasn't ignorant enough to call it love. She'd only just met the man. But some connection, some mystifying force of gravity, was pulling her in, grasping tiny pieces of her soul, and one by one, tying them to his.

"You must have run through a mud puddle," Andrew said gently, hesitating just slightly before he raised his hand and ran his finger across a smudge of dirt on Kate's cheek. His hand lingered on the square of her jaw. Kate's heart quickened, an echo of the pulse beating visibly in the hollow of Andrew's throat. They stood there, frozen in the intensity of the moment, and listened to the rain pounding on the metal roof of the porch overhead. Kate remembered words she'd read in Ian's journal the night before when describing his relationship with his wife: *Our souls are bound, hers and mine . . . our hearts beating as one.*

Just as suddenly as the storm had started, the rain slowed and softened. Andrew tore his gaze away from Kate and shook his head as if to work himself out of a trance. He stepped away from Kate and took a deep, audible breath.

"I have to go," he said simply.

"What?" Kate questioned, glancing quickly around her to see if something triggered his retreat. "You can't run home soaking wet. Let me get you a towel, and then I can drive you home."

Andrew thanked her for the offer but insisted he was fine and hastily took off down the driveway. Kate shook her head as she watched him disappear around a curve and into the trees.

Kate went inside and headed upstairs. There wasn't an inch of her that wasn't saturated with rain. A long soak in a warm bathtub was exactly what her body needed, but it was going to take more than warm water to make sense of her thoughts. She couldn't shake the image of Andrew's hasty retreat from her front porch. He had wanted to kiss her. She was nearly certain of that. The moment had been perfect, the charge in the air almost visible. And then he'd left.

As she slid into the tub, the frustrating scene replayed over and over in her mind. Clearly, he was running away from something. But what?

Kate soaked until the water started to cool, and then she climbed from the tub. As she wrapped her hair in a towel, she thought again of the words from Ian's journal that had punctuated the moment she'd experienced with Andrew. She slipped into her bathrobe and padded down to her bedroom, where she found the journal and flipped to the entry she had read the night before.

*14 November 1826*
*I know many a man marries for convenience, for practicality rather than love. I respect the necessity for these unions, but,*

*oh, how grateful I am that I married for love. I love Jennie more every day. We've only just begun our journey together, yet I already fear what my life would be without her. I pray that God will give us many beautiful years together, and though I know not what the next life will hold, perhaps God may be merciful and allow her to be mine into eternity as well. Jennie knows me like no other . . . deals with my moods, tempers my spirit. Our souls are bound, hers and mine . . . our hearts beating as one.*

It was ridiculous to even consider such love when thinking about Andrew. They'd only just met. But there was something there—something different from anything Kate had ever experienced before.

## Chapter 15

KATE PUT THE JOURNAL BACK on her nightstand and pulled her favorite blue jeans out of the bottom of her suitcase. She should probably unpack. Three weeks was too long to live out of a suitcase, but she decided she would have to do it later. The warmth of the bathtub and her early-morning run had completely sapped her energy. Feeling wickedly indulgent, she pulled on her jeans and an old sweatshirt and stretched out on her bed to take a nap.

She was startled awake when the doorbell rang.

Kate looked at the clock on her nightstand and realized she'd been asleep for three hours. It was just past noon, too early for Leslie to be arriving. Besides, Leslie wouldn't have knocked. Kate hurried downstairs, wondering who could be at the door. For a moment, she hoped it was Andrew, come to explain his hasty departure and ask her to dinner. But then she caught a glance of herself in the mirror that hung at the foot of the stairs. Maybe she didn't want it to be Andrew after all. She looked very much like she'd just woken up, her eyes heavy with sleep and her face pale. She pinched her cheeks and rubbed her eyes, then pulled her hair into a messy ponytail. The improvement was only minimal, but when the doorbell rang for a second time, she decided her appearance would have to do.

Instead of Andrew, she found two men, or boys rather, standing at her door. Kate immediately took them to be representatives from some sort of church—probably Jehovah's Witnesses come to tell her about some event they would like her to attend. They'd visited her at her home in Atlanta as well. She would take the pamphlet they would offer and send them on their way. She stood with her hand still on the knob of the large wood door and, without opening the screen door, said hello.

The tallest one spoke first. "Hello," he smiled broadly. "I'm Elder Christianson, and this is Elder Peterson. We are missionaries from The Church of Jesus Christ of Latter-day Saints, and we are hoping we can share a message with you about Jesus Christ and His gospel. Would it be all right if we come in?"

That wasn't what Kate had expected. "I, um, I don't know. What church did you say you were from?"

"The Church of Jesus Christ of Latter-day Saints," the missionary responded. "A lot of people know us as the Mormons?"

"Mormons? Really? There are Mormons in Rose Creek?" Kate had certainly heard of the religion, had even known a few Mormons when she'd been in college, but here . . . in Rose Creek? It was such a small town.

The missionary smiled at her reaction. "We get that a lot. There aren't many of us, but, yes. There are Mormons in Rose Creek."

Kate knew very little about the Mormons—only what she had learned from the media, which wasn't all that much.

"I'm sorry," Kate said. "I appreciate you coming by, but I'm not really interested. Thank you though." Kate stepped back, not wanting to shut the door in their faces but wanting to be clear about how she felt.

The missionary who had spoken, Elder Christianson, looked at his companion and briefly shook his head. They looked back at her, showing no sign of departure.

Kate sighed. "Good-bye, then," she said with a little more emphasis as she pushed the heavy door closed—except it wouldn't close. The door bounced off the dead bolt that had somehow twisted open to prevent the door from latching into place. Kate caught the door and untwisted the dead bolt, shocked to see the two young men still standing on the other side of the screen. She went to close the door again but stopped as Elder Christianson, trembling with nerves, started to speak.

"Ma'am, Jesus Christ has restored His Church. He has called apostles, who live and serve today under proper authority, to lead His Church and teach the true gospel of Jesus Christ. There has been a restoration—a unification of purpose and spirit. May we please share our message?"

Kate froze. She had heard those words before. This man she'd never seen or spoken to in her life was repeating the very words she had read in Ian's journal. He had mentioned a restoration—a unification of purpose and spirit. Those were *his* words. She walked onto the porch and gently pulled the door closed behind her.

"Maybe we could just sit here on the porch," she said softly, motioning for them to join her.

## Chapter 16

"I DON'T UNDERSTAND," KATE SAID, looking at the missionaries—elders, they called themselves—sitting in front of her. "If this church, this restoration you speak of, is what Roger Williams was waiting for, what my ancestor Ian Wylie was waiting for . . . if this is it, the real deal, so to speak, why isn't it being shouted from the rooftops? Why aren't people all over the world jumping on the bandwagon, Christians everywhere recognizing it for the truth that it is?"

Elder Christianson leaned forward and looked at Kate, focused and sincere. "That's a great question, Ms. Sinclair. Remember that in many respects, it *is* being shouted from the rooftops. All over the world, thousands of missionaries like Elder Peterson and me are taking the message of the gospel to any and all who are willing to listen, and many have accepted and embraced it. But there must be opposition in all things. People follow the traditions and beliefs of their fathers, they question change, shy away from anything that challenges what they've believed in the past, anything that may require their lives to be different. It's human nature to do so."

Elder Christianson looked at Elder Peterson, nodding his head in encouragement. Kate could tell he seemed more at ease in his role as a missionary and thought perhaps he had been preaching a bit longer than his companion. Yet when Elder Peterson spoke, he had a quiet simplicity to his explanations that resonated with Kate. She found it easy to accept and believe his heartfelt words.

"Remember that when Jesus Christ walked the earth, there was still great opposition. People saw the miracles, saw Jesus raise the dead, heal the sick and afflicted, and yet, some still didn't believe He was the Son of God. They refused to see what they did not want to see."

"So how do I know?" Kate asked. "How do I see?"

"You ask," Elder Christianson responded. "We told you of Joseph Smith, of his desire to know what God would have him do. He read the verses in the Bible that said, 'If any of you lack wisdom, let him ask of God, that giveth to all men liberally, and upbraideth not.' So he prayed to ask God what he should do. Just as God gave Joseph an answer, He will give you an answer too." He reached for the Book of Mormon he had given Kate earlier in their discussion and flipped to the back, looking for a particular scripture.

"And here, in the Book of Mormon, the prophet Moroni makes a promise that if you read these words with sincerity and a full purpose of heart, God will reveal the truthfulness of it to you." He read, "'And when ye shall receive these things, I would exhort you that ye would ask God, the Eternal Father, in the name of Christ, if these things are not true; and if ye shall ask with a sincere heart, with real intent, having faith in Christ, he will manifest the truth of it unto you, by the power of the Holy Ghost.'"

Kate took a deep breath and leaned back in her rocking chair.

"Ms. Sinclair—Kate?" She had insisted they call her Kate, but neither seemed capable of doing so. Did she really seem that much older than they were? Elder Peterson leaned forward to ask her a question. "Do you ever pray?"

Kate looked down at her hands. It wasn't that she hadn't thought of praying, especially this past week, with all that had happened, but it seemed such a foreign concept to her. To think that God would listen, would hear her, when so many better suited to the act were out there praying all the time—it didn't seem right for her to try.

"I . . . no. Not really," she finally said.

She listened as the elders taught her about prayer, giving her simple advice about what she could say and how she could address her Heavenly Father. Then they encouraged her to read the Book of Mormon and pray to ask to know if it was true.

The familiar chime of the old grandfather clock in the front room of the farmhouse reminded Kate that she'd been sitting on the porch with the missionaries for nearly two hours.

"I should let you go," she said, glancing at her watch as she stood up. "I didn't realize we'd been talking so long."

"We don't mind a bit," Elder Peterson assured her.

"We'd like to invite you to church next Sunday. Would you be willing to come?" Elder Christianson asked as he gathered together his things.

"Oh, I don't think I'm quite ready for that yet," Kate responded. To attend church with the Mormons seemed a bit overwhelming.

"That's perfectly okay," the elder responded. "I do think it would be a great idea for you to come to the family history center this week. There are volunteers there who can help you search for additional information about your ancestors, maybe even find something specific about Ian."

"I would like that," Kate said. "It was Wednesday morning, right?" She walked the missionaries to their car, thanking them for their time and assuring them that she would read and call if she had any questions. As they walked, she wondered, of all the places in Rose Creek, how they'd wound up at her door. She looked at the elders.

"How did you find me?" she asked. "Did someone send you here, or was it just chance that turned you down my driveway?"

Elder Peterson looked at Elder Christianson, silent communication passing between them. "We were certainly sent by someone," Elder Peterson said. "Though not someone local." He smiled at Kate and looked at his companion.

"I was driving," Elder Christianson said. "God might as well have dropped a bowling ball on the brake pedal for how sure I was we needed to turn down your drive. He wanted us to find you. I'm sure of it."

Kate nodded her head. "Thank you for coming."

"We'll meet you Wednesday morning, then, 10:00 a.m. at the church building. You're sure you know where it is?"

"I know the area well," she responded. "I'm sure I'll find it."

The missionaries paused before climbing into the car and watched as Leslie's van pulled down the drive.

Kate had been so distracted by the missionaries' visit that she had completely forgotten Leslie was coming and had no idea how she would respond to her Mormon visitors. Leslie walked over from the van, Tommy on her hip and Emily and Nicholas following close behind.

"Hello," she said curiously, looking at the strangers standing before her.

"Hi, Leslie," Kate moved over to meet her. "This is, uh, Elder Peterson and Elder Christianson. They're missionaries from the Mormon Church here in town." She looked at the elders. "This is my cousin Leslie, and her three kids: Nicholas, Emily, and the baby, Tommy. The missionaries were just leaving," she added.

The elders took turns shaking Leslie's hand and saying hello to each of the children. They turned to Kate one last time. "We'll see you Wednesday morning, then," they said.

Leslie watched the missionaries' little car incredulously as it wound down the gravel drive. When they were finally out of sight, she turned to her cousin. "Seriously, Kate? Mormons?"

"They were just visiting, Leslie. It doesn't mean anything," Kate said, climbing the porch steps and opening the door for the children.

"It doesn't mean anything," Leslie commented, "but you're seeing them again on Wednesday? The Mormons have been in Rose Creek awhile, Kate. They're persistent. You're nice to them once, they won't leave you alone."

"You talk like you've had personal experience with them. And what is all this 'them' talk? The missionaries seemed like perfectly normal people."

"Huh!" Leslie laughed. "Mormons are not normal people." Leslie turned to her kids. "Run on into the family room, guys. Nicholas, will you put a movie on for Emily and Tommy?" She lowered Tommy onto the floor, and Nicholas took his hand, leading him into the family room.

"Here," Leslie said as she handed Kate a plastic to-go box from a local restaurant. "I tried to call your cell phone to see what you wanted, but you didn't answer. I just got you a grilled chicken salad. There's salad dressing in the bag. Shall we get started on the pictures?"

"Wait," Kate demanded. "I want to know why Mormons aren't normal people."

Leslie sighed. "They're just . . . different."

Kate looked at her expectantly, waiting for more explanation.

Leslie sat down at the table and reached for a stack of pictures, slowly looking at each one. "The pastor at Tom's church preached about the Mormons a few times, talked about the importance of guarding yourself against them. They have strange beliefs about marriage, about how to raise your children, and the pastor said they follow a false Jesus, talked about all kinds of weird things, about God being from another planet and whatnot. It was just weird, Kate. That's all."

"But you don't actually know any Mormons yourself?" Kate asked.

"Well, no," Leslie answered. "I guess not. Do you?"

"Just the two I met today." She paused for a moment, reaching for her own stack of pictures. "It doesn't matter," she finally continued. "I'm not even sure I'm going on Wednesday. Even if I do, it's not even church, just some sort of a history library they want me to see."

They worked in silence for a few moments.

"I didn't realize you were going to church, Leslie."

"Who, me?" Leslie asked. "I don't really, though before Tom died, we went every now and again. I've been back a few times, but it's miserable having all of those old ladies asking me how I'm holding up all the time, telling me it would be easier if I would come to church more. Really, it would have been easier if God just hadn't let Tom die."

"Yeah." Kate sighed, agreeing softly with her cousin.

"Nice of God, though, to take Mother as well, wasn't it?" Leslie continued, her voice laced with bitterness. "You know," she said sarcastically, "raising three kids isn't already hard enough. Let's try it with your support network ripped completely away." Tears spilled over onto Leslie's cheeks. She angrily wiped them away. "Ohhhh!" she said, voice full of frustration. "I have cried too many times this week. I really don't want to do it again."

Kate moved closer to her cousin and reached for her hand.

"It stinks, Leslie, and it isn't fair—not to you or your kids." Kate had certainly shed her share of tears over losing Aunt Mary, but she felt her grief was but a drop compared to what her cousin was enduring.

"I just don't think I can keep doing this by myself," Leslie said softly.

"I'm here, Leslie. I can help," Kate offered sincerely.

"You're here, Kate? For how long? For a few more weeks until work calls you back and you return to Atlanta and forget about your family here in Rose Creek? I know you mean well, but you don't have the best track record. I tried to rely on you once, and we both know how well that went."

Leslie's words stung Kate to the core. This was not where she'd imagined the conversation going. She didn't want to be angry, but she couldn't keep the words from tumbling out. "How many times do I have to apologize, Leslie? You want me to say I was wrong? I was. I know that. If I could go back and change the choices that I've made, I would. But I can't. All I can do is apologize and try to be different from now on. But that's going to be really hard if you're going to be angry at me forever for my past."

Leslie took a deep breath. "I know you've apologized. I'm sorry. But seriously, Kate, even if you have changed, if you do visit more, call more, you still live in a different city. And you shouldn't feel guilty for that. But I'm here, and when you're gone in two weeks, I'll be here, without Mom, without this house to come to when I need someone to talk to, someone to help with the kids. I'm so terrified of that—so terrified of being alone."

Kate closed her eyes as she listened to Leslie, her heart breaking for how overwhelmed she must feel.

"You'll have Linny," Kate suggested.

"I know I have Linny, and she's wonderful. But she's just one person, and she stays so busy with all of her volunteer work and taking care of Charles."

"She'd put all that down in a second if she thought you needed her. You know that."

"You're right. I do know that, but I can't ask her to give up what she loves doing to help fix my kids Hamburger Helper so I can stay in my room and cry for one more night."

"Yes, you can. If that's what you need. You know she would," Kate insisted.

Leslie still gripped a stack of pictures but finally relaxed enough to put them down. The picture on top was of Aunt Mary, holding a new baby—Sam, if Kate had to guess, based on the length of Mary's hair and the smooth planes of her young face.

"I just don't get it," Leslie said softly, shaking her head as she looked at the picture of her mother. "Why does life have to be so hard?"

## Chapter 17

LATER THAT NIGHT, KATE LAY in bed, unable to sleep. The various conversations she'd had throughout the day kept playing over and over in her head. The Book of Mormon the missionaries had left lay unopened on the nightstand by her bed. She didn't think the missionaries had seemed unusual in any respect. She was actually quite impressed with how well-spoken they'd been and with the respect and intelligence they'd demonstrated. At the same time, a pastor of another church surely wouldn't stand at the pulpit and lie to his congregation, telling them things about the Mormons that weren't true. Or would he?

She wondered for the second time that day how she was ever supposed to know what to believe. Elder Christianson's words echoed in her head. "You ask." Sure. Asking was easy for someone who knew how to pray and felt comfortable with the notion of communicating with God. But Kate didn't pray. The idea of it felt awkward, almost silly. And really, did she actually want to be a Mormon herself? Her life had gone just fine without any kind of religion. She was happy, successful, well connected . . . lonely, empty, and not really that happy after all.

Still, she had no idea what being a Mormon even involved. Would she do something so drastic just because her ancestor, dead nearly two hundred years, had written in a journal that he sought a restoration? What if it was the wrong restoration? And what good would it do him for her to join the Church anyway? He'd still be dead. She sighed in frustration and rolled over. She fluffed her pillow and collapsed onto her stomach, burying her face in the soft fabric of the sheets.

"Oh, sleep already," she said, frustrated and annoyed by her insomnia.

But she didn't sleep. Instead, her thoughts turned to Leslie. She hated to admit it, but what Leslie had said was true. Kate would go back to

Atlanta in a few weeks and leave Rose Creek behind. Certainly, she would visit and call more frequently—she would have to just to take care of the house. But there was little, other than moral support, that she would be able to offer Leslie. And that wasn't what Leslie needed. She didn't need a long-distance friend—someone good for phone calls and moral hoorahs. Leslie needed someone close, who could help with the kids and help her cope with the desperation of her situation. Leslie was a fighter, and Kate didn't believe she would ever give up, but she was standing on a very slippery slope. Without enough support to keep her going, Kate could see her rapidly sliding into some very dark emotional places.

It was her. It had to be her, Kate realized. There really wasn't anyone else besides Linny who could be here like Leslie needed. Sam had his wife and baby and perhaps even another baby on the way if they would ever get around to telling everyone. And he and Teresa both had great jobs in Asheville. And Bryan—Kate didn't know what to think about Bryan, but she didn't see him moving back to Rose Creek anytime soon. As great a guy as he was, he wasn't what Leslie needed either. Leslie needed Kate.

Leaving her job would be easy. She even thought that with a little bit of persuasion, she could convince Mr. Blanton to let her work from Rose Creek, consulting and analyzing contracts. It would mean a huge cut in salary, but she could still make more than enough to take care of her needs—especially the simplified needs that accompanied small-town life. Her mind raced as she continued to make plans. Her condo would sell in weeks, if not days. Even in a slower market, it was in a prime location just outside the business sector, with convenient parking and a great balcony. If it were priced reasonably, someone would snatch it up right away.

It surprised Kate and even saddened her a bit that moving seemed like such a simple decision. Really, her job and condo were the only loose ends she would need to tie up. A handful of friends might be sad to see her go, but there really were only a few. Steve would probably rejoice at her exit—a cat ready to pounce on her client list and corner office. He could have it. Suddenly, there seemed much more important business to attend to—business like Leslie and business like Andrew.

Kate sighed. She'd had the conversation with herself far too many times throughout the day, but she still wondered. Why had he left so quickly? What was he running from?

Eventually, Kate started to drift off, but just before sleep finally claimed her, a memory—years, even decades old—crept to the surface of Kate's consciousness: an activity bus driving the swim team to a regional meet in Charlotte, and Tracy Spencer, Andrew's cousin and Kate's fellow teammate, pulling out a little blue book, softbound with gold lettering across the front. She'd given the book to another teammate, explaining what it was and offering to answer questions if any arose. It was a Book of Mormon. Tracy Spencer was Mormon.

Kate sat up, heart racing as she realized what this meant. If Tracy was Mormon, then Andrew was quite possibly Mormon himself. It ran in families like that, didn't it? At the very least, Andrew would know something of the Mormon faith, perhaps even have some insight to share with Kate. Remembering the Book of Mormon sitting on her nightstand, she rolled over and turned on the lamp, opening the front cover of the book. There she saw the missionaries' contact information, a telephone number, and the street address and telephone number for the branch building. Then, down at the bottom of the insert: *Dan Spencer, Branch Mission Leader*, with a home and cell number. Dan Spencer—Andrew's uncle and the branch mission leader. Kate had no idea what the title actually meant, other than the general assumption that he had something to do with the efforts of the missionaries. She wondered if the missionaries knew Andrew. If they went to church with his uncle, they probably had some awareness of who he was. She lay back on her pillow, mentally exhausted. She put the Book of Mormon back on the nightstand, on top of Ian's journal, and noticed the two letters tucked neatly into the back of the book. Kate realized she'd only read one before she'd lost herself in the pages of the journal. Curious about the contents of the second letter, she reached for it and delicately unfolded the ancient paper.

> *My Dear Ian,*
> *I've just received a letter from Jennie telling me of your dear father-in-law. I'm sorry to hear of his passing, as I know he meant a great deal to you. I am forever grateful for his reaching out to you and caring for you in your time of need. Though I never met the man, I will honor him always, for your sake. Now, I must ask you to bear with me because I fear I may sound like I'm trying to tell you what to do. You must remember that the Ian I remember was just a boy the last time I saw him, and though I know you've grown into a man, it's hard to really know you as such through letters. So if I sound like I'm writing to you like you are a child in need*

*of guidance from his mother, just sit down and take it like a man. Perhaps you are in need of guidance. Jennie tells me of the disagreements you find yourself in with your mother-in-law regarding matters of religion. It appears you don't worship as she pleases? Your wife seemed compassionate to your cause, though expressed concern that your stubbornness was perhaps inhibiting you from complying in the least degree. Jennie seems to think that if you would just attend Sunday services, even if in your heart you disagree with what's being taught, you might perhaps preserve the peace at your hearth. And now she appeals to me. I wish I had an easy answer. You've made your own feelings of religion known to me in past letters. I know you to be a religious man and have no doubts that you honor God—that you praise Him and recognize His many works and miracles. I taught you as a child to study the Good Book, to learn from it, to follow the examples of those within, and I believe you have done so. And I recognize that you don't have to worship with the Methodists or the Presbyterians or Baptists or even the Catholics to live a life patterned after God, though the opportunity to learn from those who've given their lives completely to God, who preach in His name, certainly can't do us any harm. I guess all I can tell you, Ian, is that you must follow your heart. Pray for guidance, and the good Lord will lead you in the ways you should go. For you, perhaps that is staying home on Sunday, reading the words of your Roger Williams, waiting for this restoration you claim must come about. But remember, Ian, it is also your responsibility to lead and guide your family. You want your children to respect God and learn the good word, and the best place for them to learn it is in a church. I know their mother takes them, but they will always question if their father is not there, will they not? Only you can determine such a thing, and I trust you will forever turn to God and make the right decision. Beware of your pride though, my dear boy. You're just like your Da in that regard, and you best not stay home just to spite that mother-in-law of yours, no matter how tempting it is. I love you and will pray for the peace and comfort of your family.*

*Your sister's condition grows worse every day. The doctors still call her the miracle child. They never imagined she'd reach her fifteenth year, and yet here she is, nearly twenty. She's still so tiny though—looks more like a mere child of eight or nine rather than the blossoming young woman she should be. Just the same, I'm grateful for every day I have with her. She has blessed my life in so many ways. Truly, when she is gone, the happiest part of my life will be over. Yet, perhaps not, if the future allows me the opportunity to come see you and meet your sweet children and wrap my arms around that wonderful woman you call wife. And best of all, to see my young Ian grown into manhood, into fatherhood. I can't imagine how truly lovely you must be. God be with you, Ian. Think about my words, and be smart. I know you will.*
*Love,*
*Mother*

Ian must have felt strongly about this restoration, strongly enough to have written home to his mother and even argue with his family. He seemed so certain about how he felt. The story the missionaries told her, if true, was clearly what Ian had been waiting for. Kate thought it seemed so simple and yet so completely fantastic. Would God really show Himself to a simple farm boy still clinging to the last of his boyhood for something as important as the restoration of His Church?

Kate also struggled with Leslie's reaction to the Mormons. What on earth could one church do that would cause such contention from members of other faiths? Kate sighed and pushed her thoughts and questions aside, desperate to climb off the mental treadmill she'd been running on all evening. Finally, just before 2:00 a.m., she slept.

## Chapter 18

KATE SPENT ALL DAY TUESDAY and the earliest hours of Wednesday morning debating whether or not she should actually meet the missionaries as she had planned. In the end, her curiosity about Ian outweighed any concerns she had about the Mormons, and she went, journal in hand, to the church building the elders had described. Perhaps, though she wouldn't admit it out loud, curiosity about Andrew motivated her as well.

The church house sat on a small rise right off the side of the highway. A large grassy field lined with trees provided a lovely backdrop for the little building. It looked perfectly at home nestled into the side of the mountain. Kate wondered how she'd driven the road countless times before and had never managed to notice it. She pulled into the parking lot and noticed a large white truck with Spencer Contracting written on the side parked next to the missionaries' small sedan. Kate was immediately nervous. She had entertained the possibility of Andrew being Mormon, but why would he be here, at the church building, on a Wednesday morning? Kate pulled into a parking space and tried to remind herself that Andrew was not the only person who drove a Spencer Contracting truck. Even still, she was suddenly grateful she'd taken extra care in getting ready that morning. She'd chosen a light sweater that was a nice complement to her eyes and had spent a few extra minutes fixing her hair. She climbed out of her car and greeted the missionaries.

"Are we not the only ones here?" she asked, motioning to the truck.

"Oh, no," Elder Christianson said. "That must be Andrew Porterfield. He's the family history center volunteer on Wednesday mornings. Shall we go in?"

Kate's emotions must have shown plainly on her face.

"Are you all right, Ms. Sinclair—Kate, I mean?" Elder Peterson quickly asked her. "You look terrified."

Kate smiled and shook her head. "No, I'm fine, I was just . . . I'm fine."

Elder Peterson looked at Elder Christianson and shrugged his shoulders then led the way into the building. The inside was lovely in its simplicity. The walls and furniture were soft, muted colors, the only decorations a series of large framed paintings depicting the life of Jesus and His followers. The largest painting hung just inside the door. It was a picture of the Savior with His arms extended and a serene and welcoming expression on His face. Kate did feel welcome as she paused and looked up at the painting. She thought back to that childhood moment in the Methodist church when she'd gazed on the stained-glass depiction of the Savior in a similar pose.

"It's lovely," she said softly.

"It's one of my favorites," Elder Peterson said, stopping behind her.

Elder Christianson wasn't far behind. "The family history library is just down the hall. We'll introduce you to Brother Porterfield, but we won't be able to stay long. We've got an appointment in a few minutes, if you don't mind us leaving you, that is."

Kate murmured a hasty consent as she followed Elder Christianson down the hall. She paused outside the library door, allowing both of the elders to enter first.

"Good morning, Brother Porterfield," Elder Christianson said, smiling broadly. "Thanks for coming out this morning. This is Kate Sinclair, the woman we mentioned yesterday."

"Kate?" Andrew said, his voice incredulous. "What are you doing here?" He looked back at the elders. "You didn't tell me the woman was Kate Sinclair."

"You two know each other?" Elder Christianson looked from one to the other. They both started speaking at once—words bouncing around the room until finally it was decided that, yes, they did know each other, just not very well, but they were, nonetheless, happy to see each other again. With that settled, the missionaries left, promising to call Kate later that afternoon.

"Wow," Andrew began. "I just . . . It's good to see you. I really didn't expect to see you. Not in general, but just here, at the church. You're, uh, you're not Mormon, are you?"

"No," Kate answered. "I just met the missionaries on Monday. You are a Mormon?"

"All my life," he said with a smile.

Oh, how it killed Kate when he smiled like that.

"So what are you doing here?" Andrew asked. "Are you looking for something specific?"

"Indeed, Brother Porterfield. I'm looking for *someone* specific. What's with the *brother*, anyway?" Kate asked as she pulled the journal out of her shoulder bag.

Andrew shrugged his shoulders. "I think it helps us remember the relationship we have with each other within our Church family. There's a great support network within the Church."

"Hmm. What about the elders? Why are they both called elder?"

"Elder is their current office in the priesthood. Generally speaking, young men are ordained to the office of elder just before they go on a mission, so on their mission, they go by elder. It's good for them too—helps them leave their first name at home and focus on being the Lord's servant for two years," Andrew explained.

"Priesthood, offices, ordained . . . You're losing me here," Kate said.

Andrew gave her a brief overview of offices and responsibilities within the Church. He was enthusiastic and extremely knowledgeable. Kate decided it might dampen his excitement if she told him most of what he was saying was going over her head. She was sure there would be time for clarification later. But she was curious about the missionaries.

"So let's go back to the missionaries. They serve for two years? Do they do anything besides preach?"

"They preach and provide service to those in the communities where they are serving, but that's pretty much it."

Kate could tell Andrew was in his element. He seemed comfortable and open, almost like he'd taken down one of the walls Kate had imagined between them when they'd last seen each other on Monday morning.

"Did you serve a mission?" Kate asked.

"Aye . . . I served in Scotland," he answered in a surprisingly convincing Scottish brogue.

"Scotland? Really? Do you get to pick where you go?"

"Nope. It's more like an assignment. You go where God sends you."

"It's interesting that you served in Scotland," Kate said, holding up the journal. "That's where Ian is from."

"Ian? A relative of yours, I take it."

Kate looked down at the journal, reverently running her hand over its cover. Though she'd made reference to Ian and his journal to the missionaries, she had yet to actually share it with anyone else. She'd enjoyed the privilege of connecting with him and his family on her own. Just the same, she couldn't keep it a secret forever, and she was curious to know what this little library might help her discover. She handed the book to Andrew, urging him to be careful with the delicate pages. He opened the cover and scanned the first few entries.

"I just found it in the attic of the house. I don't think anyone's looked at it in a hundred years. Ian Wylie is my grandfather five greats up the line," Kate offered.

"That's a great house, by the way," Andrew said as he looked through the pages. "It was built when? 1905? 1910?"

"1907," Kate responded. "How did you know?"

"I recognize the architecture," Andrew answered. "There are a lot of old buildings and houses in Rose Creek, but not many that seem to be in such great shape and that demonstrate such classic elements of turn-of-the-century architecture."

"Well, you're welcome anytime if you'd like to see more than just the front porch," she said, blushing as she thought of their last encounter.

He looked up, his eyes sincere. "I'd like that." He turned back to the journal and glanced at a few more pages. "Kate, do you realize how extraordinary this is?" he said. "To have this kind of a record from so many years ago . . . documents like this just don't exist anymore."

"I've been doing my best to make it out, but some of the entries are near impossible to decipher. Oh, and look, there are two letters from his mother in Scotland. They seem a little better preserved." She pulled out the letters, carefully handing them to Andrew. He looked them over, shaking his head in wonder.

"My older sister is a history professor at UNC-Charlotte. She would love this."

The two spent the next half hour poring over the pages of the journal as Kate pieced together what she knew of Ian's story for Andrew.

Finally, Andrew said, "You already know so much about Ian, Kate. I'm not sure we could learn anything from the kind of records we have here." He motioned to the room around him.

"I want to know whether or not Ian's mother ever made it to the US," Kate said. "Did she ever get to hold her grandchildren, see Ian as a man? And what happened to Ian's sisters back in Scotland?"

Andrew nodded, his brow wrinkled in concentration. "Well, let's see if we can piece together some dates, and then we'll see what we can find."

Kate pulled a copy of the family history recorded in the old Bible out of her bag. She'd copied it down by hand that morning, expecting the dates and names to be of use in her searching. "This will probably help," she said, handing it to Andrew.

They started with census records, searching all of the Charleston area townships for any record of an Ian or Jennie Wylie. "Prior to 1850," Andrew explained, "US census records listed only the name of the head of household and then a list of the number of females and males, white and black, who lived within. They didn't include names of the household members in addition to the head of household until 1850."

Kate did some basic calculating in her head. "What about the 1860 census? In 1860, Ian, if still living, would have been fifty-nine. It seems likely he could have lived that long."

They did not find a record of Ian Wylie, but they did find a record of a Jennie Wylie, fifty-six years old, living with James and Lavinia Wylie and their six children, ranging in age from thirteen to three.

"There, Henry Wylie, thirteen years old," Kate said, looking back to the scanned family tree. "He's my great-great-great-grandfather."

"And this must be Jennie MacDonald, Ian's wife, probably widowed and now living with her children," Andrew said.

"That must have happened a lot," Kate remarked, remembering Ian's journal entry about his own mother-in-law moving into his home.

When they searched the 1840 census, they were able to find an Ian Wylie in the same township in which they'd found his family in 1860, but the generic information included with the listing provided little information Kate didn't already know. Simply searching for Ian's mother was pointless. While she knew Ian's father's name was James, Kate didn't know his mother as anything other than Mother, or perhaps Ms. Wylie. It would certainly make it more difficult to find her. Andrew suggested they search the Scottish census to see if they could find record of Ian's father, perhaps then finding his mother's first and maiden name, but they found nothing specific. Wylie was not the least common name in eighteenth-century Edinburgh, and it seemed to Kate that every third person in the census was named James. She sighed, temporarily discouraged but still, on the whole, hopeful that answers would come. At the same time, she wondered what it was she was looking for in the first place. Why did she feel such a need to locate as much information as possible, to connect with these people who had been dead for so many years?

Kate reached for the journal, searching the pages for the entry near the back where Ian discussed the tenets of Roger Williams and his own personal desire to wait for a restoration of apostolic authority. She handed it to Andrew.

"Read this one," she said simply. She hadn't told Andrew about her meeting with the missionaries a few days before, and though she could tell he was curious, he hadn't pushed her for information. She watched as he read, wondering what he thought of Ian's heartfelt words.

When he finished, Andrew looked up, eyes shining. "Kate, this is remarkable. What he sought . . . if only he'd had the opportunity to learn of the gospel. There were missionaries then, all over the southern part of the United States. He must not have ever heard them preach. If he had, he would have been baptized."

Kate looked up. "I didn't realize the timing was so close. When was Joseph Smith's vision?"

"The spring of 1820, but the Church wasn't actually organized until 1830. Even ten or fifteen years later, there were missionaries all over the United States, and many people had heard of the Mormons. But still, information traveled so slowly back then. There would have been many who never heard—your ancestor Ian, for example."

"But how can I be so sure this is what he sought?" Kate questioned. "He was so adamant about his feelings. How could I ever have the same certainty?" Kate stood up. "I can't know, and yet, for whatever reason, I can't seem to let it go. I feel almost tormented by this Ian Wylie. He's almost constantly in my thoughts, urging me to keep reading, keep digging for information. Why Andrew? Why does it even matter?"

Andrew circled his chair away from the computer and leaned forward, looking at Kate.

"It matters," he said softly. "There are certain ordinances that, as God's followers, we can receive. Baptism, for example, is an ordinance. When we are baptized, we make promises to obey God's laws and follow His commandments. We can also make additional promises designed to bring us closer to our Father in Heaven and give us the knowledge and experience we need to live with Him again. It is these promises that allow us to live with our families forever in God's presence."

"I still don't understand what that has to do with Ian," Kate said.

"There are promises we make to prepare ourselves to live with our Father in Heaven, but we can also make these promises for people who have already passed on. We do work by proxy for the dead—for our ancestors."

"Wait. Back up," Kate said. "Explain this to me one more time."

"The ordinances God requires are earthly ordinances," Andrew explained. "They must be completed on this earth. But with so many, like Ian, who lived without the opportunity to hear of Heavenly Father's plan, God created a way for the ordinances to be completed on behalf of those who are already dead."

"So if Ian were to have an eternal family," Kate reasoned, "someone would have to do these ordinances on his behalf?"

"Exactly," Andrew said. "There are millions upon millions of names of people still waiting for their work to be done. And they will continue to wait until those of us here on the earth get it done. It's an individual process for each person who is waiting. Perhaps Ian doesn't want to wait anymore," Andrew reflected.

Kate leaned back in her chair, her heart nearly pounding out of her chest. Suddenly, so much seemed to make sense—the house and Mary's unknown reasons for leaving it to Kate; the journal, words so amazingly preserved; and the missionaries showing up on Kate's doorstep, repeating the very words Ian had written so many years ago. Her mind raced back to another journal entry, one of the first that had truly touched Kate, where Ian lovingly described his sweet wife and spoke of the agony he felt at the thought of losing her. She remembered his hope that God would allow him to be by her side beyond death and into eternity. It was Ian—all this time the pull she felt to read, to search, and to listen—it was Ian reaching out to her.

Andrew spun around in his chair and reached for a Bible lying on the shelf next to the computer. "It's here, Kate, in the scriptures." He flipped open the book, turning the pages until he found what he was looking for.

"In Malachi: 'Behold, I will send you Elijah the prophet before the coming of the great and dreadful day of the Lord: And he shall turn the heart of the fathers to the children, and the heart of the children to their fathers, lest I come and smite the earth with a curse.'" He looked up at Kate. "You've felt the spirit of Elijah . . . Your heart is turning to your fathers, to your ancestor. He needs you to do for him what he didn't have the opportunity to do for himself."

Kate took a deep breath. She shook her head, biting her lip as she pondered what Andrew was telling her.

"So what do I do now?" Kate finally asked.

Andrew smiled. "Well, there's a lot to learn. What you do is completely up to you, but I can certainly recommend a place to start."

Kate looked at him encouragingly. "All right, then. Where do I start?"

"Before you do anything else, if you haven't already, that is, I think you ought to read the Book of Mormon."

# Chapter 19

KATE STOPPED AT HER FAVORITE café on her way home and ordered lunch to go. She didn't drive home but sat in the parking lot to eat her sandwich and think about the morning's events. She felt completely overwhelmed and unsure about her future. There was so much she didn't know—so much that seemed confusing and almost impossible to understand. As much as she wanted to trust what Andrew and the elders had shared with her, she had nothing beyond their word to back up her feelings. Deep down, she knew she needed to read and ask for herself, but something was holding her back: fear of change, perhaps, or the ridicule of others? She'd gotten a small taste of how Leslie would react if she were to become a Mormon. And with their relationship just beginning to mend . . . Kate sighed. Suddenly, everything seemed so complicated.

She stopped at the end of the driveway and got the mail she'd had forwarded from Atlanta, as well as Aunt Mary's mail. She sat in the car and shuffled through it all, weeding out the junk mail. One letter in particular from the county commissioners office caught her attention.

> *Dear Ms. Walker,*
>
> *As we have been unable to reach you regarding the negotiations of the land purchase of your property, 728 Red Dogwood Lane in Harrison County, North Carolina, we hereby send this letter to notify you of the state's petition to exercise eminent domain in the taking of said property. The hearing regarding such action will be held Friday, June 1, at 7 p.m. at the Harrison County Commissioners Office. Should you wish to file a petition against said action, you must do so by 5 p.m. on the day of the scheduled hearing. If*

*you have any questions regarding this notice, you may contact the county commissioners office at (828) 555-6789 from the hours of 9 a.m.–5 p.m. Monday through Friday.*

*Signed,*
*Douglas B. Bradley*
*Chair, Harrison County*
*Board of Commissioners*

Kate reread the letter three times. Over the past week, she had convinced herself the attorney's concern for the house was based on old information—it was all a miscommunication, a simple mistake. But Mr. Marshall's concerns had not been ill founded. The letter was dated just two days earlier. The house really was in danger, and Kate had no idea what she needed to do.

She felt foolish for having ignored the possibility of a problem. She should have called and verified with the state department that her house was no longer an issue in the highway project, but her cousins' reassurances had lured her into a false sense of security. When she heard nothing from the attorney, she had explained away his silence with the old saying "No news is good news." But this time, no news was not good news. Kate was angry at herself for having so acutely dropped the ball. Still sitting in her car, she pulled out her cell phone and looked at the date mentioned in the letter. The hearing was three weeks away. She called Mr. Marshall's office first.

The receptionist was not moved by Kate's hasty explanation and demand to speak with the attorney immediately. "I assure you, I will not interrupt him when he is in a meeting," she said sweetly. "But he will call you back."

Kate hung up the phone then dialed the number listed on the letter for the Harrison County Board of Commissioners. By some stroke of luck, she got through to Chairman Douglas Bradley himself.

"Ms. Sinclair," a stuffy, annoyingly Southern voice said over the phone. "The letter is legitimate. Numerous properties stretching through that part of town have been in negotiations for quite some time. The state DOT is building a bypass to get over to the university without having to drive straight through the heart of Rose Creek. It really is an excellent plan and will do much for our economy. But the road will infringe on the Walker property. This plan has been in the works for over a year. I daresay I'm surprised this is the first you've heard of it."

Kate pressed her forehead against the steering wheel, eyes closed in frustration.

"I told you I just arrived in town last week. Even still, my aunt Mary received notification that her house was no longer in jeopardy. A different route was chosen, and it didn't involve our house."

"Ah, yes. There were many potential routes," Mr. Bradley said. "We discussed numerous possibilities at a series of town meetings, which, I believe, Ms. Walker attended. She was a vocal participant, if I remember correctly."

"She would have been at all of the meetings, Mr. Bradley, which helps prove my point. She would not have settled, would not have relaxed until she knew her home was going to be okay. Why was she told one thing and now we're being told something different?" Kate tried to maintain her composure. She'd spent the last week falling in love with the old farmhouse all over again. The thought of losing it now made her sick with fear.

"Ms. Sinclair, any number of things can alter the construction of a highway this size. Perhaps a route was determined and then, for whatever reason, an additional change was made that pulled in your property after all. I assure you, whatever the reason for the change, your aunt would have been notified. You'll have to contact the DOT directly to verify that with them."

Kate shook her head. None of this made any sense. She ended her conversation with the county commissioner and called Sam. She quickly explained the letter and subsequent phone call.

"Kate, he can't be telling you the truth. Why wouldn't any of us know about this?"

"I don't know, Sam. I'm hoping the attorney has some answers. I'm waiting for his call right now. What else can I do? The hearing is just three weeks from now. That's so little time."

"Go see Mr. Marshall, Kate," Sam responded. "Go see him and don't leave his office until you have some answers."

She pulled out of the driveway before she and Sam were even off the phone. She could not lose the house. It killed her to think of so much history and family experience bulldozed for the sake of a bypass. She felt sick just thinking about it. And what of her plans? What of her decision to move back, help Leslie, live in and take care of the old farmhouse? The questions filled her mind as she parked her car in front of Mr. Marshall's office.

*Don't be busy*, she thought as she entered the dreary waiting room.

"Well, aren't you persistent," the secretary said when Kate insisted she see Mr. Marshall. "He's handling a real estate closing and won't be done for another twenty minutes. Since you drove all the way down here, I suppose he can squeeze you in before he leaves for the day. Just have a seat, and I'll let him know he's got someone here to see him."

"Please tell him it's urgent," Kate said, annoyed with the little woman and her syrupy sweetness. She sat on the end of the stuffy, leather sofa and drummed her fingers nervously against her knee. As the minutes ticked by, Kate grew impatient and stepped outside to call Linny, filling her in on the afternoon's events. Kate glanced back into the attorney's office and noticed the secretary was away from her desk. She darted back inside, not wanting to miss her opportunity with Mr. Marshall. It was nearly 4:00 when she finally got in to see him.

"Ms. Sinclair, it's clear the property is meant to be included in the land purchase. All of my inquiries haven't given me any reason to think differently. I'm trying to find out why your aunt was given the impression the house was all right if it was still under consideration, but these things take time. Our state government is such a jumbled series of telephone extensions and secretaries and voice mailboxes that one can never just call up and ask a simple question."

"But what am I going to do?" Kate asked, annoyed that he seemed so powerless. "They plan to initiate eminent domain! How can they do that when we didn't even know the house was in danger?"

"Well, we suspected the house was in danger. What we don't know is why Mary didn't know, or if she did, why she didn't tell anyone."

The thought never occurred to Kate that Mary might have known. She wouldn't have kept it a secret, but what if she had run out of time before she could let anyone else know?

It felt terribly unfair that the state could simply claim property that a family had owned for generations. Sure, they would buy the property, but Kate couldn't think of a price high enough that would even begin to compensate for a century of lost family history and experience.

"How can they just take someone's house like that?" Kate asked. "How is it legal?"

"There are a lot of things that are difficult to handle, but that doesn't make them illegal," Mr. Marshall responded, pushing his glasses back onto his nose. He stood from his desk, obviously ready for their meeting to end. "It's been a long day, Ms. Sinclair. Give me more time to make further inquiries. I'll contact the state transportation department, go over the information with the county commissioners, and do my best to find out if your aunt was sent a notice of any sort regarding her property. I will call you as soon as I know something. If anything comes up before then, you'll call me?"

"What will I do until then . . . just wait?" The idea did not excite Kate. She stood and followed Mr. Marshall to the door.

"There's nothing else you can do. As I said before, things like this take time. You will have answers as soon as I have answers, I assure you."

"Mr. Marshall, please be honest with me. Is it possible that I may lose this house?"

He paused in the doorway. "Yes, Ms. Sinclair. It's a very real possibility, even likely at this point. The most I can hope to do is buy you a bit more time or perhaps, considering the death of your aunt, encourage the state to reopen negotiations allowing you to get a much better price for the property. Your hope basically rests upon the possibility of her not having been appropriately notified. But again, discovering that may only buy us more time. I do not believe it will actually change the fate of the property. I will try, but I don't expect to accomplish much."

Kate nodded and thanked him as they left his office. She returned home, discouraged and emotionally spent. But her spirits lifted a bit when she found a note taped to the front door. It wasn't signed, but Kate knew who it was from.

> *I meant to get your cell number this morning*
> *but didn't. Here's mine . . . will you call me?*
> *828-555-6464*

Kate was disappointed that she'd missed Andrew but was touched by the simplicity and sweetness of his note. She most definitely would call him, but not until she'd called Sam back to let him know about her visit with the attorney. In the end, Kate talked to Sam and Linny one more time as well as to Leslie and Bryan. No one was happy about the idea of losing the house. The conversations were emotionally draining for all involved. When Kate finally hung up, the situation had been hashed and rehashed, turned upside down and inside out so many times she thought her head might explode if she had to discuss it again. Her ear was hot from the cell phone battery, and she was hungry. She hadn't eaten since lunch, and it was already near 9:00. It was almost enough to make Kate put down the phone and simply call Andrew the following day. Almost.

He answered his phone after one ring. Kate smiled at the thought of him waiting, anticipating her phone call.

"Have I not heard enough from you today?" Kate teased after Andrew said hello.

"Apparently not, since you called me," Andrew teased back. "How are you?" Just like that, he'd replaced his teasing with genuine concern. Kate wondered how he could make a three-word question sound so sincere.

"Oh!" Kate groaned. "It's been a long day. Don't ask me about it though. I've been talking about it for four hours, and that's already three hours too many."

"Oh no," Andrew said. "I hope everything's okay."

"I think it will be," Kate said, though she hardly felt certain. "How are you?"

"I'm good. Hey, listen . . . Monday, two weeks from now, my sister is coming into town, passing through on her way home from a conference in Atlanta. I was hoping we could all have dinner. It would be a family thing, really, over at the Spencers' house."

"Is this the sister who's the history professor?" Kate asked.

"The very one," Andrew responded. "I was hoping you could show her the journal. I know she would love to see it."

"That sounds great. I'd love to hear what she thinks. So," she continued, "will it be two weeks, then, before I see you again?"

"I hope not," Andrew answered. Kate could hear the smile in his voice. "Will you have dinner with me tomorrow?"

# Chapter 20

KATE PACED BACK AND FORTH across the worn linoleum in the kitchen, drinking her second cup of coffee. She was drinking decaf on purpose; she hadn't been sleeping very well and, for once, thought the caffeine might not do her any good. Fear and worry about the house had eaten at her all night for several nights now. Three days had passed since her initial conversation with Mr. Marshall, and yet she still felt no closer to a solution. She'd called the attorney every day, and every day he had told her he was still waiting for answers. Two nights before, over dinner, Kate had told Andrew everything. It had helped to discuss it with someone else, but words alone weren't getting her any closer to saving the house. Fortunately, their discussion had been the only dark spot in an otherwise blissful evening.

Kate couldn't get enough of Andrew's company. Something had happened that first morning when he'd come so close to kissing her. They had connected on a level far deeper than anything she had ever experienced before. The more she got to know him, the more at ease she felt in his presence. Her only hesitation was his work. He didn't hide the fact that he was an architect, but clearly, that wasn't the kind of work he was doing for his uncle at Spencer Contracting. Even when Kate probed for more detail, Andrew tap danced around any conversation that involved his employment history. She could tell there was something he wasn't telling her. But then, there was plenty she wasn't telling him either. It was too early, she decided, to stress over any potential skeletons in his closet.

Kate heard gravel crunching in the driveway and walked to the porch to meet the missionaries, who were just arriving for an appointment. Kate was grateful for the distraction—anything to help pass the time until she heard from Mr. Marshall.

An attractive woman in her mid- to late fifties accompanied the elders. Something about her seemed familiar, though Kate was fairly certain they hadn't ever met.

"Good morning, Kate," Elder Christianson said. "This is Caroline Spencer. I hope you don't mind her joining us this morning."

"Not at all," Kate said, smiling, now making the connection. Caroline Spencer looked familiar because she looked just like her daughter Tracy, Kate's teammate from so many years ago.

The small party moved into the family room, Caroline choosing a seat right next to Kate.

"It's so nice to finally meet you, dear, though now that I look at you, I do remember you from Tracy's team."

"How is Tracy?" Kate inquired. "Andrew tells me she has four children now."

"Oh, she's doing just fine," Caroline answered. "I wish I got to see her more often. Those kids grow up so fast! And yes, she does have four children. Her oldest is seven, and then, believe it or not, she had a set of twins just like I did, except hers are a boy and a girl, and then the baby, who is almost two."

Kate smiled. "That's really wonderful. I hope you'll tell her I said hello."

"I'd be happy to." Caroline reached over and squeezed Kate's hand, lifting her shoulders and leaning in as if to tell Kate a secret. "You're even prettier than Andrew described."

Kate blushed at the thought of Andrew describing her to anyone. She wished for a moment that he were here and wondered why he hadn't volunteered to come. After thinking about it, she decided it might actually be better if he wasn't around. She couldn't guarantee that with Andrew in the room she would be truly honest with herself about how she felt about this church exclusive of him. It was true his affiliation with the Church certainly hadn't hurt her opinion, but Kate knew her faith needed to be based on her own convictions and not just a desire to relate to Andrew.

"So, Kate, before we do anything else," Elder Christianson began, "we want to make sure we address any questions you may have. Has anything come up in your reading or in your own personal thoughts that you would like to discuss?"

Elder Christianson was well over six feet tall and was all arms and legs and skinny awkwardness. When he sat on the old couch in the family room, he sank so low it seemed his knees nearly reached his earlobes. It was a peculiar sight, yet when he learned forward, looking at Kate with such earnest intention, she couldn't help but be touched by his sincerity. He really did want to help, to share with her something that obviously meant a lot to him.

"I want to know why you're here and why you are serving a mission," Kate said, looking at Elder Christianson and then Elder Peterson. "What does this mean to you . . . to be here, to be away from your family and your life for two years—why do you do it?"

Elder Christianson answered first. "Returned missionaries get the best chicks." He grinned.

Kate rolled her eyes. "So that's what it's all about, huh?" She laughed, and Elder Christianson's companion punched him lightly on the arm.

"Your mission may be the only thing that saves you," Elder Peterson joked. "What girl would want you otherwise?"

The laughter continued until Sister Spencer looked at the young elders with eyebrows raised, calling their attention back to Kate and her question.

Elder Christianson held his hands up in apology. "I'm sorry." He smiled. "I can be serious now. I'm here because I know this gospel to be true," he continued. "I've studied and prayed and asked the Lord for confirmation, and He's mercifully given it to me. I cannot deny it, so I go and do whatever it is He asks of me." He looked at Elder Peterson.

"What my Savior did for me when He died on the cross, when He suffered in the Garden, I can't ever repay. What's two years of my life dedicated to the Lord's service when the Lord gave His entire life for me? And the message of the gospel, it changes people's lives. It uplifts, it enriches, it redeems. Why would I ever want to keep such a gift to myself? It's much more rewarding to share it." Elder Peterson leaned back on the sofa and looked at Kate. "What's next?"

She laughed. "It just strikes me as unusual to see such dedication from young men. The last time I spent any time with nineteen- and twenty-year-old boys, I was at a frat house in college and they were all drunk and ridiculously juvenile. You are both so refreshing."

"We have our moments," Elder Peterson responded, casting a furtive look at Elder Christianson, "but we try pretty hard not to embarrass ourselves."

"My cousin made a comment to me after you left on Saturday morning," Kate said. "She said that Mormons aren't 'normal' people. If not normal, what are Mormons actually like?" Kate wanted to understand the lifestyle and culture of a religion that nurtured such dedication and commitment as demonstrated by these two young men and, from what she had observed, by Andrew as well.

The elders looked at Caroline, encouraging her to join the conversation.

"Well," she began, "I guess Mormons aren't normal people. Our lifestyle is different in many ways from what one might consider typical. We don't smoke or use any other kind of tobacco. We don't drink alcohol, coffee, or tea . . ."

"Wait, what? No coffee?" Kate asked, alarmed that a drink as insignificant as coffee might be excluded.

Caroline smiled. "Oh, it isn't that bad. It's part of something we call the Word of Wisdom. The Word of Wisdom is a revelation Joseph Smith received regarding our health and how we can best take care of ourselves. It speaks of eating grains and fresh fruits and vegetables and abstaining from things that may be addictive or harmful to our health, things like alcohol or tobacco or coffee," she gently added. "We also teach the importance of marriage and family. We practice the law of chastity, teaching abstinence until marriage, fostering a respect for the sacred relationship between husband and wife. While these principles certainly aren't unique to the Mormon faith, and we all stumble and bumble our way through at times—making mistakes then working to correct them—we believe that living these principles allows us to have a more godly life—to be more like God and to respect what He has given us: these bodies, the opportunity to be married, and the blessing it is to have children."

"But none of that seems like it would make you odd enough for a pastor of another church to preach a sermon about you and warn his congregation to be cautious when interacting with you," Kate interrupted.

"The Church has suffered persecution of all kinds from its earliest days," Elder Peterson offered. "The early Saints were driven from New York, Ohio, Missouri, and Illinois in search of a home where they could worship as they pleased. The persecution they received was not fair, but it passed them through the refiner's fire just as any ridicule or ill-placed judgment we may receive will do for us."

"But why?" Kate asked again. "Why so much persecution?"

"I've asked myself that question many times," Elder Christianson answered. "And I'm not sure there's a good answer for it. I think perhaps it's intimidating to people for us to say that this is God's Church restored on the earth—that our church is the only one with the fullness of Christ's gospel and the authority to initiate the necessary ordinances and covenants for eternal progression. And I think perhaps it's hard for someone to accept the story of Joseph Smith's vision. That God the Father and Jesus Christ literally appeared to a mere boy is incomprehensible to many. But the Lord has promised, Kate, if you read and study His words and then ask with a sincere heart, He will make the truth known to you."

The missionaries stayed for over an hour, teaching Kate the plan of salvation and about temples, expounding even further on Andrew's comments at the family history library earlier in the week. Whenever they brought up the temple, Kate's thoughts turned to Ian. She imagined him there, listening, waiting, and hoping. Before leaving, the elders encouraged her again to read and pray and, of course, call if she had any questions.

Kate sat on the porch for a long time after they left. For the first time, she thought of eternal families and how the sealing ordinance could affect her own more immediate family as well. It wasn't a principle that applied to just Ian. Her own parents could also have the opportunity to be sealed together in the temple, and she to them. It was such a wonderful idea. And yet, it would require so much change. It still seemed foreign to her to imagine having a personal relationship with God in which He would hear and answer her prayers. She went back inside and picked up the Book of Mormon.

"No time like the present," she said out loud. She took the book back to the front porch, sat down on the swing, and started to read.

*Chapter 21*

"KATIE . . . KATIE. WAKE UP." LINNY nudged Kate with her arm, urging her to sit up and make room for her on the swing.

Kate did sit up, disoriented and momentarily confused by her present surroundings. "I must have fallen asleep," Kate muttered, stretching and blinking her eyes in the late-afternoon sun. "What time is it?"

"It's 5:15," Linny responded. "How long have you been out here?" She looked at Kate, who was totally disheveled and had indentations down the side of her face from where she'd lain on the slats of the swing for so long.

"5:15? You can't be serious," Kate said, looking at her own watch. "I, well, it was noon. I guess I read for a few hours, and then, I don't know. I guess I didn't sleep very well last night."

"Well, you must not have," Linny said sarcastically. "You were snoring like a stuck pig when I found you."

"Gee, thanks, Linny."

"What are you doing with this rubbish?" Linny asked, picking up the Book of Mormon from the seat of the swing.

"It isn't rubbish," Kate said defensively, hastily retrieving it from Linny's grasp. "This is what I was reading."

"Now, Kate, you ought to stay away from those Mormons. Have they been coming around here?"

Kate was annoyed at Linny's reaction. "So what if they have? Why does everyone seem so shocked?"

"Now, child, don't get upset," Linny soothed, altering the tone of her voice. "I'm sure the Mormons are decent enough, but what would you want to get mixed up in such an odd religion for? I know death can shake people up, make them feel like they need to find God, but there are other churches. You and I will go together to the Methodist church down the road this Sunday if you want."

"You didn't answer my question." Kate looked at her aunt, determined to get to the bottom of her biased opinion. "What's wrong with the Mormons?"

Linny leaned back on the porch swing and lifted her injured ankle up to rest on the small wicker table beside the swing. "When I was secretary of the rotary club a few years back, a woman serving with me, Nancy Freeman, was the treasurer. One afternoon she was giving out copies of these movies all about cults and weird religions. I didn't take one, as I've never been too interested in picking apart one religion or another, but she talked a lot about it, and working side by side at so many events and functions, I heard a lot about it. I don't know, Kate. She talked about brainwashing and female oppression. It just sounded weird. And all those people out there in Texas or Arizona or wherever with the fifteen wives and what not. They're Mormon, aren't they?"

"Linny, you should be ashamed of yourself, basing your opinion on such generalizations and falsehoods, and no, the polygamists you see on the news are not Mormons." Kate had asked the same question of Andrew point blank when they'd had dinner, and his answer had been very clear. "They don't have anything to do with the Mormon Church," Kate told Linny. "If you would meet these missionaries I've been talking to, and Andrew too, you'd see they really are just normal people," Kate finished.

"Who's Andrew?" Linny asked, eyebrows raised in interest.

"He's just a friend," Kate said as lightly as she could manage. "Just someone I met."

"Katherine Sinclair," Linny said. "If you join some crazy church for a man, you're not the woman I thought you were."

"It's not like that, Linny. He didn't have anything to do with it. I didn't even know he was Mormon when this all started."

"Hmm," Linny mumbled. "Well, just use your head. Don't jump into anything too quickly. I daresay I can't imagine you getting a favorable reaction from your cousins. Just be careful, child. You'll do that, won't you?"

Kate nodded her head. "Of course I will, Linny. Don't worry."

"How are things with the house?" Linny asked, changing the subject.

Kate shrugged. "Nothing's changed since yesterday," she said flatly. "I just have to wait for the attorney to call. Thing is, I don't even really know what I'm waiting for him to tell me. He told me he didn't think there was anything he could do. I just hate feeling so useless, like I ought to be doing something—protesting, making posters."

Linny laughed. "Posters, huh?"

"Ugh! I hate waiting."

"Don't worry," Linny said. "Things have a way of working themselves out."

"I sure hope so," Kate said, looking at the house and property around her. "I couldn't bear anything happening to this house."

"Well, lest you thought I came by just to wake you up," Linny said, rising from the swing, "I'm on my way over to Leslie's to watch the kids. I thought you might want to come along and kidnap your cousin for a little while to get her out of the house."

"I'd love to," Kate answered. "Is Leslie okay?"

"She's had a rough day today, I think, though I couldn't get her to come right out and admit it. It isn't easy losing your mother, especially as close as they were."

"I miss her every day, Linny."

"Who, dear? Your mother, or your aunt Mary?"

"Both," Kate answered. "It's different with my own mother. It's more the idea of her that I miss. But with Mary, it's everything—the way she smelled, the sound of her laugh. I can imagine it so clearly I can almost feel her right here beside me. It's so hard to believe she's really gone."

"You're right about that," Linny said. The women sat in reflective silence for a few minutes before Linny moved to get up. "Well, come on, then," she said, extending a hand to pull Kate off the swing. "Let's go see what we can do for Leslie."

"Linny, did you drive over here with that ankle?"

"Oh, pooh on my ankle. This here walking cast lets me get around well enough."

"Against doctor's orders, I'm sure," Kate said. "All right, we can go. But I'm driving."

# Chapter 22

"So, I think I've met someone," Kate said casually as she looked at Leslie across the table.

They sat in a corner booth at Flannigans, Leslie's favorite restaurant and the purveyors of the best cheesecake east of the Mississippi. It hadn't taken much persuading to get Leslie to leave the kids with Linny and join Kate for dinner and cheesecake. The two had talked comfortably for most of dinner, and Kate was feeling surprisingly open. She wanted to trust Leslie and be honest with her about what was going on in her life. She also hoped their evening would lend an opportunity for her to tell Leslie she was moving back to Rose Creek. While she was ultimately moving back for Leslie, Kate didn't want her to think so. Leslie would feel guilty, regardless of Kate's assurances, but by mentioning Andrew, Kate hoped to present at least a bit more motivation to up and leave her old life behind. She scraped up the last bite of cheesecake from her plate with the back of her fork and waited for Leslie's reaction.

Leslie looked at her, eyebrows raised inquisitively. "Who . . . a guy?"

"Well, of course, a guy. What else would I be talking about?"

"Sorry. I just didn't think single, datable men existed in this town. Who is it?"

"His name is Andrew. Actually, you remember Tracy Spencer from high school? She and I swam together. Andrew is her cousin, though he didn't grow up here. He's working for his uncle's contracting company in town."

"Contracting? Doing what? Like manual labor?"

"I don't think so. He does a bit of everything, I think. It's just temporary though; at least, I think it is. He's an architect and is sort of in between jobs right now." Kate was nervous talking about him. She had yet to voice her interest in Andrew to anyone. To acknowledge it made it seem especially real.

"Kate, are you nervous?" Leslie said, smiling. "Look at you fidgeting. You *are* nervous!" She playfully tossed her napkin at Kate. "You really like this guy, don't you? How'd you meet him?"

Kate summarized her interactions with Andrew, from the running and the hardware store to their dinner date two nights before. And then, finally, Kate mentioned their time together at the family history library and told Leslie Andrew was Mormon.

"Ha! So that explains why those missionaries were at the house on Saturday. Seriously, Kate, you can't join a religion for a man."

"It's not like that at all!" Kate said. "I didn't even know Andrew was Mormon until after the missionaries had come over. It was just coincidence, really. And come on, Leslie, you know me well enough to know I would never do something like that, something I didn't believe in just to make a man happy."

The waitress came and removed their dessert plates, offering coffee.

"I'd love some," Leslie said. The waitress looked expectantly at Kate. She thought for a moment then shook her head no.

"Just some more water would be great."

"Oh my gosh!" Leslie said, her eyes wide. "You're not drinking coffee. You really are becoming Mormon, aren't you?"

Kate's cheeks flushed with color at Leslie's accusation. "No! I mean, I don't know. Maybe, but that isn't why I didn't get any coffee. I just . . ." She searched for an explanation but found none. "Would it really matter if I was?" she finally asked.

"Yes, it would matter, Kate." Leslie didn't even hesitate. "Everything is different about the Mormons. They're just not like everyone else. All the stories about golden Bibles and angels and secret temples, it all just seems crazy. What would I tell my kids about their aunt Kate's crazy religion?"

"But it isn't like that, Leslie. It isn't crazy. It makes sense, and it . . . well, it's just really wonderful." Kate wondered how she had been spared any exposure to the crazy ideas about Mormons that Linny and Leslie seemed to wholeheartedly embrace.

"Wow. I guess you've spent a lot of time thinking about it. I didn't know you thought about religion much at all." Leslie leaned back against the faded vinyl of the booth, holding her coffee cup in both hands.

"What about when you go back to Atlanta? I guess they've got Mormons there too?"

"Oh, well, I'm sure they do. They pretty much have churches everywhere, but it actually doesn't matter. I don't think I'm going back to Atlanta."

"What?" Leslie nearly dropped her cup onto the table, sloshing coffee over the sides of her cup and onto her fingers. "Why? For this guy? You've only known him a week, Kate! Be serious about this."

"I'm not doing this for Andrew, at least not completely. I want to be here, Leslie. I want to be here with you, get to know your kids, be here for Linny. I've been living for a long time with a heart full of nothing but myself. I'm tired of that. I'm tired of being alone. Even as hard as this week has been, as much as I miss Mary every day, I'm finally starting to feel like me again. The farmhouse, you, your kids . . . I need this. I really want to be here. I want to be here for you," Kate said simply.

Leslie slowly exhaled and set her cup down. "What about your job? You would really just walk away from it all?"

Kate hesitated. It was the hardest hurdle in her plans to move home. She had worked so hard to get where she was, to prove to her boss that she deserved her most recent promotion. She shook her head. "Work isn't everything," she said, "not anymore, anyway."

"Kate," Leslie said calmly. "The only thing worse than moving away from your job and your life in Atlanta for a guy you've only known a week is doing it for me—because you think I'm a mess, that I might not make it if you're not here to pick me up and keep me together. Please don't do this if you're only doing it for me."

"Why not, Leslie? Why not do it for you? I just told you why I was moving back. Obviously, it involves more than just wanting to be here for you. But I can't say you don't have anything to do with my choice. I *do* want to be here for you. I've let you down too many times. We need each other . . . this, us . . . this is what we've got. And we've got to hold on to it."

Kate watched as a tear spilled over onto the soft porcelain of Leslie's cheeks. "Emily just said to me last night that she wished you would move into the farmhouse for good so that anytime she wanted she could go over and remember Grandma's smell."

"She can come over every day," Kate said. "Every day."

Later that evening, before going to bed, Kate sat on the overstuffed couch in her living room and read an entry in Ian's journal that felt particularly relevant, considering the conversations she'd been having with Linny and Leslie. It was funny how frequently Kate found herself turning to Ian's journal. It often seemed like he had insight into just what Kate was feeling. Somehow, she felt as if Ian would understand exactly what she was going through. She read the entry one more time.

*7 August 1844*
*I never thought I'd see the day that here in this place, this*
*land formed by those seeking religious freedom—a nation*
*founded under God Himself—people would be scorned for*
*honoring God. But there are those who do not seek Him, nor*
*do they care for His commandments and teachings. It even*
*seems a spirit exists in this place to urge men not to follow*
*God, to abandon principles of regular worship and instead*
*seek things of the world: material wealth, the adoration of*
*others. Indeed, it might seem easier to walk the wider path*
*and blend in among the crowd, but the reward will not be*
*found on such a path. As the scriptures teach us, straight*
*is the gate and narrow is the way that leads to truth and*
*salvation. Though there be few who find such a path, the joy*
*that comes, oh, the immeasurable joy, would be worth even*
*walking that narrow path alone.*

Her family members might think she was making a mistake, but Kate felt more and more certain that she was finding the path Ian had mentioned.

She stood and stretched, then walked through the house, turning off lights and checking the doors to make sure they were all locked. When she got to the sunroom, she had a sudden thought. She walked over to the desk and turned on the small lamp in the corner. She'd looked through the contents of the desk numerous times, gathering information for Sam, who was working to finalize the execution of Mary's estate, as well as familiarizing herself with the ins and outs of keeping up with the house. She hadn't seen anything recent from the state DOT or from the county commissioners office, though she did find the file of correspondence accumulated in past years. Still, something niggled at Kate's mind. She knew she was missing something. She searched through the desk again and found nothing. Then, on a whim, she lowered herself to the floor and looked under and behind the desk.

There was something there.

She pulled a sheet of paper out from under the desk. It was a letter dated April 22, just three days before Mary had died. Under the letter, Kate found an envelope marked certified mail. A carbon copy receipt was attached to the front, with Mary's signature dated April 25. Kate started to tremble and lowered herself into the desk chair. It was here, in the sunroom, that Leslie had found her mother . . . right here, beside the desk.

"Goodness gracious, Mary," Kate uttered softly. "Did this letter kill you?"

Kate thought of Leslie and Sam relating how hard Mary had fought for the house, how much effort she'd put into saving it, to fighting the highway project from the very beginning. If she was under the impression that she had won and that her house was secure, it must have been a shock to get this letter. Kate quickly read through its contents. It was just as she had expected—a notice from the state DOT informing Ms. Walker of a change in route that would better serve the community as a whole and have less environmental impact—a route that would now include the Walker family property. Kate shook her head in disgust. It didn't make sense that after years and years of planning, the state could just swoop in and say, "We've made up our minds. It's your house we want." The letter advised Mary to contact the department by the following Friday to sign her compliance and enter into negotiations for the purchase of her property. If they did not hear from her, their next step would be contacting the county commissioners to schedule a hearing and initiate the process of eminent domain.

"Well, of course you didn't hear from her," Kate said out loud. She dropped the letter on the desk in frustration.

* * *

Kate called the attorney first thing Monday morning and read the letter aloud.

"It isn't good news, Ms. Sinclair," Mr. Marshall responded. "Ms. Walker signed for the paperwork. As far as the state is concerned, they fulfilled their obligation to notify the property owner of their intent. There is little we can do to fight it."

"There must be something we can do," Kate insisted. "Can't we take them to court? Protest in some way?"

"Court cases have been filed, and some have been ruled in favor of property owners, but in your case, I'm not sure there is a justifiable claim. Yours is one of many properties involved, Ms. Sinclair. And numerous studies have been done to determine the best possible route for this highway. I fear a judge would not be sympathetic to your cause, not to mention the tremendous expenses involved with bringing a case before the court."

"I'm not worried about the money," Kate interrupted. "If there is any chance, even a small possibility that I could save this house, I have to do it, whatever it takes."

Mr. Marshall sighed heavily into the phone. "I thought you might feel that way. We will go to the hearing and file an official protest to the seizing of your property, notify the board that we intend to prepare a court case, and ask for an extension of time to allow us to get ready. That may at least buy us a few months' time. If there are other property owners at the hearing, we can see if anyone else is filing a similar protest. Strength in numbers might help your case. I have to warn you that this will be a long and drawn-out process. I daresay, if you want my honest opinion, I think you may be better served by simply negotiating an acceptable sale price with the state and cutting your losses."

"I beg your pardon, Mr. Marshall. This house has been in my family for over a century. I cannot give up without a fight. Aunt Mary would have fought. I have to do this for her."

*Chapter 23*

OVER THE NEXT TWO WEEKS, Kate spent a great deal of time on the phone with Mr. Marshall. He was not optimistic and was still in favor of cutting a deal, but he was not completely unsympathetic to Kate's wishes. Even still, it was hard for Kate to shake the feeling she was living in a ticking time bomb. The anxious annoyance that accompanied an unknown outcome was wearing on her nerves. The hearing was on Friday, just four days away, and Kate felt it could not arrive fast enough.

In addition to her worry over the house, Kate had long since exhausted the gracious offer of "extended" vacation time from her boss. She had been out of the office for nearly a month and was constantly fielding phone calls from coworkers expecting and needing her back at the office. Mr. Blanton had even called himself, more than once. His patience and tolerance for Kate's absence was running thin. Mentally, Kate had all but handed in her resignation. She knew she could work remotely. She and Mr. Blanton had discussed the possibility several times. But doing so would drastically change her responsibilities for the company. It was a major change, and something kept holding her back. Even when Mr. Blanton pressured her, she kept insisting they didn't need to make any changes just yet. She would be returning full time. She wasn't sure why she didn't tell him the truth. Perhaps because she found herself doubting her decision, wondering if she really could leave her job and her old life. Leslie was the only person she'd told of her decision to move to Rose Creek. While she still felt it was the best thing to do, she hesitated to change things at work, not until she was sure.

"I'm making an exception because it's you, Kate," Mr. Blanton had said. "I wouldn't normally be this tolerant."

"I know that," Kate responded. "And I'm grateful. I just need a little more time. My family still needs me."

"Your family doesn't sign your paycheck. If you're not at the meeting next Monday morning, I'll assume you have resigned and expect your office cleaned out by the end of the week," he had said.

*A week*, Kate thought. It didn't seem like enough time to make such life-altering decisions. When Kate was spending time with Andrew and with Leslie and the children, she didn't even flinch when she thought of leaving Atlanta. But then, when she talked with Mr. Blanton and heard how much he wanted her back at the office, she couldn't help but feel she still belonged there as well. The unrest and uncertainty surrounding the house didn't help her thought process. She wanted to believe she would stay in Rose Creek even if she lost the house. But she wasn't certain.

Fortunately, the weeks preceding the hearing weren't all bad. Kate spent a great deal of time with Andrew and even larger amounts of time with Leslie and her kids. She was absolutely smitten with Tommy and felt like Emily was her new best friend. Nicholas was a bit more reserved, not as openly affectionate as his younger siblings, but Kate felt the connection building. She could also tell that Leslie appreciated her being there and was grateful for Kate's efforts in developing relationships with her kids. As long as they didn't talk about religion, the two cousins got along as well as they had years before.

It wasn't an easy thing for Kate. She felt as if she were living parallel lives—the one her family was a part of, and the one that involved the Mormons. Linny and Leslie still struggled with her interest in the faith. They'd both met Andrew and agreed he seemed like a nice guy but were convinced Kate was only studying the LDS Church because of him. After several contentious discussions with both women, Kate found it easier to just avoid the subject all together. She had learned a good deal of information about the Church from the missionaries and from Andrew but still didn't feel knowledgeable enough to debate the finer points with her family, especially when they seemed so determined to believe what they wanted instead of what Kate shared from her own experience.

It was frustrating. Leslie and Linny couldn't even claim to be faithful parishioners of any congregation. Why did they care so much where she went on Sunday mornings? Kate had attended church with Andrew for the first time the previous Sunday. It had been lovely. The congregation was small but friendly and very welcoming. There was a quiet peace that ran through the meeting, a sweetness and simplicity that had touched Kate. She looked forward to going back.

She thought of Andrew walking through the halls with her and sitting with her in Sunday School. Kate couldn't help but notice the furtive glances and hushed whispers passing among the other parishioners, particularly among the women.

"Are you a celebrity or something?" Kate had asked.

"They're just excited to see me with a girl," Andrew had replied.

Kate smiled as she thought of his response again. She'd been searching her wardrobe all afternoon for something to wear to dinner at the Spencer home that evening. It was there she would finally meet Andrew's sister and show her Ian's journal. By 5:00, Kate was finally dressed, wearing a flowing knee-length skirt and a pale green sweater that complemented the rich color of her eyes.

She looked in the mirror one last time before she heard a frantic knock on the door downstairs. She hurried down the stairs and opened the front door to find Andrew standing breathless in front of her.

"Good grief, Andrew, is everything all right?" Kate asked, making room for him to enter the house. He looked excited, eyes bright and hopeful.

"I can't believe I didn't think of it before," he began. "Kate, I think we can save your house."

"Wait, what?" Kate asked. "What didn't you think of before?"

"Look around you, Kate," Andrew said, smiling broadly. "This house is an architectural relic. I remember thinking the first time I saw it that it ought to be on the historical registry. You just don't see many houses this old in such good shape."

"Okay, yes. It's an old house," Kate said. "But I don't think the state DOT really cares about that."

"That's just it, Kate. If your house is a registered historical landmark, they have to care. The house will be blanketed by the protection of the State Preservation Society. The department of transportation won't be able to touch it."

Kate sat down on the bottom step and looked at Andrew, still too hesitant to be hopeful. "Is that even possible? I wouldn't even know where to begin."

"It is possible. You just create a petition requesting landmark status for the property and turn it into the board of commissioners. I made some calls before I came over. You need an architectural survey that verifies that the house is indeed historical, and then you need a summary of the property's history—why it's significant, that sort of thing. Kate, I also called the county commissioners office, you know, to ask them a purely hypothetical question," he said, smiling. "Here in Harrison County, houses added to the historical registry are approved by the board of county commissioners. There is a separate preservation society, but it is run by volunteers, so the county commissioners office makes all of the decisions. From what I understand, when the board receives a petition for landmark status, they have thirty days to review it. At the end of thirty days, they will accept or deny it. In the case of your house, they will have to reschedule your hearing with the department of transportation for after the thirty days required to consider your petition. Any negotiations with the state cannot take place until it has been accepted or denied."

Kate still doubted. "Why would the board of commissioners approve landmark status for a house they've all but turned into an exit ramp? Maybe if it were a separate committee or a different organization that could rule the house historical and then the county commissioners would just have to comply, this could work. But why would the commissioners willingly put a kink in their own plan? I don't see that happening. Won't they see it's just a ploy to save the property?"

"Except it won't be just a ploy," Andrew said, not allowing her to dampen his enthusiasm. "This house really does deserve to be a historic landmark. It's got the architecture, the history—it would be tragic to destroy a place like this. All we have to do is convince the board to recognize the value of this place. Just think about it. If you try and you succeed, think of all the attorney fees and time and energy you could save."

"So it just has to be turned in by Friday?" Kate asked. "Do I even need to attend the hearing?"

"I'm not sure," he answered. "They just told me on the phone that your petition needed to be turned in before the close of business hours on Friday."

"I think I could handle writing a historical summary of the house, but what about an architectural survey? I don't suppose that's the sort of thing you could do, is it?"

"I absolutely could. I'm licensed to work in North Carolina and Virginia. And if that's not enough, I'm a card-carrying member of the Society of Architectural Historians. Early twentieth century farmhouses aren't exactly my specialty, but I think I could still swing the survey for you."

Kate was momentarily distracted. Over the past few weeks, she had convinced herself she didn't need to worry about Andrew's occupation that wasn't really his occupation. Surely he had a reason to be in Rose Creek, handling odds-and-ends jobs for his uncle. But whenever his career came up, she couldn't help but wonder why he wasn't practicing in his field. He'd been avoiding any discussion about his career for too long. Kate found herself growing impatient. The questions coursing through Kate's brain briefly drowned out the bigger issue at hand, and she realized how much she didn't actually know about this man. But the house deserved her attention. She tried to push away her doubts and focus on what Andrew was saying.

"It will take a bit of research, but I think I can point out the aspects of architecture and construction that set this house apart from its more modern counterparts. And really, I think it would be fascinating work to really get in and see the bones of the house, the design . . . I would love it. Only if you want me to though," he quickly added.

Kate let out a long, audible breath. "Do you really think it's possible?"

"I think we have to try," he said.

They sat silently for a few moments, the wheels in Kate's head spinning as she considered their conversation and started to make plans. She felt lighter just imagining the possibility of avoiding a long, drawn-out legal battle. Could it really be over as soon as Friday? She would call Mr. Marshall in the morning to run the idea by him and get his reaction. She knew a good deal of information about the history of the house, but she didn't think it would be enough. She thought of the Harrison County genealogy room at the public library and wondered if she would be able to find any additional noteworthy information about the house or her ancestors that might strengthen her cause.

"Isn't there a little history museum on East Main Street?" she asked Andrew. "I wonder what sort of information they have there."

"It would probably be worth checking out," Andrew said. "I think the County Preservation Society operates it. They'd at least have some information about the other homes in the area that are on the registry."

"I'll have to go by tomorrow. I don't think I know nearly enough about this house to write an entire history. I wish I knew what sort of things I ought to include."

"Well, if you find out your great-grandfather was an ax murderer, you probably ought to leave that part out," Andrew joked, smiling at Kate.

She laughed and reached over to rest her hand on Andrew's arm. "Thank you," she said softly. "I don't know what else to say. It's nice to have your support through all of this."

It touched Kate that he so naturally aligned himself to her. He was ready to help her fight her battles and offer strength and encouragement. She suddenly felt like this was no longer just her fight but that it was *their* fight.

Kate had grown quite used to Andrew's presence the past few weeks. They had spent a lot of time together, seeing each other nearly every day, and yet, save one small kiss on the cheek when he'd dropped her off after dinner two nights ago, he still hadn't kissed her. She was happy to build a friendship and was content with his company, but she had to admit she was feeling a bit impatient. They were adults, after all. What was he waiting for?

Kate's previous questions rose back to the surface. She couldn't help but wonder what he was keeping from her. And did it have anything to do with why he seemed so hesitant about their relationship progressing?

Kate didn't want to push. There were certainly things she hadn't told him about her past. Some things, even, that as she learned more and more about the lifestyles and standards of the Mormons, she thought Andrew might not actually want to know. But she was curious. She wanted to know everything she possibly could about this man, both good and bad—if bad were even possible with him. As she sat there breathing him in, feeling the warmth of him so close to her, Kate knew her feelings were rooted in something much deeper than mere curiosity. Ready or not, she was falling in love.

"I'm happy to help," he insisted, reaching over and taking her hand. "If it's all right with you, I can come over first thing in the morning and get started."

On the drive over to the Spencers' home, Kate looked around the inside of Andrew's car with a more critical eye. During the day, he drove the large white contractor's truck that belonged to his uncle's company. But when he and Kate went out in the evenings, he drove his own car. It was a nice car—an indication that wherever he had worked previously, he'd probably commanded a respectable salary. Kate wondered again why he had left. Perhaps he hadn't left voluntarily but was fired. There were too many questions. Kate's mind was doing a good job of minimizing the idea that there could be anything about Andrew that wasn't thoroughly respectable, but she also wanted him to be honest with her.

"Andrew, will you tell me about your job in Virginia? Why did you leave?"

Andrew shifted uncomfortably in his seat. "It's kind of a long story," he finally said. "I . . . Listen, I want to tell you. Just not right now. It's not, I mean, it's not anything you need to worry about. Nothing criminal— nothing even business related. I left for personal reasons."

"It's okay," Kate said, reaching out to touch his arm. "You can tell me whenever you're ready." It wasn't hard for her to see his relief.

They talked companionably for the rest of the drive, mostly about Andrew's sister and her excitement about seeing Ian's journal. A part of Kate felt guilty that she was so willing to share such a treasured item with a complete stranger, yet she still had not told her family of its existence. They were, after all, descendants of Ian just like she was and had just as much right to read the journal. Part of her hesitancy was the unmistakable connection Ian had to her investigation of the Mormon Church. She felt with great intensity that it was not coincidence or mere happenstance that brought the missionaries to her door. When Elder Christianson had boldly echoed Ian's words, mentioning a unification of purpose and spirit, Kate felt as if Ian had been calling to her, urging her to listen, learn, and read. That was something she was sure her family would not understand.

Their reaction to her interest in the Church had opened her eyes to a strain of persecution in the South she had never known existed. There seemed to be so much ill-placed hatred. Judgments and assumptions based on little fact or foundation and an attitude of fear—a wide-eyed, whisper-behind-your-back sort of attitude that irritated Kate. As Andrew drove, Kate asked him what he thought.

"There are places where Latter-day Saints aren't so much a minority," Andrew explained. "Out West in Utah, of course, then parts of Arizona and Idaho, even California. It's definitely different growing up in a place like this, where you might have five kids in your high school who share your faith and where your Sunday congregation might reach one hundred on a good day. But at the same time, I think it's worth it. When you live in the Bible Belt, you have to decide if the persecution, the questions, the rampant misinformation is going to get to you, and you have to be willing to stand up for what you believe in, regardless. You have to develop a little bit of a thick skin, I guess, but then, I think that's a good thing. One thing's for sure, your feet have to be firmly planted. Sometimes the winds of opposition can be pretty strong."

She was glad to hear Andrew offer an opinion. He'd been a little tight-lipped as of late when it came to matters of religion. At first, he had been really involved, attending her meetings with the missionaries and answering her questions. In the past few days, however, he'd pulled back, deferring her questions to the elders and frequently changing the subject. Before getting out of the car at the Spencers', Kate finally confronted him. For this question, she was sure she deserved an answer.

"Before we go in, can I ask you something?" she asked.

"Sure," he said.

"I like this. I like hearing you offer an opinion and discuss your faith with me. But aside from just now, you've totally been avoiding the subject. Why?"

Andrew sighed, looking down at his hands. "It's that obvious, huh?"

"What gives, Andrew? You've served a mission too; you've answered all the questions before. I don't mind talking to the missionaries. I like them both a great deal, but you and I can't discuss it as well?"

Andrew looked up, eyes locking into Kate's. "It's because I like you so much."

She paused and pulled her gaze away from his. "What do you mean?"

"Kate, this religion, my faith . . . it's who I am. It's priority for me, for my wife, whoever she may be, and for my future family. I had a relationship once with a girl who wasn't Mormon, and it was hard—hard to be so different, to have such different ideas about what our life together would involve. I don't want that again." The words came quickly but were focused and well thought out. "I haven't been able to stop thinking about you since that first morning we ran into each other. I tried though, because I didn't want to fall for you . . . didn't want . . . but then you just kept popping up everywhere—the hardware store, downtown. I saw you that afternoon too," he said. "I told myself that next Monday morning that I would give it one chance. If you showed up, then we'd talk. If not, I would try to stop seeing your face every time I closed my eyes."

Kate wondered if Andrew could hear her heart pounding in her chest or see the ripples of goose bumps rising on her arms.

"Kate, when you walked into the family history library and I realized you had met with the missionaries and you actually had a Book of Mormon in your hands, it almost seemed too good to be true. At the same time, this," he motioned to the two of them, "anything happening between us, has to be totally separate from what you do when it comes to the gospel. I guess what I'm saying is that I'm not sure my motives are pure enough to discuss it. I can't say I wouldn't largely be thinking about what it would mean for me if you were to join the Church. And I shouldn't have anything to do with it."

"Wow," Kate said softly. She felt him looking at her but was afraid to raise her eyes to meet his.

"I said too much, didn't I?" Andrew said.

"No," Kate quickly responded. "I mean, you did say a lot, but I don't mind. I'm glad you did." Finally, she looked up. "Andrew, I've spent a lot of time thinking about this. I'm nearly finished with the Book of Mormon. I've even stopped drinking coffee." She smiled shyly. "I can't say that I haven't thought about what it might mean for you and me if we shared a common faith. But I've been on my own for a long time. I've made decisions for the wrong reasons too many times to jump into something without knowing why I'm doing it. I like you a lot too, but I wouldn't do this just for you. Even with this," Kate picked up Ian's journal from her lap, "even with Ian searching for a truth I'm pretty sure he would have found in your church, I won't do this just for him either. I'll know for myself, or I won't do it. Not for you, not for Ian, not for anyone but me."

"That's good to know," Andrew said softly, nearly whispering.

"If something were to happen between us," Kate said, voice low to match his, "if this did work out, I think it might be nice for you to have been a part of the process, don't you think?"

"I think I'd like that," he said, smiling one more time. He offered his hand to Kate, palm up. "But for the right reasons."

She slipped her hand into his, surprised by how well it seemed to fit.

# Chapter 24

CAROLINE SPENCER MET THEM AT the front door. "Good heavens, Andrew, what took you so long? I thought I'd have to hold dinner till tomorrow."

"Sorry, Aunt Caroline, it wasn't intentional."

"Is everything all right?" she asked, looking first at Andrew then over at Kate.

"Everything's fine," Andrew said. "We were just talking." He smiled at Kate, and a faint blush crept up her cheeks.

"Uh-huh," Caroline said. "I'm sure that's all you were doing. Let's go eat, then; everyone's waiting on you."

She bustled off to the kitchen, motioning for them to follow. "It sure is nice to see you again, Kate," she called over her shoulder. "You look just lovely this evening."

"Thank you," Kate said as Caroline disappeared into the kitchen. They followed after her, passing through the kitchen into the dining room. The table was set, with Dan Spencer, a woman Kate assumed was Andrew's sister, and Elders Christianson and Peterson already sitting, waiting for them to arrive.

"Oh, Sister Spencer, I'm so sorry," Kate offered. "I didn't realize we were keeping you."

"Nonsense," Dan said. "We just sat down." He stood and extended his hand to Kate. "It's good to see you again," he said warmly. "Hope you don't mind the elders joining with us tonight. Whenever they don't have anywhere to eat, they come crawling here like lost puppies."

Kate shook her head and laughed. "No, I don't mind at all." She smiled at the elders and said hello, shaking their hands as they stood to greet her. She turned to Andrew's sister. She guessed she was in her late thirties, maybe early forties. Her hair was short, a spiky cut that accentuated her prominent cheekbones and near flawless coloring. She had the same chocolate-brown eyes Andrew had and a warm, welcoming smile. Overall, Kate thought her to be quite lovely.

"This is my sister Valerie," Andrew said as he wrapped his arms around his big sister. "How are you, Val?" he said softly. "It's good to see you." He stood back and extended a hand to Kate, pulling her forward. "This is Kate."

The way Andrew said it made Kate feel silly, like she was being presented at court for the grand duke's approval.

"It's nice to finally meet you," Valerie said. "I've heard a lot about you."

"Likewise," Kate said, casting a sideways glance in Andrew's direction. She couldn't help but wonder what he had told his sister. Sometimes she forgot she'd really only known this man for a few weeks. It seemed odd that she cared so much what he thought of her and what he might be saying to others when so little time had transpired.

"Well then, we've all been introduced, and I would imagine we're all hungry," Caroline interjected. "Let's eat, shall we?"

Andrew had mentioned his aunt's ability to cook when he'd offered the invitation, claiming the food was good enough to make up for the worst kind of company. He had not exaggerated. The food was delicious. Kate was equally delighted with her dining companions, though, and was seated comfortably in between Andrew and Valerie. Kate and Valerie talked for much of dinner. Kate told her all about Ian's journal and pieced together as best she could what she knew of her family's history all the way back to Ian Wylie. Valerie was intrigued and was obviously anxious to finish her meal and get a firsthand look at the journal.

Andrew spent a good bit of time talking to his uncle about a construction job that was giving the company a bit more trouble than they had originally planned. Kate was much too involved in her discussion with Valerie to follow all that was said, but she did remember noting how intelligent and well spoken Andrew seemed. He had a quiet confidence that was puzzling to Kate, almost inexplicable. He wasn't trying to impress her by using big words and wasn't trying to be something he wasn't; he was just himself. Kate had met men in Atlanta who dropped their education and career in her lap in the first five minutes of conversation in an effort to impress, yet Andrew had almost made an effort, it seemed, to *not* discuss what he did for a living. She had her reservations about that but was still pleased that he didn't seem the kind of guy that would flaunt it, constantly playing the how-much-do-I-earn, how-much-do-I-spend, how-big-is-my-house game that had so frequently fogged the dating scene in her previous life.

It most certainly was a previous life—a life where she never would have imagined staying in Rose Creek and eating dinner with a room full of Mormons she hoped to spend the rest of her life with. She laughed silently to herself—and she'd thought all she was coming home for was a funeral.

After dinner, the small party moved into the family room. Before Kate had the chance to retrieve the journal from her handbag in the foyer, the missionaries engaged her in conversation, asking if she had been reading the Book of Mormon like she had promised.

"I've nearly finished it," Kate said, excited to tell them. "It's been so fascinating; it's filled almost every moment of my spare time."

Elder Christianson was beaming. "That's really wonderful. Do you have any questions?"

"I don't think so," Kate responded, sitting down in a soft overstuffed arm chair. "Though I still feel like there is so much I need to learn."

Elder Peterson, normally quiet, spoke up. "Kate, have you taken the opportunity to pray about what you've read?"

Kate looked down, her face flushed with embarrassment. The missionaries had asked her to pray before, and though she'd certainly thought about it, whenever she told herself she was going to, she seemed to come up with some reason why she shouldn't. She felt silly, inadequate, and completely incapable of saying a prayer worthy of God in the first place.

The quiet tones of Elder Peterson's voice were soothing to Kate's nerves. "It's all right," he said, not waiting for her to answer. "You don't have to be an expert to say a prayer worth hearing. Whenever you feel ready, just do your best, and your Heavenly Father will hear you."

Kate looked up and saw Andrew listening to their conversation. She smiled, and he came over, sitting on the ottoman next to Kate, opposite the missionaries.

"When I was on my mission in Scotland, there was a man, a convert to the gospel, just like you," he said, looking at Kate, "who was serving as stake president." Kate nodded her head in understanding, and Andrew continued his story. "He shared his conversion story at a conference I attended. I've never heard such a powerful testimony of conversion and of the efforts the Lord makes to touch our hearts. This man talked about how there came a point in his conversion where his mind knew all he could about the gospel. He'd read the Book of Mormon, he'd asked all the right questions and thought the gospel, as he had been taught, made sense. But it wasn't until he knelt down and asked God to let him know if all he had learned was true that he really felt converted to the Lord. After he knelt down and prayed, he got in his car and was driving home. He was touched so deeply that he had to stop the car. At that moment, he felt the Lord's presence, felt His love and awareness, and knew that he had to be baptized. You are entitled to that same witness, Kate. It isn't just principles and logic. You can receive spiritual confirmation if you seek it. The Lord will make Himself known unto you."

Kate knew what Andrew said was true, and she knew if she was going to join this Church, she would have to ask. It just seemed so overwhelming and a bit impossible, if she was completely honest. She had a hard time wrapping her mind around the idea that God would speak to her and reach out to her individually. She, who had never reached out to God, had never relied on Him; she, who had spent so many years doing as she pleased, thinking about herself, breaking even the most basic commandments. And then there was a part of Kate that was simply frightened by the changes that such personal revelation would bring about. It felt right, and it made sense, but it was still scary.

"Will you pray about it?" Elder Christianson asked gently.

He wasn't pushing Kate. She knew that. She could hear the sincerity in his voice, and she felt love and concern fill the room, touching her inside and out. But they couldn't understand. "Why would God want to speak to me?" she asked simply. "I'm not anyone special. My life, the way I've been living, I just . . ." She struggled to translate her feelings into words, her emotions so close to the surface. "I'm not good enough. I've made so many mistakes."

"We all make mistakes," Andrew said gently. "But the power of the Atonement extends to everyone. Christ suffered so we don't have to—so you don't have to. Though you may not feel you've been aware of God, He's always been aware of you."

Kate wanted to believe him and the missionaries. It just wasn't that simple. "I'll try," she said. "I promise I'll try."

"I hate to interrupt," Valerie said, coming in from the kitchen. "But the dishes are done, and there's a piece of history I'd like to get my hands on before I get back on the road." She smiled at Kate. Kate quickly stood and retrieved the journal from her handbag. She sat down next to Valerie on the couch and gently handed the book to the historian.

Valerie was silent as she turned the brittle pages, shaking her head in wonder and amazement.

"It's remarkable, isn't it?" Andrew had moved to stand behind the couch, looking over his sister's shoulder as she examined the journal.

"It's amazing," she said. Valerie looked up at Kate. "It's really wonderful to have a record from so long ago, especially one that is so well preserved. The conditions must have been perfect in your attic—no moisture, no heat—journals like this don't always survive."

"There is a lot I wasn't able to read," Kate said. "I tried to piece together what I could, but there were some pages that were so faded or so blended together I couldn't figure it all out."

"There are specialists who could help with that. It's amazing what they can discover with a bit of special treatment," Valerie said. "But still, there are pages here that are near perfect. You can read it as if it were written just yesterday. Look at this entry. It sounds a little like our dinner here tonight.

> '*14 January 1845*
> *I felt great joy this day as my family and friends gathered*
> *around my table for a meal. It is God's design, I think, for us*
> *to have one another—to have family that fills and enriches*
> *our lives. Jennie made an amazing meal, as always. I pray*
> *that all who left our hearth this night did so full of food and*
> *full of goodness. May God's blessings be upon them all.*'"

Valerie asked if she could photocopy a few of the pages to show her colleagues back at the university. She also suggested a number of things Kate could do to help preserve the journal so it wouldn't deteriorate any further than it already had. The conversation eventually turned to Kate's house, and Kate, with Andrew's help, detailed to the small party the struggles she was facing. They were all very compassionate, Dan even offering to make a few phone calls to contact people he knew who worked for the county. Kate was grateful for any positive efforts on her behalf, but it was Valerie who gave Kate the most hope.

"Kate, was it in the farmhouse that you found Ian's journal?" she asked.

"It was," Kate confirmed. "The lineage is direct, father to son, from Ian all the way down to my grandfather George Wylie, who built the house."

Valerie's eyes glowed with excitement. "To have housed such a historic document as this, your house is almost guaranteed to be granted landmark status. When did the Wylies first come to Harrison County?"

Kate pulled a copy of the family tree she'd copied from the Bible out of her bag and handed it to Valerie. "According to birth location listed here, Ian's great-grandson was the first to be born in North Carolina. I assume it was his father who made the journey."

"That's long enough. The Wylies have been a long-contributing part of Harrison County history. In the summary you're putting together, talk about this, perhaps even offer to donate the journal to the local preservation museum, and be sure you mention you will allow the farmhouse to be included in their brochures and on their tours."

"Do you think that would make a difference?" Kate asked hopefully.

"It won't hurt," Valerie said. "The house has a lot of history, and if Andrew can back up the architectural end of it, I think you have a pretty good shot. Have you thought about calling the preservation society? You said they can't approve the petition, but if they can give it their stamp of approval, the commissioners might be more prone to lean in your favor."

"They have a small museum downtown," Kate said. "I was planning on stopping by tomorrow to see what help they can provide." Kate looked up as a pair of headlights shone through the window, meandering down the drive toward the house.

Caroline rose from her chair and looked out the window. "Dan? We weren't expecting anybody else, were we?" She must not have meant for the question to be answered. She hastily left the room, moving to the door to greet the unknown visitor. Kate heard a woman's voice float in from the foyer. She watched as Andrew's face turned to stone, a pale, chalky shade of white spreading all the way into the collar of his soft blue shirt. He stood, rigid, eyes fixed on the entryway to the family room. Kate followed his gaze and watched as the woman from the foyer pushed past Caroline into the family room.

"I saw his car, Caroline. I know he's here. I just need to speak to him." The woman's words trailed off as she looked in on the happy scene. Andrew didn't move.

"Ashley, what are you doing here?" he said, still motionless.

"You weren't in Charlotte, and you weren't at the cabin here in town. I just thought you might be here."

"You went all the way to Charlotte?" Andrew questioned.

"Well, if you would answer your cell phone, maybe I wouldn't have to track you down in person," Ashley fired back. "Can we just talk? Please. I came all this way."

Kate watched their conversation in shocked embarrassment. It didn't take a relationship specialist to figure out what Ashley was to Andrew. Obviously, they had a history. Whatever it was, Kate was sure she did not fit anywhere into the equation.

"Kate," Andrew said softly.

She couldn't look at him. Instead, she turned to Valerie. "Since you're on your way out, Valerie, perhaps you could drop me off at home?"

"Kate, wait," Andrew said, though he already sounded defeated.

"Wait a minute," Ashley interjected. "Is she here with you?" Her voice was thick with disdain, her words fiery darts piercing directly into Kate's heart. "Bet you didn't tell her about me, did you, Andrew? Didn't tell her what you did. You didn't mention you had a fiancée, did you?"

Kate shook her head in disbelief. How had she been so dense? No matter her embarrassment, she was determined to leave with her head held high. She would not walk out of the room like a wounded, gullible new girlfriend. She took a deep breath and stood up, crossing the room to gather her things. She stopped in front of Ashley. "I'm sorry, we haven't met," Kate said. "I'm Kate Sinclair." She held her hand out to Ashley, who hesitantly took it, face smug and obviously distrusting. "I was just here meeting with the missionaries, but I can see our time is up." Kate looked at Valerie. "I've got to make a quick phone call, so I'll just wait for you outside?"

Valerie silently nodded her head. Kate said good-bye and thanked the Spencers, then quietly let herself out.

If she had known which car belonged to Valerie, she would have climbed inside, desperate to hide her face and get as far away from the house and from Andrew as she could. How could she have been so stupid? A part of her had always thought he had to be too good to be true. He was simply too perfect. But she'd fallen for him anyway. She thought back over their conversations—the moments when he was obviously uncomfortable talking about his past—but a fiancée?

Valerie came up behind Kate. "Are you okay?" she asked gently.

Kate smiled as best she could. "Of course I am. Why wouldn't I be?"

Valerie gave her a knowing look. "This is my car right here," she said, pressing her key fob to unlock the doors. Kate climbed inside, desperate to hold on to her dignity, clinging to what small bit of composure she could. Valerie started the car and turned around in the narrow gravel drive, working around the shiny black Mercedes parked directly behind Andrew's car.

Kate shook her head, a sarcastic laugh escaping her lips when she noticed the car. "Figures," she said softly to herself.

"It isn't what you think, Kate."

"Valerie, you don't have to explain anything," Kate said quickly. "I have no claim on Andrew's affection. We've only known each other a few weeks."

"Don't be stupid," Valerie said with enough force to surprise Kate. "I watched the two of you all evening. You couldn't stop staring at each other. There's something going on with you guys, and you know it."

Kate chuckled. "And there's obviously someone who can get in the way. Oh, I don't know—a fiancée maybe?"

"She isn't his fiancée anymore," Valerie said. "It's over between them and has been for almost a year."

"A year?" Kate asked. "She wasn't acting like it ended a year ago. And why hasn't he been answering her calls? Did it really end that badly?"

Valerie drove in silence for a moment. "It was bad," she finally said. "He left her at the altar—literally just didn't show up for the ceremony. We were all there at the temple in DC. We had a rehearsal dinner, took all the pictures, and then, when it came time for the ceremony, he just didn't show up. None of us understand how he'd let it go on for so long if he was so sure she wasn't the one, but who knows what he was thinking? He's refused to talk to anybody about it since."

Kate sat speechless, suddenly feeling very sorry for this Ashley woman and all that she must have endured. Valerie's car slowed, nearing the driveway to the old farmhouse, and Kate snapped to attention, wanting a few more answers before Valerie dropped her off.

"This happened a year ago?" she asked again.

"It was July of last year. So I guess it's been almost that long."

"That's when he left his job, isn't it? It's all connected."

Valerie nodded her head. "Ashley's father is Russell Westonhouse. He was Andrew's boss. That's how he met Ashley, actually. Moved up to Richmond to take the job, and well, the rest is history." She paused for a moment, then hesitantly added, "And it's Andrew's history. You'll have to talk to him about this if you want to know more."

Kate sighed, nodding her head. "Thank you, Valerie. You've been very kind tonight."

"It was my pleasure." Valerie smiled. "Good luck with the house, Kate, and with the journal. You'll take good care of it, I'm sure."

Kate thanked her again and climbed out of the car.

"Oh, and, Kate," Valerie called, leaning over to look at Kate through the open car door. Kate paused.

"Give Andrew the chance to explain, would you? He isn't a bad guy; he just got himself into a bad situation."

Kate managed a weak smile. "I'll try," she said. She closed the car door and walked to the house, suddenly feeling very, very weary. The tears started flowing before she hit the front steps, her hands trembling as she searched clumsily for her keys.

"This isn't what I need to be focusing on!" she muttered angrily to herself.

The house was perched on the very edge of safety, just waiting for one singular decision to either save the house or pummel it into a splintery heap. And all Kate could think about was Andrew.

To leave someone at the altar on your actual wedding day seemed a cruel and horrible thing to do and very unlike the Andrew Kate had gotten to know the past few weeks. How did something like that happen? How did it go on for so long without him realizing and admitting that she wasn't the person for him? It was frustrating to imagine that Andrew was capable of such deception and inflicting so much pain on someone who obviously cared about him a great deal. She had always thought so highly of his sense of honor and decency. It was disappointing to be so boldly confronted with such a stain on his character.

At the same time, Kate was happy to know that it was Andrew who had left Ashley, not the other way around. He didn't want Ashley, which meant there was still room in his heart for Kate. But then, Kate was sure that at some point, he had wanted Ashley enough to propose marriage. What guarantee did Kate have that he wouldn't change his mind about her too? Would he walk away from her the same way? The frustrating circle of reasoning continued well into the evening. Finally, Kate pushed it from her mind, focusing instead on her house and the creation of its worthy history.

She worked late into the night, relying heavily on Ian's journal, the front page of the family Bible, and what little bits of the story she'd been told growing up. With a few phone calls to Sam, she was able to put together a substantial summary. She planned to go to the library in the morning to search the county history section for any mention of the Wylie name. Hopefully her ancestors had all been fine, upstanding citizens.

She was grateful to have had a distraction to occupy her thoughts for so long. Trying to sleep, however, was a challenge of the worst sort. As she lay in bed, tossing and turning, she imagined Andrew and Ashley discussing their relationship, heads close together, perhaps her hand resting gently on his arm. Ashley, from what Kate had seen of her, was lovely. She was much shorter than Kate—no taller than 5'2" or 5'3"—with soft blonde hair and baby-blue eyes. In a way, she reminded Kate of Leslie, though she didn't think Ashley was quite as pretty as Leslie. And she was young. Or at least, she came across as being young, much younger than Andrew. Kate groaned and flung her pillow across the room. The entire thing was ridiculous. No matter how much she liked Andrew, she reminded herself he wasn't the reason she was here in Rose Creek. She came home for Aunt Mary, and she was staying for Leslie and their relationship. Andrew certainly made life in Rose Creek a bit more interesting, but it wasn't about him, or at least, it shouldn't be.

Kate sighed.

Deep down, she knew Andrew most definitely played a part in her decision to stay in Rose Creek. If she lost the house and she lost Andrew, would she still have it in her to stay?

## Chapter 25

KATE WOKE WITH A START, her heart nearly pounding out of her chest when a car door slammed just outside her bedroom window. She scrambled out of bed and peeked into the driveway, fearing yet still expecting to see Andrew. Sure enough, he stood in the driveway, leaning against the hood of his car, legs crossed casually as he studied a clipboard in his hands. Kate moved away from the window, not wanting to attract his attention, and hastily pulled on a pair of yoga pants and a zip-up hoodie. She glanced at the clock and was surprised to see it was already 8:30, much later than she normally slept.

She had known he would still come. Even if he and Ashley had reconciled their differences and eloped to Vegas, she didn't believe Andrew was the kind of guy who would leave her in a lurch after so readily agreeing to help the day before. It didn't make it any easier to face him. She stood in the bathroom and studied her reflection. She looked tired, eyes still a little puffy from last night's tears but, all in all, not that bad. She splashed some water on her face and pulled her hair back into a ponytail then descended the stairs to greet Andrew. She had already determined that she would get through this. For the sake of the house, she had to. And while she imagined herself being tough, resisting Andrew's attempts to explain and justify the events of the previous evening, Kate knew if Andrew wanted to talk, she would listen. She was angry and a little hurt that she hadn't known about Ashley, but Valerie was right. Andrew was a good guy, and he deserved the opportunity to explain himself. Kate stopped at the door and took a long, slow breath.

She could have stood there breathing all morning and still wouldn't have been prepared for what she saw when she opened the front door. The last thing she expected to see was a fresh-faced Ashley standing in her driveway.

But there she was, right beside Andrew, with a smug look of ownership on her face. It wasn't enough for her just to win. She had to come over and rub it in Kate's face as well.

It was too much for her to comprehend. To bring her here, to Kate's own home—what was Andrew trying to prove? She looked at him, eyes wide with disbelief. He looked back, face pained and uncomfortable. A brief shrug of his shoulders seemed to indicate that he wasn't happy with the situation either. Why was she here, then? Realizing she couldn't stand there silent forever, Kate descended the porch steps and greeted the couple.

"Good morning," she said coolly.

"Hello, Kate," Andrew said wearily. "You remember Ashley from last night. She was just on her way out of town."

Kate looked up and noticed for the first time that Ashley's car was parked off to the side behind her own.

"Hope you don't mind me stopping by," Ashley said coyly. "Andrew had such wonderful things to say about this old house, I wanted to see it before I left town. I have such an appreciation for old architecture," she added, as if that made a difference to Kate.

*Where did this girl come from?* she wondered to herself.

"Ashley followed me over," Andrew said flatly. "She insisted on coming."

Kate didn't know what to say. The entire situation seemed so ridiculous, so preposterous—she shook her head, trying to make sense of what was happening. "It's fine," she said to them both. "You're welcome to look around. I actually need to get to the library, but I'll leave the house open. The two of you can talk old architecture all morning."

"Kate, I'm sure I'm going to have some questions about the house," Andrew said. Her look stopped him short. He wasn't asking her to stay around for this nonsense, was he? "You won't stay gone all day, will you?"

"I'm not sure how long it will take," Kate said. "If you'll excuse me, I need to get dressed." She turned and walked toward the house. Andrew walked after her.

"Kate, please," he said, gently grabbing her arm. She stopped and turned. He stood close to her, speaking low enough for Ashley, despite her best efforts, not to hear. "I'm so sorry, Kate," he whispered. "Please, just tell me you'll let me explain. Let me make this right."

"I don't know what you want me to say."

"Just say you'll listen," he pled. "She'll be gone soon. When she is, when you come back from the library, promise you'll listen."

Kate silently nodded her assent then turned and went into the house.

*Unbelievable*, she thought to herself as she climbed into the shower. Did things like this really happen anywhere but on daytime television? She showered and dressed quickly, mind racing the entire time. Ashley obviously had some sort of an agenda. Why else would she have followed Andrew to her house when he so clearly didn't want her company?

When Kate came out of the bathroom, her suspicions were confirmed. Ashley was sitting on her bed, arms folded across her chest, obviously waiting for Kate. Kate stopped, unable to hide her surprise and downright irritation that Ashley was in her bedroom.

"You said I was welcome to look around," she said tartly.

Kate sighed. "We both know you're not here to look at architecture. What do you want with me?"

"I saw the way he looked at you last night," Ashley said hotly, apparently grateful for the opportunity to get right to the point. "I thought it couldn't be true, that he couldn't have fallen for someone so quickly, so I wanted to come here to see him with you again. It's so obvious, Kate. He's totally in love with you. He watches your every move. And when he looks at you . . . it's just . . . He's different."

"We've only known each other a few weeks, Ashley. We're just friends," Kate insisted.

"Oh, don't be ridiculous," Ashley said. "You know it's more than that. And that's why I came up here to talk to you. Believe it or not, Kate, I'm not an awful person out to sabotage your relationship. I just think you need to know what you're getting yourself into. You need to hear firsthand what kind of man Andrew really is."

"I'm not sure this is a good idea."

Ashley continued anyway. "You think a guy like him wouldn't already be married now if there wasn't something wrong with him? He can't commit! He does everything right, makes you think he walks on water, and then . . . nothing." Ashley stood up, her hands lifted in frustration. "Do you realize how horrible it is to be sitting, surrounded by your family, your friends, waiting for the man of your dreams to walk through the door and vow to take care of you forever, to wait and wait and wonder why he isn't there? And then his old college roommate, someone you don't even know, comes in and whispers the single worst thing you could ever imagine. He isn't coming. He's left, gone . . . run out of your life forever, just like that."

Kate sat down on the bed, silent while Ashley continued.

"I didn't deserve it. I didn't deserve to be left like that." She turned and looked at Kate, eyes brimming with tears. "All I can tell you is to be careful. You better guard your heart. I never knew. I never knew that anything was wrong until it was too late." She stood silently, lost in her own memory. "I'm sorry, Kate. I'm sure you're a very lovely person. You don't deserve to be hurt like I was."

She turned and hurried from the room. Kate sat motionless on her bed, listening as Ashley descended the stairs. Andrew was still outside. She heard a few muffled words between them, and then Ashley's car roared to life. She waited until the sound had faded before she stood up and, retrieving her own keys and handbag, walked out the door. She passed Andrew and, without a word, climbed into her car and left.

## Chapter 26

"IT'S AMAZING, REALLY," KATE SAID, talking on her cell phone with Linny. She stood in front of the library, a large stack of photocopied information about her family in her hand. "The Wylies really played a big part in the establishment of Harrison County, and yet we never knew any details of their history. I think there might be enough to save the house, Linny. If I can pull it all together in time, it just might work."

"You'll get it together in time," Linny said. "It's a marvelous idea, Kate. I'm sure it will work."

Kate appreciated Linny's unfailing optimism. Linny was happy to oblige when Kate asked her to fill the rest of the family in on this new idea. They were all planning to attend the hearing on Friday, but if the petition was turned in before that, it wasn't necessary for them to be there. Kate had called the county commissioners office just before calling Linny to confirm that point. Once the petition was in, the farmhouse would be taken off the list of properties involved in the Friday-night hearing. After thirty days, the board would vote on the petition at one of their regular weekly meetings. Kate would be notified when the vote would take place so she could be present. If the petition was denied, she would then be given a new hearing date with the department of transportation.

Linny listened as Kate explained all of the details and then readily agreed to call everyone. Kate had wanted to wait to tell her family about the journal until they were all together so they could see and experience it firsthand, but it was too difficult to keep it out of her conversation with Linny. It was, after all, an integral part of the house's history and something she hoped would heavily contribute to her petition for landmark status.

"Well, I'll be," Linny had exclaimed when Kate told her of the journal. "How many years old is it?"

"Nearly two hundred years, Linny," Kate said. "It's remarkable. I can't wait for you to see it." Kate still got goose bumps whenever she thought about the journal. She felt such a strong sense of kinship with Ian and his family. She wondered if any of her family would feel the same way.

Kate had also called Mr. Marshall that morning on her way to the library. When she explained her desire to register the house as a landmark, he was enthusiastic.

"It's a wonderful idea, Ms. Sinclair!" he said. "And with the knowledge that you are prepared to take legal action if your petition is denied, they may just rule in your favor after all. Even better is the news that now we will have thirty more days to prepare for legal action in the event that your petition is denied."

Kate was encouraged and, despite the rough start to her morning, found herself almost in a good mood. Her trip to the library had proved highly successful. John Wylie, Ian's great-grandson, had moved to the mountains of North Carolina sometime after the Civil War. Kate found record of his marriage to a Charlotte Willson in 1885 just a few counties over from Harrison. And then in the Harrison County Historical Almanac, she'd found a record of a land donation—two acres in the heart of Rose Creek, purchased and then immediately donated to the First United Methodist Church for the construction of a new sanctuary. John Wylie and his wife, Charlotte, made the donation. Ian must have done well for himself, Kate realized, and his children as well.

The gesture of goodwill and faith also said much about the spiritual climate in the Wylie home. Faith and respect for God hadn't been important just to Ian. His mother had warned him of the necessity of raising his children in the church, and whatever he'd decided to do, it had obviously worked quite well. With a bit more digging, Kate imagined she could find more on John and Charlotte, but time was of the essence, and she still had much to do to prepare her petition before Friday. After her conversation with Linny, Kate left the library and drove to the Harrison County Preservation Museum to see what help they might be able to offer.

The museum was located in an old Victorian-style house just down the street from the courthouse. A dusty plaque sat beside the door, the words "Where being old is a good thing" etched on top. Kate pushed open the heavy door and adjusted her eyes to the dimness within. A tiny man, at least eighty years old, sat behind a tall counter, reading a newspaper from 1964. He wore oversized glasses perched on his oversized bulbous nose. Thick, bushy eyebrows stuck out from behind the glasses in such a wild frenzy that Kate found it difficult not to laugh.

"Was it a good year?" she asked, motioning toward the paper.

"What?" The man asked, obviously confused by Kate's question.

"1964," she said, pointing to the newspaper.

"Oh," the man said. "Well, that makes sense. I didn't think we were still at war in Vietnam."

Kate raised her eyebrows, suddenly wondering if coming here had been a good idea.

"Would you like to look around the museum? It's free," the man said, smiling broadly. His eyes disappeared into the wrinkly folds of his aging face. Kate liked him already.

"I would love to, but I was hoping you might be able to help me first."

Kate thought it best to ask if he knew anything about her family, specifically John Wylie's donation of land to the church.

"Oh, I am quite familiar with the history of the Methodist church," the man responded. "They were in quite a financial pickle when Mr. Wylie gave them that land. You say he's an ancestor of yours?"

"Yes, my great-great-grandfather," Kate acknowledged. "Do you know anything else of his history?"

"Hmm. A bit off the top of my head, but I'd guess there's even more about the Wylies in the museum." He motioned to the room around him. "They were a wealthy family, I can tell you that much," he said as he stood up and slowly moved out from behind the counter. He shuffled toward a back corner of one of the rooms. "It was all in land—they never had much liquid wealth."

"I'm surprised you know of the Wylies. They're my family, and I didn't even know about them until this afternoon."

"Well, you might have just gotten lucky with me. The Wylies were part of my own history, so perhaps I know a bit more than your average museum volunteer."

Kate smiled, enchanted by the little man. He was local, his voice rich with Southern influence, but there seemed a cadence to his voice that was different than just classic Southern speak. When she really listened, she thought he sounded a bit Scottish.

"What do you mean?" Kate asked.

"Old Ike Wylie—he would be your great-grandfather, no? He owned near two hundred acres out in the valley. He farmed a good portion of the land himself, and then he leased the lower portion of his farm to other farmers, anyone, really, in need of a leg up or a place to start. Leased farms weren't all that rare, but Old Ike was different. He never asked for much rent, though a lot of people insisted on paying more than he required, whatever they thought fair. And he never expected a portion of the crops come harvest time. He could have. It was his land, after all. But he was a generous man. I think he liked to help people."

Kate shook her head. "I had no idea."

"My own father lived on old Ike's land for near two years before I was born, farming, working, saving money until he could afford his own piece of property. He came over from Scotland with my mother and didn't have a penny to his name. But he got along quite well after Ike offered help. He always talked about him, talked of how many found help at Ike's door." The old man stopped and pointed at a large photo in the corner. "Here, a picture of Isaac Wylie's homestead. You can see it wasn't very grand, but it held his family, no doubt."

Kate looked at the photo, a hazy capturing of the very farmhouse she had lived in most of her life.

"That's my house!" Kate said, reaching forward, tracing the outline of the photo. "It looks different," Kate said. "It's been renovated and expanded many times, but it's still there. And much of it is still the same. We have a garden here," she said, pointing behind the house. "And a row of apple trees here. It's funny to think there's a picture of my house in the local museum, and I don't think anyone in my family has ever seen it."

"Life keeps us busy," the old man said. "Sometimes we are so occupied with looking forward, we forget to look back." His eyes twinkled as he looked at Kate. "But there's pleasure in looking back, isn't there?"

Kate shook her head in wonder. "It's amazing."

"So your family has always lived on the land?" the man asked.

Kate nodded. "The land was divided up between Isaac's sons, one of them my grandfather. It was all sold, except for the portion my grandfather kept, the house and surrounding six acres. He raised his family there, and I grew up there too."

"Oh, family history is such a lovely thing!" he said. "I love it when connections are made and cherished. You will cherish these connections, I can already see."

With such enthusiasm, Kate had no doubt he would appreciate Ian's journal. She pulled it out of her bag. "Can I show you something?" she asked.

"This is Ian Wylie's journal. He was Isaac Wylie's great-great-grandfather."
She handed him the book.

He flipped through it gently, stopping here and there to read a few
lines. Without prompting, he adjusted his glasses, cleared his throat, and
started to read.

> *13 November 1848*
>
> *I find great sadness in Jennie never having had the
> opportunity to meet my father. He was a good man—an
> honest, kind, generous man. And he would have loved my
> Jennie. I think of him often and hope that I've done right by
> the Wylie name. It is a good name, one I'm proud to have and
> I've tried to honor throughout the years. I hope I've taught my
> own children well—to honor their name and remember who
> they are and all that they stand for. I hope their grandfather
> Wylie, if he has the opportunity to look down upon them, will
> always be proud of the individuals they've become and, of
> course, that I've become as well.*

"Well, that's a nice thought, isn't it?" he asked, looking back up at Kate.
"You're a Wylie! It's quite a legacy."

Until Kate found Ian's journal, she had often wondered if her own
parents watched over her, but she'd never extended that thought to include
anyone else. It brought surprising comfort to consider her ancestors—
grandparents, great-grandparents, and beyond—watching over and taking
an interest. She'd never really thought about what it truly meant to be a
Wylie.

"Yes, it is quite a legacy," Kate agreed. "I'm sorry, you've been so helpful
and I didn't even catch your name."

"Angus McFinley, at your service," he said. The man took a deep bow,
and Kate smiled at his old-fashioned sincerity.

"Mr. McFinley, I'm Kate Sinclair. I'm happy to make your acquaintance."
She paused then said, "Perhaps there is something else you can help me do."

Kate quickly explained about the hearing at the end of the week and
her hope to turn the old farmhouse into a landmark. Mr. McFinley, in all of
his ancient appearance, was a wealth of information regarding the county
preservation society and their role in the establishment and maintenance
of historic landmarks. The more they discussed the process, the more
confident Kate became, especially when she considered the impact that

two of her ancestors had made on the fellow citizens of Harrison County: first the land donation to the church and then Isaac's generosity on his farm.

Kate soon found herself overwhelmed by the sincerity and kindness of her new friend. Once Mr. McFinley started looking for information regarding Kate's family, she could hardly get him to stop. When she told him it was time for her to go, he made her promise to come back the following day to see if he'd learned anything new that might help. He also agreed to make copies of anything Kate might be able to use in her petition, including the old photo of the farmhouse. He invited her to pick those up the following afternoon as well.

Kate asked Mr. McFinley if he would come to the hearing, perhaps even share a bit of what he knew of the Wylie family's history.

He readily agreed, taking Kate's hands into his own and smiling broadly. "I would be delighted to assist someone as lovely as you."

Sitting in her car in front of the museum, Kate hesitated to go home. She had nowhere else to go and assumed Andrew would be waiting for her. After hearing Ashley's side of the story, she was a little less enthusiastic about hearing Andrew recount the tale. She wanted to believe she would understand why he had behaved the way he did, and, of course, there were always two sides to every story. But she was afraid, nonetheless. She was afraid she would learn something about him that might affect the way she felt, and she didn't want that. She wanted to believe Andrew was better than all of the shallow, self-serving men she'd dated in the past. She *had* to believe he was better.

She reached for Ian's journal and casually flipped through its pages, stopping on the passage Angus McFinley had read inside the museum. She read it again and smiled. *I am proud to be a Wylie*, she thought. A few pages later, another entry captured Kate's attention.

*16 December 1848*
*I learned today that old man Patterson has been stealing from me. I've always trusted and respected Patterson and find it difficult to now have such cause to question his character. Jennie thinks I ought to write off the man, cease all business with him so as to avoid any further consequence of his dishonesty. I wonder what my Savior Jesus would do. Would He extend an arm of forgiveness? I think there must have*

*been reason for this man's blunder. Surely he found himself
in a bind most desperate for him to resort to such measures.
My heart tells me I should not condemn him, and though I
cannot convince my brain to trust him fully just yet, I feel I
ought to give him the chance to redeem himself.*

Kate closed the book with a little more force than necessary and placed it on the seat beside her.

*You would say that, Ian Wylie, wouldn't you?*

She sighed, knowing it was time to give Andrew a chance to redeem himself.

*Chapter 27*

KATE PULLED UP IN FRONT of the farmhouse and saw Andrew sitting on the front porch steps, head resting in his hands. He looked up as she approached and stood as she got out of the car.

"I've finished the survey," he said, head low, both hands in his pockets.

"And?" Kate said.

"It's definitely an old house." He smiled timidly. When Kate didn't respond, he continued. "The original structure was no bigger than fourteen or fifteen hundred square feet, which is actually still a good-sized house considering the year it was constructed. The house has had several additions, including the incorporation of modern day amenities, but the core of the house, the unique characteristics of early twentieth-century construction are still present—high ceilings, narrow stairs, the livable attic space, as well as many superficial elements based on style alone that directly reflect the building styles and influences of the house's original era."

"That's good news." Kate sighed. "Thank you for your help."

The silence stretched on for a few awkward moments until Andrew finally spoke. "Kate, I should have told you."

She shook her head. "We've only known each other a few weeks."

Logically, it made sense that he wouldn't have told her. Leaving your bride at the altar wasn't exactly an experience one clamored to tell a new acquaintance. And yet, Kate thought he should have told her. The emotional investment in their relationship already seemed much larger than anything typical. But then again, maybe Andrew would have told her, that very night even, if Ashley hadn't so inconveniently arrived on the Spencers' doorstep. Most likely, this was the long story he had alluded to the previous afternoon in the car. Kate looked at him and saw his distress.

"Please, just let me explain," he said softly.

Kate turned around and sat down on the top step, motioning for Andrew to join her.

He sat down and dove into his story before she could stop him. "I got a job right out of school working for a design firm in Richmond. It was an all right job, but it wasn't exactly what I wanted, so after a few years, I started looking and found Westonhouse. It was a great firm, exactly what I was looking for. The company had a great reputation, great location, and the guy was Mormon, so I couldn't really ask for a better situation. Within a few weeks, I'd met Ashley. She was Westonhouse's daughter. Her father orchestrated everything . . . bought us dinner, tickets to shows, sporting events . . . It almost felt surreal, like I was on some reality dating show, except there was only one girl. Everyone but me was convinced we were perfect for each other." Andrew pressed his forehead into his hands, elbows propped up on his knees. Kate could tell the story made him tired.

"Ashley was—still is—a lovely person. She was kind and compassionate, faithful in the gospel, but it just wasn't there. I knew it, and I think deep down, she knew it too, though I'm not sure she ever would have admitted it. Eventually, I started to tell myself that there's more to love than just sparks and good chemistry. There's the kind of love bred from commitment, endurance, a shared faith. I could see Ashley and me working toward those things. We dated for almost a year, all while I worked for her dad. I advanced up a line of promotions so fast it would make your head spin. It wasn't because of me though. It wasn't based on my performance or skill. It was for Ashley. I was being polished to marry daddy's little girl. I mean, don't get me wrong, it's not like I was manipulated. I made all my own choices, but it just seemed like everybody made it so easy to make certain choices and follow this predetermined path. Before long, I was convinced it was the path I wanted too. So I asked her to marry me, she said yes, and we planned a wedding . . . D.C. Temple, big reception, everything . . ." He paused, fidgeting, uncomfortable. "I'm not proud of what I did, Kate," he said firmly. "I never should have let it go so far. I think I really believed that if we were faithful, if we made good decisions, God would bless our marriage and everything would work out. But I sat there in the parking lot of the hotel the morning of the ceremony, and I was suddenly terrified at how long eternity seemed. I wasn't even married yet, and I was already looking for a way out. Everything about our marriage was practical and logical, obviously the best thing to do. But my heart wasn't in it. I just didn't love her like I needed to."

Kate finally spoke. "But why run away? Why not discuss it with Ashley? Break it to her gently. I mean, to have an old roommate slip her the news . . ."

"Ah, Valerie told you," he said.

"Ashley told me," Kate said. "When she came upstairs this morning."

"To warn you, I guess," Andrew said. "I shouldn't have run away. I was wrong, and I know that. But I was running scared. Essentially, I knew I wasn't just walking away from Ashley. I was walking away from my job, the company, from my home in Richmond. It just . . . I don't know."

"Ashley told me she had no idea," Kate said. "She thought you were her prince charming. She had no idea anything was wrong."

"I don't know if that's completely true," he responded. "It wasn't always an easy relationship. You know, I think about it every day. Every day I could kick myself for being so stupid, for carrying on for so long, living, waiting, and hoping for that one moment when I might wake up and suddenly find that I loved Ashley the way I was supposed to, the way she deserved. I didn't want to hurt her; I just . . . life just got ahead of me. And I made a big mistake."

Kate took a slow, deep breath. Hearing Andrew's side of the story, it was easy to have compassion for him. She could tell he was still struggling with conflicting emotions over hurting Ashley. His distress was clearly sincere. And yet, it was difficult to accept that there was a side of Andrew—a career, a life, a history—that she knew nothing about. It led her to question what she did know about him.

"When were you going to tell me?" she asked. "We've been pretending this entire time that your life is here—living in Rose Creek, working for your uncle—but it's not."

"Except it is, Kate. I know I walked away from a lot when I left Richmond, but I'd be kidding myself if I thought life up there was any more meaningful than helping out my uncle down here. I should have told you sooner. I wasn't trying to mislead you, but what was I going to say? It's not exactly something I'm proud of." Andrew was more emotional than Kate had ever seen him. His face was flushed with intensity, and his arms were tense.

Kate softened. "We all make mistakes," she said. "We've all done stuff we aren't proud of. Andrew, I didn't go to my brother-in-law's funeral. Did I ever tell you that? I didn't go because I had a presentation at work that I didn't want to miss. It was horrible and selfish, and it ruined my relationship with Leslie. It was the biggest mistake I've ever made, and I'm still trying to pick up the pieces. We aren't perfect, but we learn, we grow, we move on."

"It's different though. What was I supposed to say to you? Yeah, I almost got married. I had a different job, a house, a different life. I spent a year pretending, a year trying to make myself accept and love a life I didn't want. How was I supposed to tell you that I spent a year trying to feel for a girl what I felt for you after five minutes?"

Kate closed her eyes, his words echoing softly in her ears. She reached out and lay her hand gently on his forearm. "I would have understood," she said.

"It was so hard, so hard to be around you at first." His voice was soft now, full of tenderness. "I just felt so dumb. Had I known what this felt like, what it was to be around someone like you, I never could have pretended with Ashley for so long." He wrapped his hand around Kate's and pulled himself across the step so they sat side by side, then turned his body so he was facing her. "I'm so sorry, Kate. I'm sorry you had to deal with Ashley this morning, sorry that I didn't tell you about all of this before."

Kate leaned forward, resting her head on Andrew's shoulder. "I'm just glad you've told me now," she said.

Andrew sighed with relief and wrapped his arms around Kate's back, pulling her close.

"How is she?" Kate asked after a few moments of silence.

"Who? Ashley?" Andrew asked. "I guess she's okay."

"That's a long way to drive. What did she need? Closure, I guess?"

"We never really talked after I ran," he said, voice a little distant. "I called once, just after, to apologize and try to explain. But she didn't really want to talk then. I tried one more time, and she wouldn't even come to the phone. I didn't see or speak to her again until yesterday."

"She said she'd called though. You didn't answer her calls?" Kate asked, not wanting to sound accusatory but still trying to make sense of his actions.

He let out a frustrated sigh. "She just started calling a couple of weeks ago. I should have answered, but to be perfectly honest, I was spending a lot of time thinking about you. I didn't know how to handle it. I was going to call her. I knew we needed to talk. But before I could get up the nerve, she just showed up."

"But you've talked now," Kate reasoned. "That's good, right?"

Andrew stifled a laugh. "Yeah," he said sarcastically. "We talked. Or rather, she talked and I listened while she called me a self-centered jerk who broke her heart, ruined her life, ruined her wedding plans, and ruined all of her dreams of happiness. And let's not forget her telling me that she hoped I never found happiness again."

"Ouch," Kate said. "That had to hurt."

"Really, it's just frustrating," Andrew said. "The thing is, with Ashley, it wasn't ever about me. It was about the dream. The perfect pictures, the four-layer wedding cake, the temple wedding . . . It was as if she were in love with the idea of me and the idea of wedded bliss. But I don't know that I ever felt she was really in love with me, with who I am. I was just a player, a pawn in her great orchestration of happiness. I don't know; it doesn't really matter," Andrew said. "She seems to have her closure now, I guess. I don't want to think about her anymore."

Kate smiled. "I don't really want you to think about her anymore either." She leaned against his shoulder, feeling the soft exhale of his breath as it blew gently through her hair. It sent shivers up her spine, the light hair on her arms standing on end. He shifted, and she lifted her head off his shoulder, her face just inches from his.

Andrew tucked a loose strand of Kate's hair behind her ear and then cradled her face with his hands and tenderly kissed her. She had experienced a lot of first kisses but none quite as emotional as this. She nearly cried as her heart seemed to open and pull him close.

*It's love*, she thought. *Three weeks and one first kiss later, and I'm fully persuaded.* She had dated a lot of men, kissed a lot of them in the seven years she'd lived in Atlanta, but it had taken only one kiss to convince her that this was very, very different.

Andrew pulled away, still holding her face in his hands. Then he leaned in again, kissing her forehead and the top of her head as he pulled her tightly against him. She pressed the side of her face against his shoulder, just below his collar bone, which seemed to be carved specifically for her.

"We fit," she said softly.

Andrew smiled. "Yeah," he agreed. "I think we do."

Dusk settled around them. The sinking sun was quickly ushering in the chill of a May evening in the mountains.

"Can you stay?" Kate asked, feeling the cool breeze cut through the thin fabric of her shirt. "Come in, and I'll fix us something to eat. Then I'll tell you what I learned about my family today."

"Cooking for me already?" Andrew teased.

"Ha! Don't get your hopes up," Kate said as she stood up from the porch. "I claim nothing beyond mere adequacy when it comes to the kitchen."

"Maybe you should let me cook." Andrew smiled, standing up as well. "We can have waffles or scrambled eggs or french toast . . ."

"Wow. What do you eat when it isn't breakfast time?" she said playfully, nudging Andrew as they moved to the front door.

Andrew caught her arm and pulled her into him once more. She was drunk with the closeness of him, soaking in the lingering traces of his aftershave, the hint of clean laundry scent from his clothes, and the overlying muskiness from a day's work on his skin. "Cereal," Andrew joked in response to Kate's question. "And a lot of take-out."

"I can at least do better than cereal," she assured him. She looked up, leaned in on her tiptoes, and kissed him again.

## Chapter 28

INSIDE, KATE STARTED TO CHOP vegetables for a Bolognese sauce and set water for the pasta on the stove to boil. While she worked, she told Andrew about her trip to the library and the county museum, detailing the specific things she'd learned about her ancestors.

"I really didn't expect to find anything so positive," she said. "From land donations to rent-free farming, that's got to influence the board of commissioners." Kate's positive mood filled her with more optimism than she'd experienced since she first learned of the highway plan.

"And the farmhouse itself should contribute nicely as well," Andrew added. "Whoever did the expansions, remodeling, and modernizing took great pains not to disturb the integrity of the architecture. From the roof line to the wooden columns along the porch, it's the kind of house any architectural history buff would love to see. The house even has its original siding, though it has been covered with something else. But the bones are still there, and it's an old set of bones."

Kate listened to his words and thought about all of Aunt Mary and Uncle Grey's efforts to take care of it. "I don't want to lose this house, Andrew," Kate said, overcome with emotion.

"Don't give up yet. You've got a good story. If we can get it all organized, I think you've got a good shot at beating the highway," he said.

"Thank you for your help with this," she said. She truly meant it. She didn't know where she would have been if Andrew hadn't been willing to help, had he not conveniently turned out to be an architect. If it was coincidence, it was certainly remarkable. If it was fate or destiny that brought this all together, then Kate was grateful God was looking out for her.

They kept talking as she continued preparing their meal. They talked about their families and their work, and Andrew told Kate a story about rolling bowling balls down Main Street that had Kate laughing so hard she cried. When dinner was over, their conversation eventually turned to their faith.

Kate had just finished the Book of Mormon the evening before. Logically, she wanted to believe and accept the goodness the religion had to offer, but something was still holding her back. She feared what her family would say. She was convinced Linny and Leslie simply thought this was a passing phase, a response to Mary's death and a broad search for meaning that, when no longer motivated by Andrew, would fizzle out and die a quick, painless death. She did not know how they would react when they realized how serious she was.

She also struggled with guilt made worse when she contemplated the nature of her relationship with Andrew. It wasn't something she could easily vocalize. Kate knew what the standards of the Mormon faith were—the sacredness of the marital relationship and the importance of abstinence before marriage. She didn't know for a fact that Andrew was a virgin but felt reasonably safe, with her knowledge of his background, including his near-miss temple marriage, in assuming he probably was. If he and Kate wound up together, would he be bothered by the fact that she wasn't? It wasn't as if she'd been with a lot of men, but her life had been very different in Atlanta, and she had been single for a long time. It wasn't something she was proud of. She wished desperately that she would have preserved her virtue for someone like Andrew. Was it too late for her carelessness to be forgiven?

Her mind jumped back to the lesson she'd had with the missionaries regarding the law of chastity. She remembered the peace she'd felt when they'd discussed the redemptive process of baptism.

"You will be clean, Kate," Elder Christianson had said. "Your sins will be washed away in the waters of baptism as you covenant and promise to live according to God's law."

The peace and assurance of his words crept slowly back into Kate's heart. Yes, God could forgive her, and He would; but what about Andrew? Did he not deserve something better than she could offer? And then there was Leslie. Kate still wasn't certain Leslie had fully forgiven her. She seemed happy when they were all together, but there was still something there, just under the surface, that made Kate uneasy. She shook her head, trying to chase away the fear and doubt that so quickly crept into her head and heart.

"What are you thinking, Kate?" Andrew asked. "I can almost see the wheels spinning in your head."

"Oh, it's nothing," she quickly responded, though the slight edge in her voice indicated otherwise.

"I don't believe you for a second," he said, rising from the table and carrying their plates to the sink. "What's on your mind?"

Kate sighed. "I was just thinking about forgiveness," she said, unsure if she could actually vocalize the true source of her worries.

"What about it?" Andrew asked. He returned to the table and sat down next to Kate.

She shook her head. He seemed so innocent, so boyish in his desire to help make her feel better. Finally, she responded, "What if I don't deserve it?"

"Have you killed someone?" Andrew teased, his voice a hushed whisper.

Kate looked up, shocked but smiling. "Just my last boyfriend," she joked. "Of course I haven't killed someone. But I've got a . . . a past, Andrew." Once she began, it was difficult to stop her spur-of-the-moment confession. "I know what your standards are, and I haven't been living them. I've been feeding a coffee addiction for nearly ten years. I know what vodka tastes like, I've been to night clubs, to bars, I've been with men I wasn't in love with, wasn't married to . . ." Kate's face flooded with color. "I've made a lot of stupid choices I'm not proud of. How can I just go to church, pretend like all of that, all of who I was, doesn't matter anymore? What if it does matter? And what if . . ." She hesitated. "What if it matters to you?"

Andrew leaned back in his chair, arms folded across his chest. He sat silently for a few moments and looked at Kate. With his lips pursed, he shook his head. "You know what, Kate, it does matter. The coffee is the deal breaker for me . . ."

He smiled that crooked half smile Kate loved, and she threw her napkin at him. "Andrew! I'm being serious!" she scolded, though she certainly felt relieved that he didn't seem bothered by her revelation. Andrew's face settled into a more serious repose. He still smiled but this time with tenderness and sincerity.

"Kate, when you are baptized, your sins will all be washed away. The Lord has promised He will remember them no more. If the Lord will remember them no more, why should I remember them?" He reached for her hand across the table. "We've all got a past, and none of us is perfect.

But we aren't expected to walk through life plagued and burdened by our past decisions, no matter how poor they are." Andrew paused, flinching slightly, and Kate knew he was thinking about his own decisions over the past couple of years. "Acceptance of the Atonement of the Savior is a hugely personal process," he explained. "But for me, true understanding came when I first thought about the Savior willingly choosing to suffer, when He felt the pains and frustrations and fears of a mortal body as He entered the garden, knowing what He would have to do yet still praying to His Father in Heaven, pleading with Him: if there's any other way, please let this cup pass from me. But there wasn't another way, so He chose to suffer. He didn't have to. Mortal in body only, He could have stopped. He could have stopped it all, the Crucifixion, the mocking and torment He endured. But He didn't. He didn't stop it because of me and because of you, because of all of us. I get overwhelmed every time I think about it."

Kate sat silently, mindlessly tracing the back of Andrew's hand with her thumb as she thought about his words. She felt something different from what she was used to. It was a small but steady feeling, a growing confirmation that what Andrew had said was true. The Atonement could and would apply to her. She needed only to accept it.

"So now it's my turn to ask you a question," Andrew said, leaning his arms on the table.

"Go for it," Kate said.

"Are you ever actually going back to Atlanta?"

*Good question*, Kate thought. In all of her conversing with Andrew, Kate had not told him how seriously she had considered moving to Rose Creek permanently. She spoke of her job as if she were simply on temporary hiatus, and he never questioned her. He knew she'd left her job and life back in the city, but then, he also realized how fiercely she was fighting to keep the farmhouse. He must have wondered if she planned to make it home for good.

"Actually, I'm not really sure I will go back," she said. "I've been spending a lot of time with Leslie, you know? She's basically on her own now. I think I should be here for her."

"You don't sound entirely convinced."

"I think I am," she responded. "I don't know. I don't know what kind of work I would do here. Mr. Blanton has agreed to let me telecommute, but I have a feeling I'd still be spending a lot of time in the city. I'm not sure it would be worth it to live here if I were still making the drive back and forth all the time. I don't know. I think I'd rather be here full time. But it's scary to just up and leave a place, you know?"

"If you kept your place in Atlanta, what would you do with the house?"

It was a good question. It was an old house, and Kate knew it needed constant care and attention. If she wasn't living in it, someone needed to be, or she felt it would quickly fall into disrepair. Leslie would probably jump at the chance to live in the house, but Kate wasn't sure Leslie would feel comfortable functioning as her renter. Aside from that, if Aunt Mary had wanted Leslie to live in the house, she would have just left the house to Leslie.

"I don't know," Kate finally answered. "It needs someone to take care of it, I know that much."

He nodded in understanding. "Would it matter if I told you I didn't want you to go back to Atlanta?"

She smiled. "It might influence my decision. What about you though? Could you work here forever, do you think? It's a small town for the kind of work you do, isn't it?"

"Rose Creek isn't exactly a hotbed of up-and-coming architecture, that's for sure. I think there is a lot that could happen here though. I've mostly done commercial work in the past, but I'd love to design homes that really feel like they belong in the mountains and use natural materials that blend in with the surroundings. And we're so centrally located here— close to Asheville and Atlanta—that if I build a name for myself, I may be able to field work from there as well."

"Why weren't you working on all of this before?" she asked. "It seems like you've just been twiddling your thumbs working with your uncle."

Andrew looked up, eyes steady. "Well, it's only recently that I considered the possibility of staying in Rose Creek on a more long-term basis."

Kate knew he was making reference to her. Of course he wouldn't be putting down roots and establishing his career if he thought his stay in Rose Creek was only temporary.

Kate looked up when she heard an approaching car and saw headlights streaming in through the soft linen curtains hanging in the kitchen window. It was Leslie. Kate had called her earlier in the day and invited her to come over to see the journal and read over the petition. She heard the chatter of voices as doors slammed and little feet climbed the porch steps. Kate smiled. "Would you like to meet my niece and nephews?" she said to Andrew.

They moved to the door to welcome the children as they tumbled into the foyer. Kate greeted Leslie with a quick, one-armed hug.

"Andrew, you remember Leslie," she said politely. "And this is Nicholas, Emily, and Tommy."

Andrew greeted each of the boys then crouched down in front of Emily. "Hello, Emily, I'm Andrew."

"Pleased to make your acquaintance, Andrew," Emily said, in line with her typical precociousness. "Are you going to marry my aunt Katie?"

Kate's cheeks flooded with color.

"Emily!" Leslie chided. "Don't ask such questions to someone you've just met."

Andrew smiled. "It's all right," he said to Leslie. "I don't mind." He leaned in and whispered something in Emily's ear, making the little girl giggle, eyes growing wide as she listened. "It's our secret, okay?" He stood up, smiling at Kate and then Leslie.

Emily, high on the importance of knowing a secret, walked smugly past her mother and aunt, nose held high in the air. "I'll never tell," she said.

"I've got to be going now," Andrew said, attention turned back to Kate. "I want to get started on typing up the final survey while it's all still fresh in my mind."

"Thank you," Kate said simply. "I couldn't have done this without your help."

"I'm happy to do it," Andrew said. "This old house has quite a history. It would be a shame to see something happen to it."

He crossed the foyer to where Kate was standing, a bit shy in Leslie's presence, and kissed her gently on the cheek. "I'll call you in the morning," he whispered. "It was nice to see you again, Leslie."

"Likewise," Leslie said. When he was gone, she looked at her cousin, eyes wide with disbelief.

# Chapter 29

"WHAT?" KATE ASKED.

"He's totally in love with you," Leslie said as they walked back into the kitchen. "I mean, I've seen you guys together before tonight, but something's different. The way he looked at you, the way he . . . Something has changed. What about you? How do you feel?"

Kate shrugged her shoulders. "Well, I don't know," she struggled. "I mean, he's . . . I guess I really feel . . ."

"Spit it out, Kate." Leslie stood at the kitchen sink, one hand on her hip, waiting for Kate to respond.

"Well, it just sounds so stupid to say it after such a short period of time," Kate said.

"You love him!"

Kate looked at her cousin. She hoped Leslie could be happy for her. It was, after all, still an emotional time for the family. But she did love him. She knew that and didn't want to hide it from her cousin.

"What are you thinking?" Kate asked Leslie.

Leslie sighed. "I think it seems really fast, but he's a likable guy . . . He has a great smile. If you like him, I can like him too, I guess. I guess the only downside is his religion."

Kate flinched at Leslie's words. "I want to show you something," she said, changing the subject.

She took Leslie into the family room and pulled out Ian's journal and the stacks of photocopies she'd made earlier in the day at the library. She quickly explained the journal to Leslie, detailing a rough outline of the Wylie family history from Ian down to their grandfather George. Leslie listened as Kate turned through the pages of the journal, pointing out certain entries and adding her own insight about what she thought Ian might have been like. She was excited, talking quickly, her eyes bright and face flushed with enthusiasm. The only thing Kate didn't share was Ian's strong beliefs regarding religion. It was a dangerous subject and one she thought was simply better avoided.

"You're really into this stuff, aren't you?" Leslie asked, voice sounding a bit incredulous.

Kate was confused at Leslie's reaction. "What do you mean?" she asked.

"Well, I guess it's neat to have found something from so long ago still preserved and everything, but . . . I don't know. What does it really matter now? The guy is still dead."

"But that's just it," Kate said. "He's dead, but we can still learn from his life and his experiences. Aunt Mary is dead, but we want to keep things that remind us of her to help us remember her life and the things she taught us."

"That's different," Leslie said. "I knew my mother, loved my mother every day. I've never met this Ian Wylie. Don't get me wrong, Kate. It's great that you found his old journal and that it may help you keep the house, but from the way you were talking about it, it just seemed like you think it's the greatest thing you've ever seen."

Kate looked at the book reverently. It sort of *was* the greatest thing she'd ever seen. Kate felt like she knew Ian—and he knew her, watched over her. To have his words about love and family and religion, as well as the details of daily life in a time so different from her own, was something she truly cherished. She was a little miffed at Leslie's underwhelming response. She thought suddenly of what might have happened had Leslie inherited the house as she had expected. What if Leslie had found the old journal in the attic? Would she have even read it? Would she have worked so diligently at decoding some of the harder-to-read passages? Would she have even cared?

*It needed to be me*, Kate thought. *I had to be the one to find it.* She sighed and gently laid the book aside.

Leslie and the children stayed for nearly two hours. Leslie contributed as best she could, despite the distraction of her kids. She had always had a good head for grammar and helped Kate revise and reword sentences and phrases that needed polishing in the summary. Of all the information included in the petition, Kate thought her case was most strengthened by the story of Ike Wylie. Kate wished she had a way to quantify his generosity. Surely there were others still living in the community— descendants of those who, like Angus McFinley's father, had farmed and rented on her great-grandfather's land. Kate also hoped the journal would appear impressive to the board, though she was a bit discouraged that

Leslie had not reacted with an enthusiasm that matched her own. All she could do was hope that someone on the board of commissioners had an appreciation for family history and might be sympathetic to her cause.

Before Leslie left, Kate went into the family room to spend a few minutes visiting with the kids. She gathered up their popcorn bowls and empty juice boxes to take them to the kitchen but paused just outside the door. Leslie was on her cell phone.

"It's funny, really," she heard Leslie say. "It's like she's playing dress up . . . playing with the kids, walking around the house like she owns the place. It's just not the real Kate, you know?"

Kate backed into the shadows of the dining room, not wanting Leslie to see her. She wondered who Leslie was talking to.

"I just don't believe she'll really stay," Leslie continued. "I'm glad she's stayed this long. I never could have figured out how to save the house without her. But once all the excitement dies down, something will happen, and then she'll bolt, just like she did before. You just watch. She'll sell me the house. It'll be mine by the end of the summer."

The bowls in Kate's hands started to slip. She tried to catch them, but they clamored to the floor, alerting Leslie to her presence. Kate's cheeks flushed with anger and embarrassment as she scrambled to pick up the bowls. She couldn't believe Leslie's comments. When she'd picked up the dishes she'd dropped, she walked into the kitchen, slamming the bowls into the sink.

"What's wrong with you?" Leslie asked, not aware of how much Kate had overheard.

Kate braced her arms against the side of the sink. "Is that really what you think of me, Leslie? That I'm pretending? That this is all just a big game to me?"

Leslie's face froze. "You were listening in on my conversation?" she asked.

"Not on purpose," Kate fired back. "I was just coming into the kitchen. I stopped as soon I heard what you were saying. Leslie, why would say those things about me? Is that really how you feel?"

Leslie was silent, her arms folded across her chest.

Kate shook her head. "I've been so honest with you. I've tried so hard to make our relationship what it was before."

"It can't be what it was before, Kate! We're grown-ups now. We have a decade of life choices and experiences that have made us who we are. We can't be like we were when we were eighteen."

"I don't want us to be eighteen; I just want us to be family," Kate said. "I thought that's what you wanted too, but maybe not. Maybe it would just be easier if I went back to Atlanta. Then you could have this stupid house all to yourself and you wouldn't have to deal with me anymore."

"Oh, come on, Kate. Let's be real. Did you really think you were going to stay? You would have grown tired of this place, and you know it. This isn't you anymore—your fancy car, your designer clothes, they just don't fit in this little town."

Kate closed her eyes, tears coursing down her cheeks. "I'm going to bed," she said simply. "You know your way out."

Kate climbed the stairs up to her room and slammed the door behind her. She was angry that even with all of her efforts, her cousin's opinion of her still hadn't changed. Of course she'd had her doubts about moving back to Rose Creek, but she was ready to do it. She had changed a lot over the past four weeks. She listened as Leslie loaded her kids into her van and pulled away. She sat at the foot of her bed, silent and still. The anger bubbling inside her turned to the bitter embarrassment that accompanied betrayal. She couldn't shake the memory of Leslie's condescending tone as she mocked and belittled her.

At 10:30, her cell phone rang. She reached into her purse and flipped open her phone without even looking to see who it was. "Hello," she said, voice short.

"Hi, Kate," Steve said.

Kate sighed heavily. "Hi, Steve."

"Listen, I won't keep you long, but something happened at work today. Blanton wanted me to let you know."

Kate glanced at her watch. She wondered why he'd waited so long to call.

"Okay," Kate said. "What happened?"

"It's the Charleston account. They called this morning and said they were going with a different firm for their newest campaign. Blanton convinced them to come in tomorrow morning for one final meeting in hopes of convincing them to give us another shot."

"I thought they loved our ideas," Kate said. "I didn't even know they were shopping around."

"I didn't know either. This sort of came out of the blue. Listen, Kate, I know they're your clients, but I don't want you to worry. I've come up with some ideas to tweak our original presentation, changes I really think they'll like. I told Blanton I would just take care of it."

Now Kate understood the reason for his late call. Blanton told him to call in hopes that she would return in the morning in time for the meeting. But Steve knew the later he called, the less likely it was for her to make the trip. If she wasn't there and he was able to secure the client himself, he would be that much closer to pushing Kate out altogether.

"You know what, Steve, thanks for offering. But don't worry about it. I'll be there in the morning. Tell Blanton I'll take care of it."

## Chapter 30

*7 June 1838*

*James ran away this afternoon. Mad at something his Ma said and angry because I agreed with her, he packed a small satchel of food and headed to the harbor to try his luck at getting work on a ship, he said. I found him there late this evening, his cheeks stained with dirt and tears, his shoulders sagging with embarrassment and defeat. I tried not to let my amusement show. I remember being a boy not much older than he and know well what it feels like to want to run away. I told him, as we sat, about the night I learned of my father's death and how desperately I wanted to run away and never look back. In that moment, I felt so lost—like there wasn't anywhere I belonged. My family was thousands of miles away, my father dead. In a sense, I was a stranger in a strange land and felt so very alone. But running didn't change what life was. The cards were dealt, and it was up to me to decide what to make of them. I hope young James knows he'll fare much better if he deals with life as it comes. Pretending, running—it does us no good.*

"When will you be back?"

Kate looked at Andrew and sighed. "I don't know that I will be back," she said softly.

"Kate, I don't understand." He stood in the driveway as she put her bag in the trunk of her car. "What about the house? You've worked so hard. You can't stop fighting now."

She slammed the trunk closed and turned to him. "I'm not stopping," she said. "Everything's nearly ready. I'll fax it into the commissioners office from Atlanta. If I come across any last-minute things I need, Linny can help."

Andrew looked puzzled. "But it isn't Linny's house. It's yours. Last night you were talking about moving here for good, and now you might not come back at all? Why the sudden change in priority?"

She'd known he would ask difficult questions if she saw him before leaving town. He was the one person in Rose Creek she didn't really want to leave, but at the same time, she needed to clear her head. She had to get away from this place, even if it meant getting away from him for a while too. She'd sent him a text message the night before, hoping to avoid a conversation, but he'd come over anyway to see her before she left.

"I don't know, Andrew." She hesitated. "Maybe Leslie was right and I've been fooling myself. Maybe this house and this town really aren't where I belong."

"That's ridiculous," Andrew said. "What did Leslie say to you? You grew up here. This is your home."

Kate shook her head. "Leslie calls it like she sees it. And what does she see? She sees me pretending to be something I'm not, that I've never been." She opened the door to her car.

"You're not pretending, Kate. People change. Life happens, and people change all the time."

"I'm sorry, Andrew," she said. "I just don't know if I can do it, if I can be the person you think I am."

Andrew pushed his hands into his pockets and leaned against the car.

"What are you running away from? Is it me? Leslie? What is it?"

"I'm not running away from anything," Kate said sharply. She slammed the car door shut in frustration and walked several steps away from the car. She turned and looked back at Andrew. "I don't even know why I'm here, Andrew. I have an entire life back in Atlanta. I mean, really, why should I stay? Because my dead aunt thinks the house should belong to me? No one expects me to stick around anyway, so why should I? Leslie wants the house. The more I think about it, the more I think that's probably the best thing for everyone. I think all this time I've just been kidding myself. I have been pretending to be someone who could change, who could have meaningful relationships with Leslie and the kids. I tried it, and it didn't work. Like Leslie said, it just isn't the real me."

"But it is you, Kate. You know those kids love you, and you love them. And I've seen myself how much you love this house and love being in Rose Creek. Whatever Leslie said, it doesn't change who you are."

"No, it's always been this way," Kate said. "It has always been them and then me, the orphaned cousin. I don't fit here. It's not who I really am."

"What about the gospel, Kate? Is that not who you are either?"

Kate looked down. "I don't know," she said softly. "I guess I just need to figure some things out."

Andrew looked at her for a moment then took a step forward and reached for her hand. He leaned in and kissed her, gently at first then with such increasing intensity she completely lost her breath and forgot for a moment why she wanted to leave Rose Creek at all.

"I may not know everything about you," he whispered, face still close to hers. "But I know that this is real. You said it yourself—we fit. You fit with me. I'll be waiting for you when you come back. Don't stay gone long, okay?"

Kate drove in silence for the full two hours it took to reach the city. She tried not to think about Rose Creek and all that she was driving away from, instead focusing on the meeting and the clients she would have to win back for Mr. Blanton. It was difficult to shift her mind into work mode after having been away for so long, but she persisted. When she reached the parking garage of her office building, she called Veronica and asked that she have the Charleston file ready so she could review it in the twenty minutes she had before the scheduled meeting. She was back in her element, her personal life drowned out by the rigors and challenges of her work.

The meeting went well. Kate managed to clinch the deal, negotiating a contract that Blanton couldn't be happier with.

"It's good to have you back, Kate," he said after the meeting. "You made me miss you . . . really realize how much we need you around this place. Don't forget that."

Kate worked at her desk straight through the afternoon and late into the evening. She fielded phone calls and answered e-mails and brainstormed ideas for the new-product pitch list. At 6:45, Steve showed up at her office door.

"Well, it didn't take you long to get back into the swing of things," he said, smiling. "Why don't you stop for the night and have some dinner." He held up a bag of takeout, his eyebrows raised in question.

She glanced at her watch. "I didn't realize it was so late," she said. "Thanks, but I think I'll just go home. It's been a long day."

"You have to eat, Kate. You haven't been in your condo for a month. You think you'll find something there? Come on, it's Antonio's—your favorite."

Kate's stomach growled. She hadn't eaten all day, and the thought of dinner was rather enticing. But dinner with Steve? She was still irritated at his subversive attempt to edge her away from one of her biggest clients. She also couldn't help but question his motives in bringing her dinner. Surely he wouldn't attempt another define-the-relationship talk. Kate was sure she wasn't up for that. The smell of Antonio's famous ravioli with meat sauce finally won her over.

"All right," she finally conceded. "I guess I do need to eat."

"So how was your time in Rose Creek?" Steve asked as he handed Kate her food.

Kate hesitated. "It was good, I guess. Hard, but good."

"Hard? What was hard about it?" Steve asked. "I mean, aside from the whole funeral and everything."

Already, Kate felt like she'd said too much. This wasn't something she felt like discussing with Steve. But then, to dance around the truth almost seemed more exhausting than laying it all on the table.

"My aunt left me the hundred-year-old family farmhouse in her will instead of giving it to her own daughter. The State Department of Transportation wants to bulldoze the house so they can build a highway, and everyone in my family pretty much wishes I'd stay in Atlanta forever. How's that for hard?" Kate said.

Steve froze midbite, his fork poised in front of his mouth. "Wow," he said. "That is hard."

He finished his bite of ravioli then set his food on the edge of Kate's desk so he could lean back in his chair. With his hands behind his head and his feet stretched out in front of him, Kate thought he looked far too relaxed to be discussing something that weighed so heavily on her mind.

"Here's the thing though," he began. "You don't want to live in Rose Creek, do you? So sell the house to the DOT, use the proceeds to buy yourself a bigger condo, maybe upgrade your car a little bit, tell your family to shove off, and stay in Atlanta. All's well that ends well, right?"

Kate was floored by his flippancy. "Shove off? This is my family we're talking about and a house that's been in the family for generations. A new car can't compensate for losing all of that."

"Oh, sure, sure," he said. "I get it. I'm just saying, you do what you got to do, you know? You do what's best for you."

Kate didn't know how to respond. She'd been doing just that for years, and where had it gotten her? She was tired, so very tired and wanted to go home. "Thanks for dinner, Steve," she said. "But I'm tired. I think I'm just going to take the rest of this home."

After a necessary run to the grocery store, Kate didn't make it home to her condo until almost 9:00 p.m. She'd intentionally left her cell phone in the car all day, and once she was settled inside, she finally pulled it out to check her messages. Surprisingly, she had only one message—a text from Andrew. *Survey is done. Fax or e-mail?*

She responded to his message and gave him her e-mail address. Almost immediately, another text followed. *You okay?* She didn't respond.

The most difficult thing about Leslie's accusations from the night before was that Kate wasn't entirely sure that Leslie had been wrong. Kate wanted to be the kind of person who could leave a high-paying job and move home to be there for her family no matter what. She wanted to be the kind of person someone like Andrew Porterfield could fall in love with. But she wasn't. Even after she had made the decision to move home, she never did quit her job, never did anything to demonstrate her newfound commitments. *Why not? Because I can't really change. It isn't me.* Just as Leslie predicted, all Kate was, was the person who ran away.

Andrew's survey was impeccably prepared. Kate was impressed as she read through it. He must have spent the entire day getting it ready. On an impulse, she reached for her cell phone to call him, wanting to hear his voice. But then she hesitated. Her mind jumped to a conversation they'd had in the car before dinner at the Spencers' home.

"*This religion, my faith . . . it's who I am. It's priority for me, for my wife, whoever she may be, and for my future family . . .*"

Kate set her phone down, frustrated. Leslie's comments had been a wake-up call for Kate in more ways than one. Andrew wanted a relationship with someone who shared his faith. He'd never hidden that from Kate. It's why he'd waited so long to kiss her and really tell her how he felt. But what if she couldn't be the person Andrew wanted and deserved? For the second time that evening, Kate felt overwhelmed with the pressure and confusion of not knowing who or what she wanted to be. She pressed her forehead into her hands and slowly massaged her temples.

For a brief moment, she considered not turning in the petition. Steve's remark earlier that evening had been callous and rude. It had upset Kate at the time, but there was a bit of truth behind his statement. She could enter into negotiations with the state, sell the house, and be finished with Rose Creek once and for all. She still resented Leslie's claim to be living in the house by the end of the summer. Her face flushed with anger every time she thought of it. Leslie couldn't live in the house if Kate sold it to the state.

But that was a spiteful thought and completely unrealistic. Even in her darkest moments of frustration, Kate couldn't bring herself to disrespect her family in such a way. There were too many reasons for the house to stay in the family, regardless of who ended up living in it.

So she worked late into the night finalizing the petition. Just before midnight, Kate finished and faxed it over to the Harrison County Board of Commissioners from her home phone line. It would be waiting for them first thing in the morning, a full day ahead of the Friday deadline. She had done the best she could, Kate was certain of that. Now all she could do was wait.

Linny called early the next morning.

"When are you coming back, dear?" she asked.

"I don't know, Linny," Kate answered. "I've been away from my job a long time. It may be awhile before I can return."

"It was nice to see you and Leslie spending so much time together. I hope you don't stay away too long."

Kate laughed. "Yeah," she scoffed. "I'm sure Leslie would love it if I came back. You told me she needed me, Linny, but it isn't true. She'd rather have the house over me any day."

"That isn't true," Linny said. "Leslie's been carrying around a chip on her shoulder against you for seven years. She doesn't want to believe you've changed, Kate, because that means she would have to change too. Old habits die hard, don't they?"

"It's more complicated than that," Kate said.

"It is not complicated. You did change the month you were here. I watched it happen. I saw the light in your eyes, the love you found for the children. Don't let Leslie push you into a corner, Katie. Don't let her convince you that all you can ever be is the person you left in Atlanta when Mary died. You're better than that, and don't you forget it when you get back to working that fancy job of yours."

But Kate wanted to forget. She welcomed the emotionally numbing sensation of losing herself in her work. She poured herself into design meetings and pitch ideas, client lunches, and presentations. She spent very little time at home and even less time thinking about her family. Her friends were glad to have her back, filling what little time she spent out of the office with social gatherings and events, after-dinner drinks, and late-night shows. Steve's attentions to Francine Weston on the third floor diminished as he opted to spend more time with Kate. She didn't necessarily welcome the attention. But being around Steve was easy. He didn't make her question things like Andrew did; he didn't require her to be anything beyond shallow. With Steve, her emotions could remain comfortably and firmly superficial. She could be present without being invested. An empty life? Yes. But it was easy. And Kate was ready for a little bit of easy.

One week back in Atlanta, and Kate's life had slipped back into all of its old patterns and habits. On the outside, all appeared to be just as it was six weeks ago, and for the most part, all was the same. The only thing different was Kate. Rose Creek had changed her and given her a glimpse of a much richer life than she had experienced in the city. When she slowed down enough to think about it, she found herself feeling detached and empty, like she was pouring water into a bottomless glass.

Andrew had called twice since she'd been gone. The first time, she answered, anxious to hear his voice. But she felt guilty encouraging any relationship. She wasn't what he needed. She couldn't be. When he called a second time, she silenced her phone and let the call go to voice mail. Linny called more frequently—almost every day. Kate ignored her calls as well. They finally spoke on Friday night, a little more than a week after Kate left Rose Creek.

She was out to dinner with a few coworkers when Linny called, and she almost ignored it just as she had all the others, but the mindless bantering of her friends was getting under her skin. For once, she actually welcomed the distraction of a phone call.

"I have to take this," she said to her friends. "If you'll excuse me . . ."

Kate grabbed her cell phone and slipped out the front door. "Hi, Linny," she said. "How are you?"

"I'm stunned that you actually answered your phone," Linny said. "Have you not gotten my messages, child? What's a woman got to do to get you to call her back?"

"I got them, Linny. I guess I've just been busy. Work has been busy."

The words felt familiar as they glibly slipped from her mouth. She'd delivered the same excuse to Mary over and over every time she'd called. She was always too busy. And then what had happened? Mary had died, and nothing Kate could do or say would ever change that fact.

"I'm sorry, Linny," Kate quickly added. "I should have called you back. How are things?"

"Well, I was at the store with Leslie's children this afternoon, and we ran into that friend of yours—Andrew."

Kate perked up. "Really? Did you speak to him? How is he doing?"

"We spoke," Linny said. "Emily recognized him and ran straight up to say hello. He seems like he's doing all right. Are the two of you not speaking anymore?"

"It's been a few days," Kate said. *Six*, she thought to herself. *It's been six days since we spoke last.*

"Well, he asked about you," Linny said. "Told me to pass along his regards the next time I talked to you. I told him I'd try, but I'd need more than a hill of beans' worth of luck to get you to answer your phone. Imagine my surprise when you answered tonight."

"How did he look, Linny? Did he look all right?"

"He didn't say as much, but I think he looked a little sad. What did you do to the poor man, Katie? Although," she added, "maybe it's better for it to end, what with his religion and all. He'll find a nice Mormon girl, and we'll find you someone right here in Rose Creek, someone to take you down to the Methodist church—"

"No, Linny," Kate interrupted her. "I'm not coming back. Not ever."

Linny was silent. "Oh, don't be so rash. You don't really mean that, dear."

"I do mean it," Kate said. "It's better this way, better for me to stay in the city."

"Don't say that. Do you know the children ask about you every day? They've had too many people disappear from their lives. Don't you do it to them, Katie. They need you. Have you thought about the children at all?"

Of course Kate had thought about the children, but the conversation was too much. She couldn't do it. She couldn't face everything and everyone who came with Rose Creek.

"I'm sorry, Linny. I've got to go now. I'm out with friends, and they'll start to wonder where I am. I'll call you another time, okay?" She hung up the phone without waiting for Linny's reply.

She returned to the restaurant and tried to engage herself in the conversation, but her heart wasn't in it. Really, her heart wasn't much of anywhere. She didn't fit in Rose Creek, but this didn't feel right either. She felt like a stranger in a strange land.

Kate had only looked at Ian's journal one time since she'd left Rose Creek. She'd read an entry about the night he learned about his father's death and how desperate he had felt. He had used those words—called himself a stranger in a strange land. But the similarities ended there. Kate wasn't strong like Ian.

As she left the restaurant that evening and drove home alone, she thought of the warmth and security she had felt in the Spencers' home—a feeling unlike anything she'd ever experienced anywhere else. She'd mentioned to Steve over lunch the previous day that she'd spent some time with a Mormon family while she was back in Rose Creek.

"The neighbors across the street where I grew up were Mormon," he had said. "Nice enough family, I guess, though if you ask me, that's a miserable way to go through life."

"Miserable how?" Kate had asked.

"Come on, Kate," he had responded. "To never get to kick back and have a drink, live it up a little? I wouldn't sign up for it."

*Miserable* was the last word Kate would ever use to describe the Spencers. In the one short evening she'd spent with the entire family, Kate had felt more support and love than she could ever really quantify. She wondered what they thought of her hasty departure. *Surely they were disappointed,* Kate thought. *Them, and everyone else in Rose Creek.*

*Chapter 31*

OVER THE NEXT TWO WEEKS, things got a little easier for Kate. Linny still called every day, but Kate didn't make the mistake of answering again. As long as she didn't think about Rose Creek, she felt like she could keep her emotions at an even keel. She wasn't happy, but the emptiness in her heart had diminished to a dull ache. She imagined with time it might subside completely.

And then she got a text from Andrew.

*In town for a job interview. Can I drop by to say hi?*

She readily agreed. How could she not? Distracted by the anticipation of seeing him again, Kate couldn't focus on her work. Instead, she turned to the little prisms of afternoon sunlight that danced across the smooth surface of her desk. Leaning back in her chair, she watched a pair of pigeons perched on the ledge outside her window. *Oh, to have your wings,* she thought.

She didn't know how she would feel when she saw Andrew again. She still thought of him all the time, every day even. But it had been weeks since they'd spoken in person. She was nervous, anxious to see him, but worried that she had hurt him and worried to hear of the disappointment that he surely felt over her recent actions.

Her phone buzzed, and she heard Veronica's voice. "You've got a call, Ms. Sinclair. A woman who says she's your aunt?"

Kate sighed. "All right," she said. "Put her through."

"Kate, is that you?" Linny said loudly. Kate wondered how many different operators Linny had spoken with before finally reaching her. She'd never called Kate at the office before.

"I'm here, Linny," Kate said. "Is everything all right?"

"Oh, well, I guess so. I thought I'd go crazy trying to get you on the phone. You know, if you'd just answer your cell, it wouldn't be such an ordeal."

"I'm sorry, Linny. I've just needed some time to think about things."

"I don't need to hear your excuses, dear. I've got you now. That's all that matters. Listen, the commissioners are going to vote on the petition tomorrow evening. Are you coming?"

Kate knew about the voting. She'd received notice from the commissioners office the week before.

"I don't know, Linny. I'm not sure I can get away from the office in time."

"Katie, now you listen to me. You've been ignoring me for three weeks, and that's fine. I'm tough and can handle it. But you need to be there for this hearing. You may have the opportunity to say something. They need to see how serious you are about saving that house."

"Linny, they'll either accept the petition or deny it. I don't see how my presence will make a difference one way or the other."

"Katherine Sinclair, that's baloney and you know it. You can tell me a lot of things, blow smoke about this or that, a meeting you can't miss or any other such nonsense. But I'm not going to buy it. It's your house, your responsibility. You have to be there!"

Kate suddenly wished she hadn't answered the phone. "It won't make a difference, Linny. They've all but bulldozed the house to get ready for that highway. It was a long shot to get them to change their minds. I just don't have a lot of hope that this will work."

"So you're giving up? Just like that?"

"I'm not giving up. It's just . . . I just have a lot to do here at work."

"Well, I guess that's how it is, then." She paused. "You know, Katie, I've always defended you, always smoothed over the ill opinions of others, but this time, it's me you've disappointed."

Kate heard a click. She closed her eyes and rested her forehead on the heel of her hand. Before she had time to really internalize their conversation, Kate heard a small knock on her door.

"It's open," Kate called.

"I hope I'm not interrupting anything," a familiar voice said from the doorway.

"Andrew," Kate said as she looked up. He was earlier than she'd expected. She stood from her desk and quickly walked to greet him. They met in the center of the room, and Andrew wrapped his arms around her in a giant hug, nearly picking her up off the ground. He took a step back, taking hold of her hands.

"It's good to see you, Kate. How are you?"

"It's nice to see you too," she said. "I'm good. Do you . . . want to sit down?"

Andrew gave a small nod. "It's a great view of the city," he said, looking out the large windows of Kate's office. He moved to the sofa pushed up against the back wall and sat down.

"You look really great," she said, motioning to his suit as she sat down next to him. It was light gray, with a hairline navy pinstripe. Kate had never seen him so dressed up.

He shrugged casually. "Dress to impress, you know? You look good too, Kate, really good."

"How did the interview go?"

"I think it went well. It's a great firm. I think I would enjoy working there."

"I didn't realize you'd thought about working in Atlanta."

Kate wondered for a moment if she'd had anything to do with Andrew's decision to take the interview, but she was nearly certain she couldn't have. He wasn't the kind of man who would go chasing after a woman, change careers, or move to a different city just to make himself available. He had more confidence than that.

He shrugged again. "They're based in Atlanta, but the position I'm interviewing for is in Raleigh. It's a firm I considered when I was finishing school, even spent a few months interning with them over the summer. It was a natural place to begin when I started looking again."

Raleigh? Kate thought of their conversation the night before she'd left Rose Creek. He'd talked of staying in Rose Creek, crossing over into residential construction and striking out on his own. Something about Andrew working in Raleigh didn't feel right to Kate. She thought the mountains suited him better than the city. She missed his rugged jeans and faded flannels.

"I guess it's good that it went well," she said. She chewed on her bottom lip, not sure what to say next.

"Have you heard anything back about the house?" Andrew asked.

"No," she responded. "The board of commissioners will vote on the petition tomorrow evening."

Andrew nodded his head silently. This was obviously small talk. He hadn't come all this way to ask her about the house.

"So, I haven't heard from you in a while," Andrew said. "I've missed you, Kate."

Kate looked down at her hands. With two hours of distance between them, she'd been able to push him from the forefront of her mind, but here, sitting next to him, she was totally consumed by the intensity of their connection and was surprised at how quickly her feelings rose to the surface.

"I've missed you too," she said softly.

Andrew took a deep breath and leaned forward on his elbows then turned his head to look at Kate. When his eyes found hers, she could not look away. It was impossible to look at him without feeling as if their souls were somehow linked, wordless communication passing from her heart to his through the intensity of their gaze. She closed her eyes and took a deep breath, trying to keep her wits about her.

"Kate," Andrew said. "I can't stop thinking about you. I don't want to give up on what I think we could be together. If it doesn't work, then so be it. But I want to try. I want us to try."

Kate turned and looked out her window and watched as the pair of pigeons on the windowsill, stationary all afternoon, finally lifted off the ledge and flew off into the late-afternoon sky.

"Andrew, I . . ." She hesitated. "I'm not that girl. I'm not the Kate you met in Rose Creek. I remember what you said that night about the gospel being a priority for you. I just don't think I can be that person. I thought I could be, that I could change, but it's just complicated right now."

"Why is it complicated, Kate? I was there with you when you learned about the Church. I saw how it touched you and moved you to tears more than once. That wasn't acting, was it?" Andrew stood and walked over to the window, hands in his pockets. He turned back to Kate.

"Exclusive of all of that, what if I care about you just because you're you? I'm not offering any ultimatums. I've thought about this situation a million different ways, and honestly, I don't know how it will all play out. But I know I'm miserable without you. No matter how I look at it, the one thing that's consistent is my complete inability to get you out of my head."

"You just interviewed for a job in Raleigh," Kate said. "I have a job here. How would we make it work?"

"It was just an interview. I've got to keep my options open, and I haven't committed to anything yet."

Kate was silent as she processed his words. Suddenly, he was beside her again, his face close. "Just tell me you feel it too," he said quietly.

She sighed. "Of course I feel it."

Kate heard a brief knock as the door to her office swung open.

"Hey, beautiful, just wanted to make sure we were still on for dinner," Steve said. "Oh, I'm sorry. I didn't realize you were with someone."

Kate looked in horror as realization flashed across Andrew's face. She shook her head, her eyes pleading with him to understand. *It isn't Steve I want. It's you. It's always been you.*

Steve crossed the room and extended his hand to Andrew. "I'm Steve Carson. I don't believe we've met."

"This is Andrew Porterfield," Kate said awkwardly. She turned to Andrew. "Steve and I work together."

Andrew stood and shook Steve's hand.

"Oh, come on, Kate," Steve said, wrapping his arm possessively around her shoulders. "You don't have to hide your social life from your clients. It might help him focus, knowing someone pretty as you already has a boyfriend." He was the only one who laughed at his joke.

Kate shrugged out from under Steve's arms and took a step away.

"Andrew is a friend, Steve. Not a client."

"Oh, well, a friend of Kate's is a friend of mine. It's almost 5:00. Shall we all get a drink before dinner?"

Andrew's cell phone buzzed, and he glanced at the screen. "Actually," he said, "I have somewhere I need to be. Thanks for the offer though."

"Hey, no problem," Steve said. "It's good to meet you, Alan, was it?"

"Andrew," Kate said softly.

"Right," Steve said.

Andrew paused at the door and looked back at Kate. "It was lovely to see you again," he said.

And then he was gone.

"Andrew, wait," Kate called after him. She pushed past Steve and hurried out of her office, chasing Andrew toward the elevators.

"Please, Andrew. Let me explain!" she called.

Heads turned to watch the commotion Kate created as she careened down the corridors of her office building, trying to catch up. But she didn't care. She had to stop him, convince him to listen. Andrew's long stride kept him several steps ahead of her. He did not stop until he reached the elevators.

He turned and looked at her, eyes distant but still warm and full of kindness.

"You don't have to explain anything, Kate," Andrew said calmly. "We haven't talked in a while. I should have realized . . ."

Kate cut him off. "Andrew, please, it's not like that," she said.

He held up his hands, palms facing out, and shook his head, rejecting any further explanation. The elevator beeped, and the doors slid open. Andrew stepped inside. "Good-bye, Kate."

Steve came up behind Kate just as the elevator doors slid closed. "What was that about?" he asked.

Kate turned on him, hot with anger.

"What is wrong with you?" she shouted. She pushed past him and stalked toward her office, raising eyebrows and turning heads for the second time in five minutes.

"What did I do?" Steve questioned, following after her. "What did I say?"

She turned on him, hands on hips. "You are *not* my boyfriend, Steve. Why did you say that? What were you trying to prove?"

An eerie silence followed her outburst as everyone within earshot stopped whatever they were doing and turned to stare. Steve nervously looked around.

"Do we have to talk about this right here?" he said, voice low.

"No," Kate said. "We don't have to talk about this at all. In fact, we don't have to ever talk again." She spun on her heel to head to her office but bumped right into Mr. Blanton. Kate didn't know how much he had observed.

"Is everything all right, Kate?" he asked, eyebrows raised.

She took a deep breath and tried to regain her composure. "It's fine, sir. I'm just fine," she said.

He looked at her for a moment then cast a sideways glance at Steve, still standing a few feet away with a wounded look on his face.

"Take a few minutes to pull yourself together, Kate, then come up to my office. I've been meaning to speak with you," he said. He looked at Steve one more time. "If I were you," he said. "I think I'd leave her alone."

Kate hurried to her office, too angry to cry. She paced around the room like an agitated cat ready to pounce on anything that even remotely resembled a mouse. She could not believe the gumption Steve had had making such an obnoxious claim. Sure, they had spent time together since her return to the city, but in no way had it constituted a steady relationship. A few nights before, the two of them had gone out to dinner just a few blocks down the street from Kate's condo with a group of coworkers. Steve had insisted on walking her home. At the door to her building, before Kate had had time to protest, he'd kissed her. She'd hastily pushed him away and told him they would only ever be friends. She thought her message had been pretty clear. In the moments right after Steve had kissed her, Kate had realized how much it paled in comparison to kissing Andrew.

Andrew.

A new surge of anger rose within her as she thought of how foolish and betrayed he must feel. She scrambled to her desk and pulled out her cell phone, hands trembling as she dialed his number. The phone rang once and then clicked over to his voice mail. She hung up without leaving a message and dialed again. He still did not answer. At least she could send him a text. She typed out a hasty explanation—*It's not what you think. He isn't my boyfriend, just a jerk I work with. Please call me.* She didn't expect him to respond right away, but she kept her phone close by anyway. When it finally buzzed with an incoming message, she was annoyed to see it was from Steve.

*So I guess we aren't still on for dinner?* She angrily tossed the phone aside. Dejected and disappointed, Kate slid into her chair and laid her cheek against the smooth wooden surface of her desk. She sat motionless until her anger had finally dissipated and she felt calm enough to talk to Mr. Blanton.

## Chapter 32

"IS THERE SOMETHING YOU NEED to tell me, Kate?" Mr. Blanton asked. He sat on the arm of the chair across from her, hands clasped in his lap, a genuine look of concern on his face.

"No, Mr. Blanton, everything is fine," Kate lied.

Mr. Blanton scratched the graying, prickly whiskers on his chin and studied her countenance.

"I don't think I believe you."

"Sir, it has been a rough couple of months for me, but I can assure you, it isn't going to affect my work here. Things should be all right now. What happened downstairs isn't going to happen again."

"The problem, Kate, is that it already has affected your work here."

Kate look confused. "I don't understand. I've been working seventy, eighty hours a week the past few weeks. I'm pouring myself into my work. I'm giving you everything I've got."

"That's true," he responded. "And yet, with all that effort, your work is still far below what I'm used to from you. Your ideas have been one dimensional and flat, your presentations listless, and your reports vague. You may be working here in body, Kate, but your mind must be somewhere else entirely."

Kate was surprised to hear that her boss had noted such changes in her performance. Her level of effort and the intensity of her work ethic had not changed. But Kate realized Mr. Blanton was right. Her mind was not as focused as it had once been; her efforts weren't as clean and precise as they had been in the past.

"Did you know I've never been married?" Mr. Blanton said.

He didn't wait for her to respond.

"Engaged once, but it didn't work out. And never married. Instead, I married my career. Poured myself into creating the best company I could ever imagine. And you know what? It worked. I did all this." He motioned to his impressively spacious office. "I built a company from the ground up and made it successful. It's a great feeling to have done that. But at the end of the day, when I leave this fancy office and go home, do you know what I feel? All I feel is alone."

He leaned back in his chair, an air of contemplative silence settling around him. Kate thought he suddenly looked tired, older. They had always had a good relationship. Kate respected Mr. Blanton, admired his abilities, and appreciated his kindness to her. He had always been supportive of her career. But this was a side of him she had never seen before.

"Don't marry your career, Kate," he finally continued. "You're too good for that. You have too much potential. Whatever's been eating at you the past three weeks, go fix it. Go back to Rose Hill or Flower Creek or whatever that little place is called and fix it."

"I don't think I can do that," Kate said morosely.

"You've been here a long time. I've seen you change and grow and get better at what you do, but it's not everything. If you hide in your work for too long, it'll be too late to fill your life up with anything else, with the stuff that really matters. There has to be a balance. And right now, for whatever reason, your life is completely out of balance."

She stood silently, still not sure what to make of their conversation.

"Look, these are just my opinions, and I may be completely off the mark, but whatever is going on in your life, if you want to keep working here, you'd better find a way to keep it from interfering with the quality of your work. I want you to take a couple of days, do what you need to do to clear your head, and then come back ready to work on Monday morning. Are we clear?"

Kate left his office weary and completely disheartened. She went straight to her office and, without a word to anyone, grabbed her purse and keys and went home.

*Chapter 33*

WHEN KATE ARRIVED AT HER condo, she tried to call Andrew one more time. Voice mail. Again.

All month long, Kate had been ignoring her feelings. But suddenly, and quite violently, Kate realized she could not pretend anymore. All the rage and disappointment she had been suppressing, in one frightening moment, came rumbling to the surface. Kate flung her purse across the room then reached for the closest dining room chair, tossing it onto its side. She moved to the window seat, picked up a stack of pillows, and threw them across the room. The largest pillow, red with gold fringe, hit a framed landscape hanging on the wall and sent it crashing to the floor. Kate stood, her breathing heavy, hot tears streaming down her face, and looked at the broken frame and glass. It was no good. *She* was no good.

And then she saw it.

On the window seat, previously hidden by the pillows but now clear to her view, she saw the leather messenger bag she had carried when she was in Rose Creek. She knew what was inside. After reading the journal entries just after she left Rose Creek that had resonated a little too well, she had decided she no longer cared for Ian's insight. She'd left the bag hidden on purpose. *Out of sight, out of mind,* she had thought. But now she opened the bag and pulled out Ian's journal, as well as the Book of Mormon the missionaries had given her nearly two months before. It seemed so long ago that she had held these books so reverently, reading them every day, cherishing the feelings they inspired. She sat on the window seat with the books on her lap and leaned her head against the cool glass of the window.

She relived the many conversations of her afternoon. From her phone call with Linny to her brief meeting with Andrew and then her final confrontation with Steve, it was almost too much for her to process. If she knew anything at all, she knew Mr. Blanton was right. Her life was out of balance. Just as she'd done so many years before, Kate was trying to hide from her life in her work. She was ashamed and frustrated over the way she had behaved in the past month but was completely overwhelmed when she thought about what she could do to fix it. She thought of Andrew's question. *Why is it complicated?* It was a good question.

Why *was* it complicated?

It was complicated because Kate was terrified of running to her problems instead of away from them. It was complicated because as much as Kate wanted to be with her family and give her heart to Andrew, she didn't really think she deserved it and wasn't certain Leslie thought she deserved it either. And it was complicated because changing her life was hard—so very hard.

Kate looked at the books in her lap. Could it really be so simple? Setting the Book of Mormon aside, she opened the journal. The book fell open to a page in the back that Kate didn't immediately recognize. She thought she'd read the entire thing, but she must have somehow missed this entry.

> *23 June 1844*
>
> *I do not know if I will ever find the truth I seek. I have grown weary of searching, the sermons, the pastors and preachers all claiming to know the way to salvation. The way for whom, I ask them. Your two hundred parishioners alone? What of the rest of us, then? When and if I find the truth, I believe I will feel peace and joy in my heart like I have never known. I will know of the truth because God will reveal it unto me. He has not let me down yet. I do not believe He will let me down this time either.*
>
> *Many years ago, when I first learned that Da was dead, old Mr. Watson, the baker, walked me down to the churchyard and pointed out his grave. It was still fresh, the exposed earth barely visible in the pale moonlight. Watson left me, I guess, thinking I needed time to cope. But he said something just before leaving that has stayed with me for years and years since. He looked at me and said, "God is aware of you, Ian. He'll not leave you alone." And He has not left me alone. I have strived to walk with Him as my father counseled, and He has been with me. Those first hours after I learned of Da's death were the darkest I experienced in my young life and the darkest*

*still today. But it was in those hours that I felt the confirming presence of my Savior. I felt Him lift me up and give me the strength to move forward. I had no idea where or what I was going to do. But I knew I would be fine. Because of God's grace and love, I knew I would be all right.*

Fresh tears coursed down Kate's cheeks as she read the entry again and then again. There *was* someone Kate could turn to, someone who would help her know what she needed to do and then help her have the strength and courage to do it. God was there for her. He knew who she was and knew specifically what she needed. She needed only to ask Him for help.

But could she do it? She thought of Andrew and the faith she knew he had in her and the person she was capable of becoming. She thought of the Spencers, the missionaries, her cousins, her aunt. She thought of Mary and Grey and her own parents. They deserved so much more than what Kate had given them.

She could do this. She could change. She had to change—for her family, for Andrew, for God. She had to change because it was the right thing to do. In her heart, she knew it.

The words came slowly at first, Kate embarrassingly aware of her solitary presence in the room. Yet she persisted, forming her sentences carefully, patterning them after the examples the missionaries had given so many weeks ago when they'd taught her to pray.

"Help me feel of Thy love, Father. Help me to feel Thy goodness and mercy. Forgive me for my sins, for being so selfish, for hurting my family. And give me the strength and the courage to be a better person . . ."

She paused, feeling foolish. "Agghh, I can't do this." She rose from the window seat and paced about the room. More tears, more frustration.

She looked upward as if to address God face-to-face. "This isn't how it's supposed to be, is it? It should be easy to talk to You and know that You're there, that You know who I am. But it's not! I don't know. I don't know anything at all." She sank back down onto the window seat, her balled fists finally relaxing into her lap. "God, help me . . ." she said softly. "Help me know You're there . . ."

The feeling was like a soft warm breeze, except it started on the inside and radiated, expanding, filling Kate to her very fingertips and quickening her heart. She closed her eyes, tears washing her cheeks as she realized what she now knew. God knew her. He loved her, and He always had loved her. And He would not, not ever, leave her alone.

Kate sank to her knees, overwhelmed with relief, grateful for the sudden peace that filled her heart. "Thank you," she whispered. "Dear God in heaven, thank you so much . . ."

Kate slept better than she had all month. She awoke with a new energy, and she was determined and, much to her surprise, happy. Her circumstances were hardly different than they had been the night before, but she was different. And that changed everything.

She dressed quickly and packed her suitcase. With the board of commissioners voting on her petition that evening, she did not have a lot of time to waste. Her mind raced as she drove back to Rose Creek. She glanced at the clock on her dashboard. She would be at Linny's house by 11 a.m. There was no question of her going there first. She owed Linny an apology and wanted to reassure her that not only would she be at the meeting that night, but she would also be in Rose Creek from now on. Linny was never one to give up on her. She deserved to know that Kate knew what she was fighting for and that she wasn't going to give up.

Linny was also Kate's most trusted source of information about the rest of her family. She would know if anyone else was planning on attending the meeting and would know what Kate might expect when she saw them there. Kate guessed Sam would drive over, and Leslie would probably be there, assuming she believed Kate was gone for good. She dreaded a conversation with Leslie but knew it would have to happen sooner rather than later. No matter how much Leslie doubted her, Kate could not—would not—relinquish her claim on the farmhouse. Leslie needed to see that and realize Kate was there to fight. She would not willingly yield to the board of commissioners, nor would she shrink from Leslie's pressure or criticism.

Kate was full of hopeful energy as she pulled down the little dirt road that led to Linny's home. Her mind was filled with more peace and clarity than she had ever experienced before, her resolve unbending to accomplish the tasks set out before her.

Kate knocked and listened, recognizing the thud of Linny's walking cast on the floor as she came to the door.

"Well, I'll be dumbfiddled," Linny said as she looked at Kate through the screen door. A wide smile spread across her face, and she shook her head. "I knew you wouldn't be able to stay away. I knew it."

Kate smiled. "Linny, I'm so sorry about our conversation yesterday. I . . . I don't know what I was thinking."

Linny opened the door for Kate and gave her a warm hug before ushering her inside.

"I know what you were thinking," she said as they walked to the kitchen. "You were scared and overwhelmed and you had your head stuck in the sand. What finally made you pull it out?"

"Let's call it a bit of personal revelation," Kate said. "How is everything? Have you been to the farmhouse lately?"

Linny nodded. "I was just there yesterday. Things are fine. The weeds are a bit out of control. You didn't go there first?"

"No. I wanted to come apologize."

Linny sighed and sat down at the kitchen table across from Kate.

"Well, I appreciate that, and I accept your apology. We're human, every one of us. We stumble, we fall, we make mistakes. But when all the sand finally clears out of our ears and we start hearing plain again, well, then we do the right thing, don't we?"

"I shouldn't have run away. I was here, I was happy, I was so close to having things worked out, and then it just got so complicated all over again."

"Leslie didn't help matters there, did she?" Linny asked.

"How is Leslie?"

"As fine as one might expect. Does she know you're here?"

"No. The only person who knows is you."

"You'd better call Sam," Linny said. "He's planning on speaking for you at the meeting tonight. I'm sure he'll be glad you can be there yourself."

"Is Leslie going?"

"I expect she might, though you'd better make certain you talk to her before you both just show up. It wouldn't do anybody any good for the board to see fireworks just before they vote."

"I don't want any more fireworks. In a way, I guess Leslie still has the right not to trust me. I'm just going to have to show her that I'm here for good and that I'm not giving up. It may take a long time, but what else can I do? She'll have to see eventually, right?"

"Of course she'll see. And she'll get over the sting of feeling slighted by her mama when that house went to you instead of her. She's still angry about that. But she can't be angry at her mom 'cause that just feels wrong, so the anger goes straight to you. It'll pass though, Katie. Everything will be fine in the end."

"It's scary to think it might not matter at all if the vote doesn't go our way," Kate said.

"It will all be fine," Linny said. "Trust an old lady. It will all be just fine."

# Chapter 34

KATE STOOD AT THE BACK of the meeting room at the Harrison County Board of Commissioners office with Sam and Linny, waiting for the meeting to commence. Mr. Marshall was also present, as well as Angus McFinley, the elderly gentleman from the preservation museum. Kate had gone to see him that afternoon, inviting him to the meeting and thanking him in person for all of the additional documents he had sent to her when she had prepared the final petition. Kate was humbled by the support her family and friends provided. In all of her fickleness, she didn't feel she deserved their consistent, unwavering faith. She never would have made it so far on her own.

Leslie was not at the meeting. Kate had called her a few hours before and tried to talk but had found Leslie cold and cynical. It frustrated Kate. She couldn't help but feel she was being blamed for things that were not her fault. She had apologized more than once and had made a valiant effort at improving and repairing their relationship. It was Leslie who had chosen to belittle her efforts and ignore her apology. Linny was probably right in that the house most certainly had something to do with Leslie's bitterness, but what else would she have Kate do?

Linny wobbled over to Kate and interrupted her thoughts. "You look nervous enough, dear. Just relax."

"Much easier said than done; I'm just ready for this entire thing to be over," Kate said.

"How many times have I told you today that things will work out just fine? For better or worse, with or without the house, *you* will be fine," Linny said. She shifted her weight and leaned against the wall behind them. "So whatever happened to that man of yours, Andrew?" she asked.

Kate's face fell as she thought of him. "I don't know," she said. "We talked a few times after I left for the city, but I don't really know if we'll be able to make it work."

"Well, like I said before, I reckon in the end, that's better for everyone, though I certainly don't relish your disappointment in the matter."

It was the second time Linny had implied her satisfaction over the potential end to Kate and Andrew's relationship.

"Better for who?" Kate asked, a slight edge to her voice. "What are you trying to say?"

"Now, now, it doesn't matter, really," Linny said gently. She fiddled with the straps of her shoulder bag, rubbing her fingers up and down the smooth leather. "I guess it just seems like with this family barely managing to get ourselves back together, throwing a new religion in the mix wouldn't really help matters. I liked Andrew just fine, but if I'm being honest, I'm relieved the two of you aren't seeing each other."

"So what if I decide to become a Mormon, regardless of whether Andrew and I are in a relationship?" Kate asked. "And what if things aren't necessarily over between Andrew and me? I'm not ready to hammer the last nail in the coffin just yet. Maybe things will still work out. If they do, I hope my family can learn to handle it."

Kate sounded more defensive than she'd intended, and Linny's eyes grew wide with surprise at her little outburst. Linny pinched her lips together and folded her arms tightly. "Well, I expect we'll handle it just fine," she said coolly. "But that doesn't mean we have to like it." Linny looked smug but did not push the conversation further. She looked over Kate's shoulder. "Well, there's Andrew now," she said. "Did you know he was coming?"

Kate spun around and watched as he moved into the room, taking a seat in the back row. "I didn't know," she said.

Nervously glancing at her watch, she walked across the room and sat down in the row just in front of his. She turned around to face him. "Hi," she said. "I wasn't sure I would see you here."

"I thought it best to be here in case any questions were asked regarding the survey," Andrew answered.

"Oh, well, thank you. I really do appreciate your help," Kate said.

Andrew's eyes darted all over the room, looking in every direction but at Kate. He was trying not to make eye contact, she could tell.

The room grew quiet as the board members took their seats. Kate looked around. She wanted to reach out and take Andrew's face, make him look at her and listen. She wanted him to see that Steve meant nothing, that from their first conversation, Andrew was all she'd ever wanted. She closed her eyes and took a deep breath. It wasn't the right time. Kate needed to focus on getting through the meeting. She turned and faced forward.

Sam and Linny came and sat down next to Kate as Douglas Bradley, chairman of the board and the man Kate had spoken with on the phone when she'd first learned of her dilemma, called the meeting to order.

Kate looked at the chairman, wondering if he would be one to support her cause. He looked nice enough—tall and thin, generally unimposing. As he welcomed everyone to the meeting and conducted a few items of unrelated business, he seemed rushed and a bit intolerant of distractions or secondary conversation. It made Kate uneasy. Finally, her petition was next on the agenda.

"Next on tap for this evening is a petition for landmark status regarding the Walker farmhouse on Red Dogwood Lane, owned by Katherine Sinclair. Ms. Sinclair, are you present?" Mr. Bradley looked up, scanning the room in search of Kate.

"I'm here," she said, forcing confidence into her voice as she stood up.

Mr. Bradley nodded. "All should have received a copy of Ms. Sinclair's petition prior to this meeting and been allowed a reasonable and substantial amount of time to review it. We will now open the floor for discussion," he said, addressing his fellow board members. Then he turned back to Kate. "Ms. Sinclair, I assume you're willing to answer any questions the board may have?"

Kate nodded.

"And I believe the architect who conducted the survey is also available should his opinion be needed as well. Mr. Porterfield, I believe?" Mr. Bradley said.

Andrew stood. "I'm Andrew Porterfield. I'd be happy to answer any questions, if need be."

Mr. Bradley paused and looked at Andrew. "I don't believe I recognize your name. Do you work locally?"

"I have family in Rose Creek that brings me here on occasion, but I haven't done any other work in the area," Andrew answered.

"Where do you work, then?" Mr. Bradley asked.

Andrew paused long enough that Kate started to feel uncomfortable.

"Actually, I've just been offered a position in Raleigh," he finally said.

Kate struggled to hide her response. She closed her eyes for a moment and forced her attention back to the front of the room.

"Ah, yes. I see your credentials listed here. Very well," Mr. Bradley said. "Now, to get us started, I'd like to make a few observations that I believe are pertinent to how we consider this case. There are, after all, special circumstances concerning this house. The board is aware that nearly two months ago

Ms. Sinclair received notice that the North Carolina State Department of Transportation was initiating eminent domain to acquire her property for construction of the Mountain Way bypass, a highway that we all know has been in the planning stages for quite some time. Now, I did a little bit of research, and it seems, Ms. Sinclair, that you've only owned this property a short time. Is that correct?"

"I grew up in the house," Kate answered. "But when my aunt Mary Walker passed away last month, she left the house to me."

"I see," Mr. Bradley said. "Ms. Sinclair," he continued, "I struggle to understand why this petition was only just filed. Obviously your goal is to create a blanket of protection for your house that will nullify the state's ability to take it. But this process, this highway has been in the works for months, years even. Ms. Walker had ample time to protest, to attend the countless meetings we've had about this, about the numerous properties involved in this project. Why have we not heard from your family before now?"

"Commissioner, I assure you my aunt was a responsible, intelligent woman. She would not have sat idly by, knowing that her property was going to be taken, her home bulldozed to the ground. My family was under the impression that the house was not to be involved in the construction of the highway. On the twenty-fifth of April, my aunt received a notice indicating a change in the proposed route that would include the house after all. It was that very afternoon that my aunt died, sir—perhaps just moments after reading the letter. However it happened, Mary did not tell anyone in the family about the letter before she passed away."

"I am sorry for your loss, but even still," Mr. Bradley said, "do you realize where we are in this process? Your property is the only one still in stages of negotiation."

"Commissioner," Kate said, "this house is not the kind of house one can easily exchange for any sum of money. As the petition states, it is rich with history and meets all requirements to qualify for landmark status."

"But the highway is a project that will benefit all citizens of Harrison County. Months and months of research have gone into determining the best possible route. Do you really feel you and your little petition are qualified to negate all the efforts and hours spent by others to get this highway built most efficiently?"

"Now wait, Douglas, let's be fair." A woman sitting at the end of the table interrupted him. The name plaque in front of her seat read *Annabelle Markham*. She was a short, round woman, with small, closely set eyes and short wispy hair that stuck out in every direction. Unimposing though she seemed, there was an element in her voice capable of commanding a room. Kate had barely noticed her presence until she'd spoken. Once the woman had Kate's attention, Kate wondered how she had ever overlooked her before.

"We can't ignore the value of Harrison County history. If the house qualifies, then it qualifies. If it doesn't, it doesn't. We need to consider this petition exclusive of how it may or may not affect the highway construction project." Ms. Markham raised her eyebrows at Mr. Bradley, daring him to challenge her.

"But this isn't an issue separate from the highway," Mr. Bradley argued. "This petition is being made only to disqualify the property from being subject to eminent domain."

Voices from several other board members, all with various opinions on the subject, started chiming in, but it was Ms. Markham's voice that overpowered in the end.

"The time when it becomes a landmark doesn't matter," she argued, "whether it happened ten years ago or it happens tonight. If the house is worthy of preservation, then it is, end of story. We are not state transportation commissioners, Mr. Bradley. We are Harrison County commissioners. And it is our job to make decisions for the county as a whole. Highways are not the only things that matter in this county. The people matter. The history matters."

The woman looked in Kate's direction, sending her a small smile of encouragement. Kate felt like giving the crazy-haired Annabelle Markham a hug.

"Mr. Bradley?" Kate said. "The petition also includes my commitment to donate the several historical items found in the attic of the home to the Harrison County Preservation Museum. I would also be willing to erect a small plaque in the yard of the property, with a brief explanation of the home's history. I believe there is a driving tour through the county already that identifies the existing landmarks. I would be happy to have the farmhouse included on the tour."

He sighed in frustration. "Does anyone have any questions regarding Ms. Sinclair's petition?" he finally asked.

Ms. Markham spoke again. "I'd like to hear Ms. Sinclair tell us a bit about her home's history here in person, if there's time for that."

Mr. Bradley turned to Kate and wearily nodded his head in approval.

Kate started with a brief outline of Ian Wylie's life, identifying the presence of his journal as well as the other artifacts she'd found in the attic of the farmhouse. She continued on through Ian's great-grandson John and his arrival in Harrison County, as well as his land donation to the Methodist church just across the street from the very building where their meeting was being held. And then she discussed the generosity and character of her great-grandfather, Isaac Abraham Wylie.

"There is a picture in the county museum that shows the original homestead of Isaac Wylie—my great-grandfather," Kate said. "His modest home sat on the northeastern corner of nearly two hundred acres—acres and acres of farmland he worked his entire life. But along the south side of Ike Wylie's property, there was farmland he didn't work himself. Instead, he parceled it off and leased it to other farmers, those who didn't own their own land. Several small homes lined the property and were constantly filled with those needing a place to live and a place to get started. Many citizens of Harrison County benefited from Isaac's generosity. He was a kind landlord and always believed the best of people. While he did require a reasonable rent, he never required even the smallest portion of the profits that came from the harvest on his leased farmland. Angus McFinley," Kate said, motioning to Mr. McFinley sitting a few seats away from her, "a volunteer for our local preservation society, told me about his own father, who came to Harrison County with a new wife and $1.25 in his pocket. He found himself at Isaac's door and wound up staying in one of his cabins for four years, farming and working, until he could save enough money to purchase a piece of property for himself. Countless others were helped in similar ways. The old farmhouse still stands today—a relic of early twentieth-century architecture and a monument to the generosity and kindness of the Wylie family and those men who made valuable contributions to the very fabric of Harrison County history."

Kate finished, looking at each member of the board, scanning their faces for some hint of a positive response.

A man sitting to Mr. Bradley's left cleared his throat and began to speak. "You've painted a pretty picture for us, for sure. But I think it's important to remind the board that the feasibility studies for this highway are complete. If this house is no longer eligible and a new route must be identified, it could set the project back weeks, even months. Countless other properties could be pulled in, new homeowners, new hearings . . . This isn't a process we want to go through again, is it?"

"That's not fair," Kate said, struggling to keep the edge out of her voice. "The preservation of my house is not just an issue of convenience—some inconsequential structure that doesn't matter to anyone. This is a century-old farmhouse that didn't see indoor plumbing for the first half of its existence, that has experienced life and death, stood through the Great Depression, the world wars. No amount of money could replace the parts of history this house has helped write and certainly no highway is worth its demise."

"She's right, Douglas," Ms. Markham said, looking directly at Mr. Bradley. "Where's the architect?" she asked, looking across the room to find Andrew. "Without all of the technical mumbo jumbo you wrote in here," she said, holding up the petition, "what can you tell us of the architectural history of the structure?"

Andrew cleared his throat and stood. "The house demonstrates ample characteristics in line with traditional early twentieth-century construction. With the exception of the major renovations that introduced modern conveniences to the house—indoor plumbing, heating, and air conditioning, that sort of thing—the changes made to the house have been very superficial. The core patterns of construction, the bones of the house, if you will, are still intact. The original plaster walls, for example, are still present, as well as the original wood flooring in several bedrooms upstairs. The exterior of the house has a large wraparound porch, with a raised-seam tin roof and slender Doric columns, consistent with the influences of the Colonial Revival style present in the farmhouse's period of construction. All in all, the house is a unique study in architecture and could be considered a valuable resource in demonstrating patterns of construction and design of that period. I would even go so far as to say that with proper marketing, the house could even pull students of architecture into Harrison County with the specific purpose of viewing the property."

Kate watched as Mr. Bradley tossed down his pen and removed his glasses, rubbing his eyes in frustration. He looked defeated, which made Kate feel even more hopeful.

"Ms. Sinclair?" he asked, still not looking up. "You've made an excellent case for the preservation of your property. In other circumstances, I have no doubt the board would be thrilled to consider your home a part of our preservation society. But I will ask you once again, are there not any other accommodations we could make? I'm sure the state, at this point, would be willing to compensate you above and beyond fair market value. Are you far beyond reach in that regard?"

"I assure you, sir, there is no sum adequate enough to compensate for losing the house."

"There's nothing left to do but vote on it, Douglas," Ms. Markham said from the corner.

"Might I say a brief word, please?" Kate turned and saw Mr. McFinley standing up, waiting for the opportunity to speak. He winked at Kate and smiled then turned his attention back to the board.

"Angus, what association do you have with this petition?" Mr. Bradley asked with an air of familiarity, indicating the two men knew each other.

"None whatsoever," the spry little man responded, "except that I'm nearly as old as that house. And I know a bit about our county's history, if you don't mind me sharing." He moved from his chair and took a few shuffling steps toward Mr. Bradley. "You know, I remember your grandfather. Walter Bradley worked at the mill with my brother for nearly thirty years. He was a good man—the kind of man who acknowledged the kindness of others and expressed appreciation whenever he could."

"Angus, I appreciate your sterling remarks regarding my grandfather, but are you going to make a point?"

"I wonder if you're aware, Doug, of where your grandfather was living when he purchased the land your family owns. You still live there, I believe— on the land your grandfather first purchased when he arrived in Harrison County." Mr. McFinley moved slowly forward and handed Mr. Bradley a single sheet of paper.

Mr. Bradley looked over the document, nodding his head in recognition. "This is the record of the land purchase," he said. "You gave me a copy when I was first elected to the board."

"Yes, I did," Mr. McFinley said. "If you take a look right here," he continued, pointing with his wobbly, crooked finger, "and then look at an old map of Harrison County, I believe you'll find that the address listed as Walter Bradley's current residence at the time he purchased the land was located on old Ike Wylie's farm. Why, it seems, Doug, that your own grandfather was a recipient of Wylie's generosity."

Mr. Bradley sighed. "I'm sure Grandfather was grateful for any assistance offered by his neighbors and friends when he was settling in Harrison County, but that's hardly a significant reason—"

"I think your grandfather might have disagreed with you there," Mr. McFinley said.

He glanced at Kate and smiled conspiratorially. She continued to watch, wondering what Angus McFinley had up his sleeve. He returned to his seat and pulled out a second document then returned to the front of the room, handing it to Mr. Bradley. He turned to address the room at large.

"When Isaac Wylie died, the mayor of Rose Creek felt compelled to express his gratitude for all Ike did for those around him. So he drafted a letter pledging his support to protect the Wylie farm as an acknowledgement of—and you'll note I'm quoting from the letter—'the significant impact the Wylie farm and family had on the growth and success of Harrison County.' It appears Ms. Sinclair's property is already protected to some degree."

Mr. Bradley looked at the letter he'd been given then passed it down the row so his fellow commissioners could see it as well. "Am I really to believe that in all the research that has been done regarding this highway project, every single person involved failed to discover this letter?"

Mr. McFinley shrugged. "It's not so hard to believe. The physical address of the property changed in 1952, so perhaps it was simply a technicality that kept the truth from coming to light. Or perhaps it was just what I always say . . . Sometimes we are so occupied looking forward, we forget to look back."

Annabelle Markham cleared her throat. "In light of this recent discovery and to avoid all the questions and red tape that might ensue if we try to validate what protection the claims of a sixty-year-old letter from the mayor might or might not entail, I motion to accept Ms. Sinclair's petition and grant official historical landmark status as dictated by our current laws today for her property located on Red Dogwood Lane. All in favor, say aye."

Kate watched as the vote moved from one commissioner to the next. She counted each vote . . . one yes, two, three, four, five, and then Mr. Bradley, the sixth and final yes.

Chairman Bradley straightened in his chair. "Well, I guess it's decided then. With six votes in favor and none against, your petition has been accepted, Ms. Sinclair. We will refer you to our preservation society, who will help you complete all necessary paperwork for submission to the state organization, as well as the list of requirements for you to comply with county guidelines."

Kate closed her eyes and released her breath, holding on to the chair in front of her for support. "Thank you," she said.

After the meeting, her family gathered around her, complimenting and congratulating.

Mr. McFinley gave her a hug. "Welcome aboard, my dear. We're delighted to have you and your lovely old house," he said, smiling.

"Mr. McFinley, thank you for your help," Kate said. "How did you find that letter?"

He smiled, his twinkling eyes disappearing in the wrinkly creases of his face. "Oh, an old man has his secrets," he said. He winked again and then left Kate to her family. She watched as he worked his way to the front of the room, where he shook hands with Mr. Bradley.

Annabelle Markham was the next person to approach Kate. She smiled warmly. "Congratulations," she said. "And might I say, a job well done!"

"Ms. Markham, thank you so much," Kate said. "I'm not sure things would have gone my way if you hadn't spoken up when you did."

"I was happy to help," she said. "Please, do call me Annabelle. Besides, we're family."

Kate was taken aback by her claim. "What do you mean?" she asked.

Annabelle laughed. "Don't worry. I wouldn't have known you from my house cat before I heard your story. But I just so happen to be a descendant of old Isaac Wylie myself. And I have the history to prove it."

Kate shook her head. "I never would have guessed," she said. "I didn't realize there were any other Wylies in Harrison County."

"Well, not Wylie exactly," she said. "Old Ike had three sons, but he also had an adopted daughter named Melissa. She was the daughter of a widowed woman who was a tenant of the Wylies. When the widow fell ill and died, Old Ike and his wife took six-year-old Melissa into their home and raised her like their own. Melissa was my grandmother." Annabelle smiled.

Kate looked at Linny and Sam, who'd just come to join her in the hallway and picked up the last details of Annabelle's story. "Can you believe we've never heard this story?" Kate asked, still incredulous. "How could Grandpa have had a sister that his family never knew anything about?"

"We were very young when Grandpa died. There's probably a lot we don't know about him," Sam said.

"Well, and Melissa was much younger than your grandfather," Annabelle said. "The three boys were long out of the house before she ever went to live with Isaac."

Kate understood how Melissa's existence could have been overlooked in her family's accounts of their history but was grateful just the same to learn about her now. She felt a sudden kinship with the woman, perhaps because they'd both lost their parents at a young age and been left in the care of someone new. She hoped Annabelle would be able to tell her more about Melissa.

"Would you like to hear the best part?" Annabelle asked, face glowing with anticipation.

Kate and Sam nodded in unison.

"I have Isaac's ledger. He kept a list of every person who ever stayed on his property, as well as the dates of their stay. I've kept it all these years, not really knowing if it would ever be of value to anyone. I wish I'd known to look for old Bradley's grandpa in there. Wasn't that wonderful how it all worked out? At any rate, I think you ought to have the ledger now. Perhaps it could be included in what you donate to the museum."

"Oh, that would be wonderful, Annabelle. I can't wait to see it." Kate embraced the woman and thanked her again, overwhelmed and grateful for her generosity. "Would you come for dinner on Sunday?" Kate asked. "Bring the ledger and come see the farmhouse and the journal."

"That's very kind," Annabelle said. "I have plans for dinner, but I'd love to come by afterward, if that's all right."

Kate and the rest of her party finally moved to the parking lot. By the time she had finished her conversation with Annabelle, she figured Andrew was probably already gone. But she saw him across the lot, almost to his car. She hurried after him. "Andrew!"

He paused and waited for her to catch up. She stopped a few feet away.

"I just wanted to say thank you again," she said. "I never would have been able to do this without you."

"I'm glad it worked out for you, Kate," he said sincerely. "It really is a great house."

"I just met Annabelle Markham," Kate said. "Would you believe she's almost my family? Isaac Wylie and his wife took in her grandmother when her grandmother's parents died. I'd never heard anything about the story before now, but Annabelle has this really wonderful ledger that recorded all of the people who ever stayed on Isaac Wylie's farm . . ."

Andrew shifted his weight from one foot to the other and pushed both of his hands deep into his pockets. Kate's nerves were making her talkative. *Get to the point*, she thought.

"So you got the job in Raleigh," she said.

Andrew nodded his head. "They called this morning with an offer. I haven't accepted it yet."

"You may not?"

"It was my first interview back in the industry," he explained. "I'd like to explore my options a bit more before making a decision."

"Oh," Kate said. She chewed on her lip and looked at her feet. Mustering one final surge of courage, she blurted out, "Andrew, I don't want you to take the job in Raleigh. I don't want you to leave Rose Creek at all."

Andrew raised his eyebrows in question but otherwise didn't respond.

"I'm not in a relationship with Steve," she continued. "I was at one point, before you and I even met, but not anymore. I don't know why he said what he did. But it isn't him I care about. It's you. It's always been you."

Andrew moved to the side of his car and leaned against the driver's side door. His hands were still in his pockets, his face looking down so that in the shadow of the late evening, Kate could barely see his expression.

"I don't know if I'm the kind of person you deserve," she said. "I have a list a mile long of reasons I'm not. But here I am. This is all I can offer—me with all of my shortcomings. I'm not a morning person. I eat too much junk food. I'm an emotional wimp. I have a short temper, and I'm prone to running away from difficult situations. My family life, at the moment, is a complete mess. My cousin won't speak to me, and my aunt thinks my religion is going to ruin the family. But I'm here. I'm here asking you to still care, to overlook all of that and love me anyway. I'm asking you to love me because I have fallen in love with you."

A soft summer breeze lifted Kate's hair from her temples, blowing it across her cheek and into her eyes. She pushed it away, tucking it behind her ear. Andrew looked up at her and smiled his crooked half smile.

"Besides," she said. "It's hot in Raleigh."

"Miserably hot," Andrew agreed. They looked at each other, and that wordless communication that mystified Kate so fully passed between them.

In an instant, he was close, pulling her into an embrace, holding her face with his hands. Suddenly, the emotional strain of the past few days, topped with the intensity of the moment with Andrew, caught up with Kate. Tears spilled onto her cheeks and his as they kissed.

"Kate, are you all right?" Andrew asked. "What's wrong?"

She smiled and wiped the tears away, shaking her head. "I don't know. I guess it's just been a long couple of days. I mean, yesterday morning I was in my office working, thinking I might not ever come back to Rose Creek at all. And now, here I am, not forty-eight hours later, back in Rose Creek permanently, with you, with the house saved . . . I guess it's just a bit overwhelming."

"So you're here for good? You're not going back to Atlanta?"

"Only to pack up and move," she said, smiling. "I'm glad the house was saved, but even if things hadn't worked out, I'd still be moving back. I need to be with my family. This is home. This is where I want to be."

"This is where I want you to be too," he said. "What happened, Kate? Why *did* you come back?"

"I wasn't happy the entire time I was in Atlanta," she said. "I was trying to be, but everything felt so empty. My heart was still here in Rose Creek, with you and my family. But I was so scared and angry and hurt by Leslie's comments; I think my pride wouldn't let me consider the possibility that I'd made another mistake by leaving again. But then I spoke with Linny, and she was so disappointed in me, and then you came and left. Seeing you walk away like that, I was a little surprised by the intensity of my reaction. I yelled at Steve for being a jerk, and then Blanton told me my work was terrible, and . . . I don't know. I was pretty low. But it was good to hit rock bottom. It was there that I realized I couldn't give up on what was most important. It was time to stop running and hiding from what's hard."

They stood side by side against the car. Kate leaned her head on Andrew's shoulder and watched the fireflies rise from the grassy hillside beside the parking lot. Fireflies were one of her favorite parts of summer. As a child, she and Leslie would stay up late on summer evenings to chase them all over the yard and capture them in canning jars with air holes punched in the lid. They would keep them in their rooms late into the night and watch their mysterious little bodies light up. Uncle Grey always told them it's how they talked to each other, how the males would find the females. The flickering lights were simply the fireflies' form of elaborate courtship. Eventually, one of the girls would feel guilty about keeping the little bugs separated from their potential soul mates and would run to the window, slide open the heavy sash, and send the fireflies dancing back into the night. The memory made her suddenly grateful that she was in Rose Creek. There weren't any fireflies in the city.

"Can I ask you something?" Andrew asked.

"Sure."

"You mentioned your religion—that your aunt is afraid it might divide your family. Is it *your* religion, then?"

Kate lifted her head and looked at Andrew. She'd never been so sure of anything in her life. "I tried not to think about it while I was gone. I was afraid to, you know? But then, when I felt so low yesterday, I decided if there was ever a time I ought to give praying a try, this was it." She shrugged her shoulders. "So I did." She smiled again when she saw Andrew's response. He was elated.

"That's really wonderful," he said. "I'm so happy for you."

"Andrew, I wanted to ask you if you would do the baptism. It can be you, can't it? It doesn't have to be the missionaries?"

Andrew was visibly touched by her request. "I would be honored to do that for you," he said. "Thank you for letting me be a part of it."

He kissed her again and said good-bye, promising to call her in the morning.

As Kate drove home to the farmhouse—*her* farmhouse—she knew everything was going to be different.

When she arrived home, she sat down at the kitchen table and soaked in the peace and stillness of her home. It was a relief, she reflected, not to have the fear of losing the house looming over her. But better still was the peace she felt on the inside. Though she was just as much alone in the house as she had been the month before, it didn't feel the same. She was alone, yes—but not lonely. Her heart, which was once empty, was now brim full.

## Chapter 35

A WEEK LATER, AFTER CHURCH, Kate worked to prepare dinner for all of her family. They were coming at Kate's invitation to celebrate the farmhouse's victory. Even Leslie was coming with the children, mostly to appease Linny, who hadn't veiled her threats in the slightest. Whatever Leslie's reason for being there, Kate was glad they would all be together. Though it made her nervous thinking about it, she planned to tell her family about her decision to be baptized. She'd hesitated at first, wondering if it would be better to wait instead of sullying the happy mood of their celebration with an announcement she was sure would leave her family in shock. But they were all together so infrequently she didn't want to miss the opportunity to let them know how she felt. At least she would have Andrew there for support.

Kate opened the oven and checked on the pot roast. It was nearly perfect, cooked just as Mary had taught her. The potatoes were boiling, the green beans cooking on the back of the stove, and the rolls rising. For the time being, there was nothing to do in the kitchen but wait.

"I couldn't have done what you did."

Kate jumped, startled by the voice in the doorway. She turned and saw Leslie standing there with her arms crossed.

"I couldn't have done it," she said again. "I wouldn't have known what to say about the house; I wouldn't have been able to stay so calm. Not like you did."

"I didn't realize you were at the meeting," Kate said, wiping her hands on her apron.

"I stayed in the back," Leslie said.

"Oh."

"I've got to bring the children inside." Leslie turned and went out to her van.

Kate moved to the kitchen table and sat down. It was the closest thing to an apology she could expect, and it was enough. In time, Kate was certain that all would be well between her cousin and her. She closed her eyes and said a silent prayer of gratitude. Andrew arrived just minutes after Leslie and the children came inside. Sam and Teresa were next, with Kenzie asleep in Teresa's arms.

"Does that child ever do anything but sleep?" Kate asked as she greeted them at the door. "I don't know if I've ever seen her awake!"

"It's the long drive on the mountain roads," Teresa responded. "Knocks her out every time."

Teresa settled the sleeping toddler on the couch in the family room then stood to greet Andrew, who was talking to Sam. The two men had met briefly at the county commissioners meeting the Thursday before, but it was Teresa's first time meeting him.

"It's nice to finally meet you," she said. "Thanks for all of your help with the house. It would have been sad to see anything happen to this place."

"The pleasure was all mine," Andrew said. "It's an amazing house that deserves to be protected."

"Yeah, old houses are pretty great," Sam said. "But it helps when you get to kiss the girl at the end of the night too, right?"

Andrew blushed as Sam slapped him good-naturedly on the back. He glanced at Kate, who was kneeling by the stairs in deep conversation with little Emily. "It certainly doesn't hurt," he said.

Linny blustered into the house and headed straight for the kitchen. There, she placed a large chocolate layer cake ceremoniously on the counter. Kate followed her in.

"Linny, you made your chocolate cake," she said excitedly. Andrew appeared in the doorway behind her. "Andrew, you will never eat a chocolate cake better than this one."

"Oh, now hush. It's not anything special," Linny said. "I just thought with us being together, the occasion warranted an extra bit of chocolate. Andrew," she continued, "can you help Sam get Charles in the house? He doesn't get around much these days and will need help from the car."

"Sure thing," Andrew said.

Kate hoped Charles would be polite, especially to Andrew. She watched as the three men slowly climbed the porch stairs and made their way into the family room. When Charles was settled into the large leather chair by the window, having greeted each of the children, he turned back to Andrew.

"You're the Mormon?"

Andrew barely flinched, taking the question in stride. Kate had a harder time hiding her embarrassment.

"Yes, sir, I am," he answered, extending his hand in greeting. "It's nice to meet you."

"I'm not sure how I feel about Mormons." Charles sat motionless, hands still in his lap. Andrew dropped his hand, sliding both of his into his own pockets.

"Well, I guess that's all right. I'm not really sure how I feel about you yet either. Are you a baseball fan?"

Charles looked at him, face still gruff. "I like baseball. You a Yankees fan?"

Andrew shook his head and cringed. "Atlanta Braves all the way."

"Hey," Charles said, smiling. "That's good. I hate the stinkin' Yankees."

Kate watched in amazement as the two men sat on the couch and started rattling off every possible statistic regarding the Braves' previous season, as well as any and all predictions regarding the upcoming year.

"Charles, you're not being mean, are you?" Linny called from the kitchen.

"Only to the Mormon," Charles called back, laughing quietly at his own joke. "Hey, Linny, this here Mormon is a Braves fan. How 'bout that?"

Kate shrugged her shoulders in Andrew's direction then went to the kitchen to finish dinner.

Bryan arrived just a few minutes later, surprising everyone by bringing a woman with him. "Everyone," he said, entering the family room. "I'd like you to meet my fiancée, Susanna."

"Fiancée?" Leslie reached them first, hugging her brother tightly. "Why didn't you tell us?"

"I like surprises," Bryan said. He smiled broadly as the family gathered around, showering the two of them with warm greetings and well wishes. Susanna seemed a perfect extension of Bryan's rugged, outdoor appearance. She wore khaki cargo pants and Tevas, hair pulled back in a loose ponytail. Kate thought she'd probably never worn a stitch of make-up, though she was still very pretty. Pretty and perfectly suited to Kate's carefree, adventure-loving cousin.

"Looks like today is a day for announcements," Andrew said to Kate, sliding his arm around her waist.

She took a deep breath. "Yeah, I guess so."

Bryan was the only member of Kate's family who Andrew hadn't yet met. After the introductions, Kate invited everyone into the dining room.

"Everything looks lovely, Kate," Teresa said. "You didn't have to go to all this trouble."

"Oh, it was no trouble at all," Kate insisted. "I'm glad you could all come."

When everyone was seated, Kate remained standing behind her chair. Andrew gave her a brief nod of encouragement.

"So," Kate began, "first of all, congratulations to Bryan and Susanna. I'm so happy for you both." She smiled at the new couple. "In the spirit of making big announcements," she continued, "I guess you've all probably guessed that I am moving back to Rose Creek permanently." She glanced at Leslie, studying her face for a reaction, but was unable to discern a lot.

"And," Kate continued, pushing forward before her courage failed her. "I've decided to join the LDS Church. I've decided to be baptized—next Sunday, actually, if you would all like to come," she added.

Kate looked around the table. Her family members were silent.

It was Charles who spoke first. "Baptized? You mean you're goin' to be a Mormon?"

"Yes, Charles, of course that's what she means," Linny hissed.

"Um, well, that's great news about you moving back," Sam said, apparently choosing to ignore the second part of Kate's announcement. "So you'll live here in the house?"

Kate nodded. "I fought so hard to keep it. It just doesn't feel right not to stay." She looked at Leslie again, this time forcing eye contact.

Leslie shrugged her shoulders as if to say, "It's your life . . . not mine," and looked away, finding some reason to tend to her children.

"What do you want to be Mormon for?" Charles asked. It was a question she was sure they all felt like asking. Kate was actually grateful for Charles's willingness to just spit it out.

Kate looked at Andrew, relying on his emotional support, and said simply, "I believe it's true."

Bryan looked at Andrew. "I guess you have something to do with this?"

"Kate and I have talked about it a great deal, and I've tried to answer her questions as best I can, but her decisions have been made independently," Andrew answered.

"Yeah. I'm sure," Bryan said sarcastically. "Worked out nice for you though, didn't it?"

"Bryan, it wasn't like that," Kate said. "I didn't even know Andrew was Mormon the first time I met with the missionaries. I'm not doing this

for him. This is for me. It's because I want this." Kate looked around the
table at her family and dropped down into her chair. "Why does it matter
anyway? It's not as if we've all been a hugely religious bunch as it is. It isn't
going to change anything." Kate was growing frustrated with her families'
lack of response.

"It's just a lot of change, dear," Linny said. "First you're home, then you
disappear and are gone again. Now you've come back, you've quit your job
. . . It's only natural for us to be a little . . . cautious in accepting your new
religion."

"I've been doing some research, Kate," Leslie finally spoke up. "I've
read all sorts of things online. I don't think you have any idea what you're
getting into. Secret temples, plural marriage—it's weird stuff. You need to
see this stuff I've read."

Andrew found Kate's hand under the table and held it tightly.

Sam finally spoke. "You're an adult, Kate. You're obviously capable of
making your own decisions. But we just want you to know we don't think
this is a good idea."

Kate shook her head. "Wait, *we*? Who's we? You're speaking for everyone,
Sam? Have you all talked about this?"

"We're concerned about you, Katie," Linny said. "Of course we've
talked about it."

"Mormons don't have the best reputation," Bryan said, reaching for
the serving spoon of the mashed potatoes. "Can I go ahead and eat? I'm
starving."

Kate rolled her eyes. "This is so ridiculous," she said under her breath.
The conversation died as everyone passed the food around the table. Kate
couldn't believe her family had actually talked about her interest in the
Mormon Church behind her back. How many times had Leslie called
Linny, she wondered? How many times had she called to read one more
story off the Internet, one more accusatory, condemning paragraph?

"We're not judging you," Sam finally said. "We just want you to open
your eyes and see beyond the here and now of Andrew and what you think
is the best choice. Will you just read some of the things we've found? It really
is quite disturbing."

Kate slammed her fork onto the table. "Is this really what you've all
spent your time doing? Researching reasons for me *not* to join a certain
church? Who asked you to do such a thing? And how do you even know
these things you are reading are true? Sam, if you needed open heart surgery,

would you go see a podiatrist? Of course not! So why, when you're looking for information about the Mormons, would you go anywhere but to a Mormon? You have questions? Ask them. Right here and now when there's someone willing to answer—someone who will tell you the truth instead of some trumped-up website trying to lead people astray." Kate sat back in her chair, annoyed with herself for getting angry and irritated at the subversive attack from her family members. She knew Leslie and Linny were leery of the Mormons from her previous conversations with them. But she had not expected anything beyond indifference from Sam and Bryan. She was shocked at how readily they'd jumped on the criticism bandwagon. Kate toyed with her food, suddenly unable to eat, wishing instead to leave the table all together.

"My best friend in high school was Mormon."

Kate looked up at Susanna, who had been sitting quietly next to Bryan. She had been silent through the entire religious exchange. But now she spoke, offering Kate a shy smile. "My best friend was Mormon," she repeated. "And there was never anything weird or unusual or disturbing about her. She's the nicest person I've ever known."

Kate immediately loved this girl—this courageous, kind person whose words were like the balm of Gilead. The rest of the family looked awkwardly at each other, suddenly aware of their judgments and criticisms.

"I've got some news, if it's all right for me to change the subject," Teresa said, tentatively looking at the others surrounding the table. When no one objected, she said, "Sam and I are having another baby."

"I knew it," Linny shouted. "Didn't I tell you that, Kate? I told you I thought they were having another one!"

Kate nodded her head and smiled, genuinely happy for baby news but really just grateful for the change of subject.

"You okay?" Andrew asked softly enough for only Kate to hear. She looked at him and shook her head.

"It's about what I expected, but it still hurts," she said.

"It will get easier as they get used to the idea," Andrew encouraged. "It may take them a long time to understand, but it will be all right in the end."

The rest of dinner progressed with little excitement, everyone making a concerted effort to keep the conversation on safe and neutral subjects. While Linny and Leslie worked to clear off the table and start on the dishes, Kate slipped into the living room to look for Susanna. She found her standing at the fireplace, looking at the scores of family photos lining the mantel.

"That's Bryan right there," Kate said, pointing to a little boy in dusty overalls. "He was probably nine or ten there."

"He was cute," Susanna said.

"Susanna," Kate began, "I just wanted to thank you for what you said at dinner. I know it wasn't easy."

"Don't worry about it," Susanna said. "I should have said something sooner. I was really surprised they all ganged up on you like that."

Kate sighed. "I think they mean well. They just . . . I don't know. This is a big change for me. I think they'll understand with time. You said you had a friend who was Mormon?"

Susanna nodded. "We haven't been in touch with each other for a number of years, but she was my best friend all through school. She had a great family and was such a nice person. We talked about her religion a lot. I'm really happy for you. I think it's wonderful you've decided to be baptized."

Kate smiled. "Thank you," she said. "I'm glad you came here today. You're going to be a great addition to the family."

Kate looked for Andrew and found him on the front porch, leaning against the railing across from Sam. She stood back for a moment, listening as the men conversed. Andrew was a likeable guy, and Kate felt certain her family would all approve of him once they got to know him—if, that is, they could look beyond religion. She decided to join them, sliding her arm around Andrew's waist as he wrapped his arm around her shoulder.

"Dinner was wonderful," Andrew said.

Sam nodded in agreement. "I didn't know you could cook like that, Kate." He smiled. "I nearly believed Mom herself was the one cooking in the kitchen. The pot roast was just like hers."

The family spent the next few hours looking through the many boxes and things Kate had pulled down from the attic and upstairs closets in the previous weeks. They forgot any prior contention as they reminisced, laughing and even crying a time or two as they remembered Mary and Grey and the many happy moments of their childhood. At one point, Kate found herself sitting on the floor across from Leslie, a box of old handkerchiefs and scarves in between them.

"So you already quit your job, then? You really are here for good?" Leslie asked.

Kate shook her head. "I didn't have to quit. Mr. Blanton has created a new position for me so I can work remotely. I'll still have to drive back to the city once or twice a month, but I'm determined not to do it more frequently than that. Leslie, I'm really sure about this. I don't expect things to be easy for you right now, but I know I'm doing the right thing. I'll be here. Whenever you need me, whenever you need to talk, I'm not going anywhere. Not ever again."

"So this whole Mormon thing," Leslie said. "You're sure about that too?"

"Yes, I am. I promise I know what I'm doing. I've thought a lot about this. I was thinking, maybe if you come, you'll realize it isn't really that strange after all."

"What? Come to church with you?" Leslie asked.

"At least come to the baptism. I'd really love for you to be there."

Leslie pulled a pale blue scarf out of the box and slid it through her hands. She took a deep breath and looked up at Kate. "I'll think about it," she finally said.

Annabelle Markham arrived at the house around 7:00 p.m. After meeting everyone, she settled on the couch next to Kate and handed her a worn leather-bound notebook. Kate opened it up, turning through the first few pages. Each page contained several entries—names and dates and a short description of the circumstances that brought people to Isaac Wylie's door. Kate looked at each entry—men, women, entire families who lived and worked on her great-grandfather's farm.

"It's so wonderful what he did," she commented, "how he helped so many."

"My grandmother always said there was never a nicer man," Annabelle said. "I want you to have this, Kate. Donate it to the museum with that journal of yours. I also spoke with a friend of mine today. I hope you don't mind. She works for the Harrison County Press and would like to write a human interest story about the farmhouse, mention Isaac Wylie and what he did, and then talk about all of this history you discovered in your efforts to turn the house into a landmark."

Kate smiled. "I think that sounds wonderful," she said. "I just had a conversation yesterday morning with the head of the preservation committee here in Harrison County. They are excited to include the house as part of their driving tour and even asked if I would host their quarterly meeting in September, a grand-opening sort of deal for the house. Perhaps the running of the story could coincide with that."

"That's a great idea," Annabelle agreed. "The thing is, Kate, I bet there are people all over this community who could look through this old book and find their ancestors' names—grandparents, great-grandparents—it could be such a wonderful resource for people, a window into history that they may not ever see otherwise."

Kate paused and thought about her own glimpse through the window of her family's history. Her heart had been touched and her life changed because of words written two hundred years before. There was value in reaching out and reaching back, remembering those who lived before.

"Thank you so much, Annabelle. Tell your friend I would love to meet her. I'll help any way I can with her story."

# Chapter 36

By the following Sunday, Kate had endured several more conversations with her family regarding her decision to be baptized. Susanna had a remarkable influence on Bryan, and while he didn't plan on driving up to be there, he had at least offered Kate his wishes of happiness and a promise to not judge her or Andrew harshly. Sam and Teresa had accepted her decision as well. Sam told her the last time they spoke that he thought Kate seemed like a different person and that it must serve her well to be so committed to something. If it was changing her for the better, he could hardly voice any opposition. Kate suspected that perhaps her cousins would have reacted differently from the start had Leslie and Linny not worked so hard to get them fired up against her. The women were obviously the ones struggling the most with her decision.

Just hours before the baptism, Kate was still unsure if any of her own family members would be there. She was hopeful but tried not to be overly concerned. Even without them there, she knew she would have plenty of support. The branch members in Rose Creek had warmly received and welcomed Kate. Dan and Caroline Spencer would be there, as well as the missionaries. Much to Kate's surprise, Andrew's family was making a special trip all the way from Charlotte to be there for the baptism as well. She'd spoken on the phone with Lindsay Porterfield, Andrew's mother, and was excited to meet her.

Kate stood in front of the mirror in her bedroom, studying her reflection. She did look different. An inner peace seemed to radiate from within—a light in her eyes that pushed any murkiness or confusion aside. The word that came to mind was *clarity*. She took a final deep breath and went downstairs, where Andrew was waiting for her.

"You look radiant." He smiled. "Are you ready to go?"

"As ready as I'll ever be." Kate smiled back.

* * *

"Katherine Isabelle Sinclair, having been commissioned of Jesus Christ . . ." Kate would never forget those words—the simple prayer Andrew uttered before lowering her into the waters of baptism. Andrew later told her when he lifted her out of the water, she'd never looked quite so lovely. But what she would remember was how she felt—clean and pure and fully sanctified.

After Kate dressed and returned to the chapel, she looked around the crowded room, searching the faces of those in attendance. There, in the back row, sitting alone, she saw Leslie. She smiled at her, touched and grateful that she had been there. It was more than she could have hoped for. Leslie smiled back, lifting her shoulders in a little half shrug of acceptance.

Caroline Spencer gave the final talk on the gift of the Holy Ghost, something Kate would receive when she was confirmed a member of the Church the following Sunday, then Dan Spencer closed the meeting.

Kate quickly pulled away from those gathering around to hug and congratulate her and ran after her cousin. "Leslie," she called, finally reaching her in the parking lot. Leslie stopped and watched as Kate approached her, pausing to catch her breath before speaking again. "Thank you for being here."

"It was nice, I guess," Leslie said. "Everyone seemed really nice."

"They are really nice. Do you want to stay? I think there's food."

"No. I left the kids with Linny. She wanted to come, but I couldn't get Beatrice to stay with the kids, so Linny came at the last minute."

"It means a lot that either of you cared to come."

Leslie sighed and looked deeply into her cousin's eyes. "I'm sorry about what I said that night, Kate. I wasn't giving you enough credit. I'm sorry, and I'm glad you're home now."

Later that afternoon, after dinner with the Spencers and the Porterfields, Andrew brought Kate his cell phone. "It's my sister," he said excitedly. "You're not going to believe what she has to tell you."

"Hello, Valerie," Kate said warmly into the phone.

"Kate, I've got the most exciting news!" Valerie said. "I did some research about Ian, and the Wylie family in general. I have this associate who was doing some field work in Scotland who agreed to look into a few things over there. He just called me back this afternoon. As it turns out, Ian's father, James Wylie, was married to Elizabeth Cochrane. Now, James wasn't really a person of importance as far as his station in life. He was the son of a merchant, middle class, respectable but certainly not nobility of any sort. But Elizabeth was noteworthy—daughter of an earl, the Earl of Dundonald, though little is written about her once she married James Wylie. I would imagine there was quite a frenzy of disapproval over their union, considering their different stations in life. At any rate, she wasn't completely forgotten, and apparently, some years after James's death, she was reconciled to her own parents. That's probably why she stayed in Scotland—life would have been much better for her once she was living under the care of the earl, now willing to accept her with her husband dead."

It made Kate sad to think that Ian's mother had never met her grandchildren or seen her son as a grown man—a man Kate was certain she would have been proud of.

"Here's the best part," Valerie continued. "There is a collection of letters in a Scottish history museum in Edinburgh—letters saved Elizabeth Cochrane, then donated by her granddaughter. There are letters in the collection from Ian that he sent to his mother. She saved them and probably cherished them for years."

"I have to read them, Valerie. I can't believe you found so much," Kate said.

"Would you believe I'm not finished yet? Listen to this. Ian was the first male descendant in the Cochrane line. By all intents and purposes, he had claim to the title of earl. The title went to another son, a cousin of Ian's, as Ian, the son of a merchantman and now living in America, was conveniently overlooked. But history didn't overlook the relationship he had with his mother. The letters were an indication of the love she had for her first husband and for her son. Everyone loves a good love story, you know? Marrying for love wasn't so common back then."

"What an amazing woman she must have been," Kate said.

"Well, and James too, to have wooed and wed the daughter of an earl without his own claim to title or fortune. I've ordered photocopies of the letters. As soon as I get them, I'll send them to you. But you should go see the letters. Tell Andrew you want to go to Scotland on your honeymoon," Valerie said enthusiastically.

Kate flushed with embarrassment at the implication of Valerie's comment and was suddenly grateful not everyone was listening to their conversation. They talked for a few more minutes, Valerie answering Kate's questions as best she could, before Kate hung up the phone and returned it to Andrew.

It was remarkable how compelling Kate found her family's history. It hadn't always been her best subject, but she felt keenly aware of the family ties that extended from her ancestors directly into her own blood. She felt the pull and wanted to make sure she didn't forget the obligation she had to take the names of her ancestors to the temple to do for them what they were unable to do for themselves when they lived on the earth.

She and Andrew had already talked about going to the temple to perform baptisms for her ancestors and had already started the process of compiling names and gathering the required information. It was an important step, but Kate most looked forward to participating in the ordinance that would seal Ian and his beloved wife, Jennie, together forever. She thought often of Ian and how long he'd been waiting for her to find him—to find the truth.

Kate imagined that if Ian had the opportunity to do so, he would thank her for accepting the gospel and for making his eternal progress possible by completing the necessary ordinances in the temple. Just the same, Kate was overwhelmed with gratitude for Ian and the spiritual leanings and intuition he had felt that compelled him to write the very words that had changed Kate's life forever. *We needed each other, didn't we, Ian?*

She felt it so clearly that she wondered if she hadn't heard a voice of confirmation. She knew in her heart that it was true and that somewhere, Ian was smiling upon her. She smiled in return, warmed from the inside. *I'll get you there, Ian. I promise.*

*Chapter 37*

IT HAD BEEN THREE MONTHS since Kate had secured the safety of the house. And she had been busy. Though she hated to be away from the farmhouse, she'd spent quite a bit of time settling her affairs in Atlanta. Fortunately, her condo sold with little trouble, and Andrew had helped her move all of her belongings from her condo into the farmhouse, a task that had created a lengthy new to-do list as she moved out some of the old furnishings to make room for her own. It was difficult to make changes at first. But Kate knew Mary and Grey would want her to make the farmhouse feel like hers.

A soft summer breeze blew through the yard and gardens, lessening the burdensome heat and humidity of the early-September afternoon. Friends and members of the community were gathered together for the quarterly meeting of the Historical Preservation Society. It was less of a meeting though and much more of a celebration. Kate looked around her home, happy to see so many gathered together in honor of her ancestors and the old house she'd managed to save. The Harrison County Press had written a wonderful story about Isaac Wylie, highlighting the many efforts he'd made to strengthen the community and help those around him. Everyone in town had been invited to visit the museum, look through old Ike Wylie's book, and see if any of their own ancestors were listed within. Many had found record of parents or grandparents, even great-grandparents, and were there at the garden party paying their respects and celebrating Kate's success in preserving the home. All of her family was there as well: Leslie and her children, Bryan and Susanna, Sam, Kenzie, and Teresa, now blossoming with late pregnancy. Kate smiled as she thought of Linny's intuitive prediction made months before. She'd known Teresa was expecting again, had called it, known it, and hadn't been shy in letting everyone know she'd guessed beforehand.

Kate wondered if Linny had a feeling one way or the other about Andrew. Could she read their relationship like she had Teresa? One thing was certain, Linny loved Andrew. Though Linny maintained her opposition to all things Church-related, Kate and Andrew had both made an effort to reach out to her to bridge the divide Kate's baptism had created. Slowly but surely it was working. Linny was there that afternoon as well, standing under the large oak tree in the front yard, engaged in conversation with Mr. Brumfield from down the street.

"Ms. Sinclair, if you don't mind me saying so, this might be the loveliest quarterly meeting our preservation society has ever seen." Mr. McFinley approached her on the porch and took her hands in his.

"You're sweet to say so, Mr. McFinley. I'm glad you're here."

"Oh, I wouldn't miss it for the world. In my heart of hearts, I always honored the Wylie name, but it's nice to have a place on the map that does so as well."

"Well, I certainly couldn't have done it without your efforts. I hope you'll still come visit once this is all over. You know you're always welcome," Kate said.

"Oh, that would be lovely. I think perhaps we may just be friends for life." Mr. McFinley squeezed her hand once more then shuffled off to get some lemonade.

Kate watched as he sat down next to Linny and pulled Leslie's youngest, little Tommy, onto his lap. It was a good day.

That evening when the party was over and guests were gone, Kate picked up the stray plates and cups that littered the porch. The sun, finally relenting, dipped low behind the summer-green mountains, leaving the yard in peaceful shadow.

"Aunt Katie," Emily called as she skipped toward Kate. Her cheeks were pink from exertion, her pigtails swinging behind her. She nearly collided into Kate as she stopped in front of her.

"What is it, child?" Kate asked, bending down in front of her niece.

"Andrew says I can tell you my secret now."

Kate looked around, searching the grounds for Andrew, but he was nowhere to be seen. She looked back at Emily. "Okay." She smiled. "What is it?"

Emily leaned in, a serious look on her face. "He says he loves you and he wants to marry you."

Kate closed her eyes and bit her lip, a smile spreading across her face. "Emily, where's Andrew? Did he just tell you that?"

"Nope," Emily said. "He told me that when I very first met him. But he just told me now that I could finally tell *you*."

"Emily, can you help me find him?" Kate asked.

Emily nodded her head and took off around the corner of the house. "He's back here!" she yelled over her shoulder.

Kate followed behind her niece. She found Andrew in the back corner of the garden, leaning against the trunk of an old cherry tree. The tree had been a customary retreat of Kate's childhood and one of her favorite spots. She stopped in front of him, heart racing.

"Hi," she said.

"I see you got my message." Andrew smiled.

She looked at his smile every day, and still, it made her heart melt. "Yeah," she whispered softly.

"Marry me, Kate," he said, dropping to one knee. "Marry me and make me the happiest man alive."

* * *

They waited until spring when Kate was able to go to the temple. On the anniversary of her baptism, Kate entered the Lord's house and married the man of her dreams. She didn't worry one single time that Andrew might not show up. After their own ceremony, the couple stayed in the temple awhile longer. Kneeling across the sacred altar for the second time that afternoon, they were sealed for Ian and Jennie Wylie, uniting the couple in an eternal union.

When they finally left the temple, Andrew paused just outside the door and looked into his wife's eyes. "That was pretty amazing," he said gently. "He was there this afternoon, Kate. Ian was there. I'm sure of it."

Kate closed her eyes, overwhelmed and grateful. "I know," she said softly. "When I rose from the altar, I couldn't help but feel he was speaking to me, urging me not to forget."

"Not to forget what?" Andrew asked.

"The others," Kate said. "There is still so much work to do. He doesn't want us to forget the others."

"We won't forget," Andrew said. "Not ever."

They walked arm in arm to the car and headed to the airport. They had a plane to catch that afternoon . . . to Scotland.

# About the Author

JENNY PROCTOR WRITES FROM HER home in the mountains of western North Carolina. She loves being a mom to six kids, loves being a writer, and loves being a Mormon in the South.

Jenny is convinced the four basic food groups should be fruit, bread, cheese, and chocolate, and she consumes plenty of each—quite often together. When she isn't writing, Jenny likes to run, swim, and bike (because it balances out the bread, cheese, and chocolate).

Her first novel, *The House at Rose Creek*, was inspired by discoveries she made in her own family history. She has always felt strongly about the importance of family history work and has experienced firsthand the joy that such research can bring.

To learn more about Jenny, visit her website at www.jennyproctor.com.